Pun...

By G. Angel

Copyright 2013 Golden Angel LLC

A huge thank you to Fifi and Katherine, without whom this book would not be what it is.

Also thank you to Lee Savino, my author sensei

Thank you, dear reader, for picking up my book!

Would you like to receive a free story from me as well? Join the Angel Legion and sign up for my newsletter! You'll immediately receive a free story from the Stronghold series in a welcome message, and as part of the Angel Legion you'll also receive one newsletter a month with teasers, sneak peeks, and news about upcoming releases, as well as what I'm reading now!

And, as always, thank you to my husband for his continued support, love, and contributions.

Table of Contents

Chapter 1

Out of all the words in the English language, Cynthia's absolute favorite was "don't."

The most interesting things to do were always "don't"s. "Don't" was how she'd learned that climbing trees was great fun and so was swimming in the lake. It was how she'd learned breeches were more comfortable than skirts, and riding astride much more exciting (and easier) than riding in a lady's sidesaddle - although she could do both. Kissing was another great fun she would have missed out on if she listened to the word, "don't."

The moment Cynthia was told "don't," she immediately felt the strong urge to do whatever it was she wasn't supposed to. It led to such wondrous discoveries!

As she'd grown older, those discoveries were what gave her life sparkle after her parents died. Of course she missed them very much, she did, but that didn't mean her life should always be sad. She was sad when she thought of them and she'd mourned them very properly, and during her mourning period had tried to behave as the perfect young lady she hadn't been during their lives, in their memory, but once she'd thrown off the black she'd thrown off the shroud of gloom as well. Life was just more fun when attempting all the things one wasn't supposed to do.

Which was how she'd ended up sneaking out of Lady Spencer's house in Bath to go meet with the scandalous Mr. Carter. According to her ladyship, Mr. Carter was a rogue, a rake, a dissolute braggart and a man completely without honor. Her ladyship's clear instructions had been "don't ever even talk to him, avoid him at all costs."

How was Cynthia supposed to ignore such temptation? Such a colorful description? Mr. Carter must know even more wonderful things one wasn't supposed to do, things Cynthia didn't know. She had to admit she thought he cut a rather dashing figure with his air of indifference, those lazy brown eyes and his mop of golden curls which were always slightly mussed. So, of course, when he'd coaxed her onto the terrace during one of the Assemblies she'd gone willingly, only to be interrupted moments later by an irate Lady Spencer.

Fortunately he'd found her in a shop this morning, her hovering chaperone nearby but not within earshot, and had murmured he'd like to meet her. She'd whispered back that she'd meet him at the nearby park in the afternoon, when she knew Lady Spencer would most likely be entertaining. At first her ladyship had tried to include Cynthia in her 'at-homes,' but Cynthia quickly grew bored of sitting, drinking tea, and listening to vicious old ladies exchange scathing observations and gossip. Although she did perk up whenever any of them had anything to say about Lady Spencer's sons.

She'd become great friends with Matthew and Vincent, and while she hadn't met the Earl of Spencer yet, she rather enjoyed hearing stories about him. Most of the best stories weren't told in Lady Spencer's presence, but a few of the old dragons would whisper the juicy tidbits to each other while the Countess was occupied, and Cynthia had managed to overhear quite a bit. Gambling, tumbling other men's wives, gallivanting about town... it all sounded quite grand to her. They said he was as handsome as the devil with a twinkle in his eye that could make the most chaste lady turn up her skirts for him.

Cynthia knew she wasn't supposed to know what that meant, but she did. She was bright enough, and listened often enough to the matrons' gossip, to at least be able to guess at some of the things men and women did together. Husbands and wives, Lady Spencer had said, but Cynthia knew unmarried couples did the same activities.

Perhaps the most delightful "don't" she'd ever received was "don't touch yourself between your legs." Combined with her observations and her natural penchant for trying anything new, she'd quickly managed to discover exactly *why* touching herself between her legs could be quite wonderful, although she still hadn't discerned why it was a "don't."

Mr. Carter had wanted to touch her between her legs today, but she hadn't allowed him to. She was wary of gentlemen, not wanting to find herself in a *situation*, although she certainly planned on touching *herself* there as soon as she was able. His passionate kisses and wandering hands had quite aroused her. But she had remained cognizant of the fact that Lady Spencer couldn't remain shut up in her room forever, even if the woman had thrown quite a fit when she'd realized her charge and the roguish Mr. Carter were standing far too close to each other in the store. She'd dragged Cynthia home immediately, told her to stay in her room until the Earl arrived there this afternoon to "deal with her," and then immediately took refuge in her own room.

Of course Cynthia wasn't going to stay in her room, not when she wanted to know what Mr. Carter could show her, but she had known she only had a limited amount of time. Then they'd almost been caught by a pair of gossiping girls who were talking in high-pitched excited voices about how both the rakish Lord Hyde and the Earl of Spencer had been seen in town.

Still, it had all been rather wonderful even if she had to rush home now.

Unfortunately, just after pushing through a group of rather rowdy young men, she ran straight into the poor man who was walking behind them. She thought it was unfortunate because he seemed like a very fine specimen of a man, even taller than Mr. Carter and with a harder body - she knew because it felt like she'd just smashed herself against a wall - and he was very handsome, but she didn't have time to make any kind of introduction or discover his direction. It also wasn't the kind of impression she wanted to make on a man as attractive as he was, but it couldn't be helped.

"Oh I'm so sorry, I beg your pardon!" she blurted out, before darting past him. Hopefully he wouldn't get a good enough look at her to remember her if they were to meet later; she'd rather he remember her as anything other than a rampaging harpy dashing through the street. Hurrying up the steps to the house she went immediately into the front door, hoping Manfred might be in one of the other rooms doing whatever it was he did when he wasn't watching her with disapproving eyes.

Unfortunately her hopes were in vain. Not only was Manfred standing in the center of the foray, there were several other servants running in and out of the room as well, including her maid Julie who looked to be rather teary-eyed. Cynthia glared at Manfred. If he'd been taking Julie to task over Cynthia's disappearance then she would have words with him. How could a mere maid be expected to keep tabs on her?

Manfred ignored her as the front door opened behind her again. Shockingly, something like relief flickered across his normally blank face.

"My Lord.... your ward has returned."

Oh dear. So not only was the Earl of Spencer certainly here, he knew she had been missing. Well, Cynthia had always been one to face up to her misdeeds without flinching. After all, they were almost always well worth whatever repercussions came from ignoring the word "don't."

Taking a deep breath for fortitude, she turned to face the Earl and gasped. It was the same man she'd bumped into outside! Now that she could get a better look at him she realized why she would have never expected him to be an Earl - he didn't at all look like one. Even though he'd been described as a rogue and a devil, she still expected him to look like the other rakes amongst the *ton* she'd met. This man had tanned skin, like a laborer, and his brown hair was long and unruly, falling in waves down to the collar of his shirt. A shirt which was anything but pristine and his cravat was crooked too. Besides which, he wasn't even wearing a waistcoat! What kind of titled nobility went anywhere without a waistcoat? He looked more like a pirate than an Earl!

She was so busy gaping at him that she missed seeing the amusement flashing across his face.

"So I see," the Earl said.

Well he might be a rogue and a devil, but he looked like a severe and unhappy guardian to her. Cynthia recognized the features of his brothers in his face, but the Earl wasn't looking at her with playful amusement or gleeful hilarity; he looked just as angry as his mother often did. And not nearly as easy to ignore.

Still. Men often thought she was beautiful, over the years she'd learned they were much more likely to grant her leeway than women. Even her father had been more easily charmed than her mother. As she regained her composure, she didn't miss the way his eyes flicked down to her bosom. Cynthia had often found that beauty and a great deal of cleavage went a long way with men.

"My lord," she said prettily, batting her eyes and dipping down into the low curtsy that often grabbed men's attention.

Wesley, being such a favorite among the *ton*'s ladies, recognized her tactics immediately. In any other young beauty he might have admired her inspiration or been amused by her obvious ploy. But this was his ward and while he might enjoy his leisure, his rakish reputation was a relief from the responsibility plaguing him.

When it came to this young woman, responsibility was to be his byword. Not only did his personal sense of honor demand it, his mother would as well. He held

Cynthia's future in his hands; he was to shelter, succor and care for her until he could get her married off in a reasonable match (his mother wanted a good match, but he was willing to settle for a reasonable one, just to speed things along and get this blatant temptation out of his life). That was his duty as a guardian.

His hardening cock and roving eyes had obviously not heeded his intentions, but he could ignore his physical reaction.

Crossing his arms over his chest, he forced himself to turn away from her and look at Manfred. "I'll deal with my ward in my study. Get the household back in order now that she's been found. Make sure no one has disturbed my mother."

"Yes, my Lord," Manfred said with a little bow; his tone and demeanor much more respectful than it usually was when he was addressing Wesley. Obviously he meant to set a good example for Miss Cynthia Bryant on how one was supposed to behave with an Earl. Wesley barely glanced at her, although out of the corner of his eye he could see she was looking rather pouty and put out at being so deliberately ignored by him. He'd wager not many men were able to overlook her abundance of charms so easily, even if they'd wanted to.

Hell, it wasn't easy for him to do and he was one of the most practiced rakes of the *ton.* There was just something about her... the slightest hint of refreshing innocence to go with the devious sparkle in her eyes and innate sensuality. As if she truly didn't know where her words and actions might lead, but was willing to explore. An invitation for a knowing man to lead her down the path of wickedness.

Was she an innocent?

Normally he would have thought the answer an immediate no. His father's friend, Lord Harold Bryant, and his wife Susannah had been very conservative. No daughter of theirs would be allowed to behave in any kind of immoral or indecent manner. And he would have banked his mother against any young woman.

Obviously he would have been wrong on all counts. How could the staunchly upright Lord Bryant have sired this seductive, brazen hussy?

Still, he'd have to protect her as if she was completely innocent. If his mother had been aware of any stain to the girl's reputation then she would have included that information in one of her letters. Going by Cynthia's tactics in trying to deal with him, if she was still an innocent it was more luck than anything else. He was going to have to keep a close watch on her. Fortunately, as a rake himself, he knew all the tricks of the trade.

"My study," he said to her, rather grimly. "Now."

Turning on his heel, Wesley stalked down the hallway, not waiting to see if she followed. He needed privacy to question her and then to tan her bottom for upsetting the household in such a manner. If she didn't follow immediately then he'd just blister her pert little bottom even more. Damn well enjoy it too.

＊＊＊＊＊＊

Sighing, Cynthia trotted gamely after Lord Spencer, frowning down at her dress as she did so. She'd never been so easily dismissed by a man, especially not with her bosom so exposed. Lord Spencer had looked, but only for a moment and then he'd moved on to other things.

Maybe he was one of those men who preferred other dishes?

He certainly didn't seem the type though. Of course, she was only going by rumors about that type of man, as she hadn't knowingly met any, but they were said to

10

dress a great deal fancier than Lord Spencer was. The Earl looked as if he didn't care a fig for his appearance. Though she thought he might still be the most dashingly attractive man she'd ever seen, and his sartorial lack of effort did have a certain appeal.

Tall, shoulders as broad as a soldiers, and those pants hugged his legs tightly enough that, unless he was wearing some very clever pads, he had most superbly muscled legs she'd ever seen. Too bad he was apparently a stuffed shirt despite his roguish reputation and dress.

Once they'd entered his study, Lord Spencer didn't turn to look at her until he'd reached his desk.

"Close the door." Once she had, he nodded at the chair in front of his desk. It was a large, cushy armchair with broad arms. More than once she'd snuck into the study for a quiet place to read, on those rare occasions when she was in the mood. The chair was incredibly comfortable, not to mention welcoming.

From his position leaning against the desk it would also give him quite a view down into her cleavage. Cynthia smiled. Maybe he wasn't as immune to her as he appeared. That was a nice thought. Although he just scowled at her even more when he saw her smiling.

With another sigh, she moved across the room and settled down into the chair. Again his eyes flicked down into her bosom and then away before coming back to her face.

Humph.

"Explain yourself."

"Explain myself?" she asked rather wonderingly. How did one explain oneself? She was just... herself.

Lord Spencer glared at her. "Where were you, who were you with and why did you go?"

Oh, explain her actions. Nearly as difficult as explaining herself when it came right down to it. "I was out, with no one, because I was bored."

She'd found, over the years, it was best to keep things simple when she lied. The vaguer she was and the less she had to remember, the easier it was to stick to her story.

Unfortunately Lord Spencer just looked even angrier at her lack of real explanation. Quicker than a snake he had his hand around her arm and she found herself lifted out of the chair, and just as quickly yanked her back down so she was over his lap. Squealing, she threw her hands out in front of her, pressing them against the ground so she didn't slide right off of his thighs. An iron bar was placed across her back, holding her securely in place, and her skirts were thrown up, followed by a quick jerk of fabric that pulled down her drawers.

SMACK!

"OUCH! Stop that!" Outraged, Cynthia bucked, but it was completely useless as his hard palm came down on the other side of her buttocks to give her a matching handprint.

SLAP!

Fire alternated back and forth between her cheeks, no matter how hard she kicked or yelled. When she tried to reach back to cover her burning skin with her hands, the iron bar across her back moved only long enough to gather her wrists in his hands and hold them securely before returning to delivering the first spanking she'd had since before her parents had died.

Tears dripped down her nose to fall on the floor and she kicked out even harder. As if he'd been waiting for her to kick, Lord Spencer's leg somehow wrapped around her calves, holding them firmly in place so his thigh was in front of hers but his calf was behind hers.

And the relentless spanking continued.

"I'm sorry!" she wailed finally. "I'm sorry, I'm sorry!"

Several more blows fell before he stopped. Cynthia found herself hiccupping, her bottom feeling so swollen and hot that she itched to touch and rub it, but his long fingers were still wrapped around her wrists, restraining them. His hand settled on her bottom, making her skin feel like it was itchy, hot and tight.

"What are you sorry for, Miss Bryant?"

"I'm sorry for going out, I'm sorry I didn't tell anyone, I won't do it again!" She hiccupped again in her rush to get the words out.

"I certainly hope not, Miss Bryant, because if you do then I will be forced to do this again."

Cynthia howled as he began to rain down blows on her already sore bottom again, her body jerking as she cried out.

Once Wesley decided he'd imparted his message onto her bottom, which was glowing a nice, hot red, he finally let her up. His cock was throbbing from the effects of having her over his lap, his hand so close to her womanhood - which he hadn't been able to keep from noticing was dripping wet by the time her spanking was over - but he ignored that. Cynthia was crying outright as he lifted her off of his lap.

She was so overwhelmed she hadn't even noticed the hard bulge at the front of pants. Staring up at him through her tears, she couldn't even find it in herself to glare. She was too afraid doing so would put her back over his knee.

"From now on you will comport yourself in a manner befitting a young lady," he said sternly. "My mother has had to deal with your antics for long enough. Any more misbehavior and you'll find yourself back in this room over my knee or worse. Do you understand?"

"Yes, my Lord." Cynthia resisted the urge to rub her bottom in front of him, her hands clenched at her sides from the effort.

"Good. You may go."

It only took her a moment to pull up her drawers and then she practically ran from the room. Wesley grinned as he watched her swift flight. She might be a recalcitrant female, but he knew how to deal with those. The chit just needed a firm hand. Surely he could have her whipped into shape and married off within the next month or two and then she wouldn't be his burden anymore.

Trying to forget how delightfully wriggly she'd been against his body and the way her pussy had creamed as he'd punished her, Wesley moved behind his desk to go through the pile of papers he'd had set there for him. As he sat, he adjusted his cock to a more comfortable position. At least, as comfortable it was going to get until he could find a willing woman in Bath.

******

Humiliated and shockingly hot and aching between her legs, Cynthia fled to her room. That did not go at all the way she had expected. She was even more embarrassed when she saw more than one of the servants witnessing her flight and snickering.

How loud had she been when Lord Spencer spanked her? Had they heard her yelling? Begging?

When she finally reached the safety of her room, Cynthia slammed the door and locked it. It wasn't

14

unusual for her. Most of the servants knew to leave her alone if her door was locked, unless the Countess was looking for her. There were moments when a girl needed her privacy so she could do the naughty things she wasn't supposed to be doing.

Hurrying over to the mirror, Cynthia lifted up her skirts and dropped her drawers. Hissing at the sight confronting her, Cynthia gently touched the bright red skin with gentle fingertips and found it was hot to the touch.

"Ouch," she muttered under her breath.

Touching the swollen heat of her buttocks made the tingles between her legs even stronger and Cynthia nearly moaned. How could she be feeling *that* way when she'd just been spanked?

Maybe it was because of Lord Spencer himself. Cynthia wondered if his hands would be as rough touching her if he wasn't delivering a spanking.

Another swipe of her fingers over the heated flesh of her bottom and Cynthia couldn't take it anymore. She let her skirts drop and scrambled over to the bed. Lying on her back hurt, but lying on her side didn't give her the access she wanted and lying on her stomach made it too hard to move her hand.

With her skirts up around her waist again, Cynthia planted her feet into the bed and lifted her weight off of her poor bottom, arching her hips up so it hovered above the bed sheets. Reaching one hand into the low bodice of her dress, she squeezed her breast as her other hand immediately went to the forbidden area between her thighs.

This might be her very favorite "don't" in all the world, she thought as she began to stroke and fondle the soft folds she found there. They were already wet, soaked in fact, from her spanking. At least his Lordship hadn't known that little secret!

Cynthia moaned as her weight trembled, her thighs burning from the effort of holding her up, and her bottom came into contact with the bed for a moment. The discomfort and burning sensation reignited, but it felt almost good now that she was touching herself. Teasing the hard little bud amidst her folds, she gasped and moaned a little louder as a flash of pleasure sizzled through her.

Her hips began to move, letting some of her weight rest on her flaming bottom before lifting it again, the pain a sharp and intense counterpoint to the ecstasy she was creating for herself. Picturing herself back across Lord Spencer's knee, she began to fantasize a very different ending to her spanking. One where, once her bottom was red and burning, his hands would go wandering.

One would slide into her bodice and begin to play with and pinch her nipple, the other would seek out the hot, wet, folds between her legs and begin to stroke her. His fingers would rub her swollen little nubbin to hardness, tweaking and pulling at it, until she was bucking across his thighs for an entirely different reason.

Letting out a high cry, Cynthia spasmed, her legs giving way as the waves of rapture rushed through her. The pain of her bottom coming down hard on the mattress only fed into her fantasy and she writhed with the intensity of her climax, so much more satisfying than any she'd had before. Moaning, her fingers finally slowed, the little circles she was making growing more languid as she moaned and panted in satisfaction.

That had been... amazing. Better than she'd ever experienced before.

Obviously this was going to be something she needed to explore. Cynthia smiled. She was quite sure she could find plenty of reasons to earn a spanking. Then she winced as her bottom throbbed slightly painfully, and rolled onto her side. She'd earn another one eventually. Once this one didn't continue to sting so badly.

Chapter 2

Ensconced in his study, Wesley was steadily working his way through the correspondence with his estate managers. It was taking a bit longer than usual because his concentration wasn't what it normally was.

He'd spent the evening yesterday with his Mother and Cynthia, ostensibly to learn more about his ward. What he'd found was she was even more distracting than just physically. Sweet, overly curious, and naturally cheerful, he'd been shocked when she'd been flitting around the house only an hour after receiving her spanking, acting as if nothing had happened. In fact, she'd been sitting quite cheerfully, gossiping with two of the maids about the doings of their next door neighbors.

If it hadn't been for her slight wince when she sat down to dinner, he might have thought he'd imagined the entire episode. During dinner she chattered quite brazenly and familiarly with him, despite his disapproving scowls and his mother's attempts to divert the conversation. Cynthia treated him just as casually as if he was one of his brothers, whom she obviously got on well with. They'd apparently sent more letters to her than they had to him, or at least more descriptive ones, as she knew far more about their recent doings than he did.

When Manfred came to announce the arrival of Lord and Lady Hyde for a visit, Wesley welcomed the break with relief. "Set them up in the drawing room please, and let Mother know they're here."

Since he knew she'd declared herself "not-at-home" today, stating she wanted to rest before they went out that evening, he figured he had a good half hour before she would be ready to make an appearance. There was no way she would miss out on seeing Edwin and Nell, even if she wasn't at-home, but it would take her at least that long to clothe and ready herself for receiving visitors.

Which was all to the good because he had a proposal he wanted to put forth to his friends, before his mother joined them. Especially as she would probably bring Cynthia with her.

Putting his signature and seal on the document in front of him, Wesley stood and hastened to the drawing room.

******

Sitting in the elegantly decorated room of cool blues and grays, Eleanor should have felt calmed. Instead she watched her husband warily. Edwin had been incensed when he'd first declared they would join Wesley in Bath; yet since the original confrontation he'd acted as if nothing upsetting had happened. She'd had to endure a rather uncomfortable carriage ride to Bath, because of her red bottom, but she thought she'd have to endure uncomfortable dinners and silences with him as well.

Instead he was somehow warmer with her than he'd been in London. He'd always been passionate, from the very beginning of their marriage, but now his entire demeanor towards her was warm and affectionate at all times. Blatantly so, although in a decorous way when they were in public. Yesterday a few of their neighbors had stopped in to see who had rented the house and Edwin had danced his attendance on her, keeping her rather distracted with tiny touches and gestures of affection until she could barely keep her head on straight. It had her decidedly off balance because it wasn't at all what she had expected from him; he'd been so very angry with her and now he was... not.

At least not as far as she could tell and she found that confusing. Even though she'd been punished, she hadn't expected such an immediate reversion to typical behavior. Although, his behavior wasn't quite typical, truly.

It was *more*.

Now he was examining the room, while Eleanor sat rather stiffly on the ornate settee in the center of the room, and she examined him from the periphery of her vision. Handsome as sin, darkly commanding, the way he moved was almost a prowling as he inspected the room and the dainty, feminine decorations.

When he turned and caught her eye he grinned, looking almost like the boy she'd once known. "I wonder how comfortable Wesley feels in this room."

A small smile split her lips. Out of the three men who were best friends, Wesley, Edwin and her brother Hugh, Wesley had always been the most rambunctious and, as such, the most dangerous to the small glass collectibles his mother favored.

"One would hope he's outgrown his affection for hearing glass shatter," she replied. Their eyes sparkled in a moment of fellow feeling and memory.

"It was never an affection, just a tendency," said a deep voice from the doorway. Wesley stood, grinning at them as he shut the door behind him.

Eleanor laughed and stood as Edwin strode forward to greet their friend. Despite the fact Wesley had only been in his mother's house for a bare twenty four hours, Eleanor thought he looked rather harassed. She wondered if his mother or his wayward ward had done the harassing. Normally Wesley was the most easy-going of the three men, but his mouth had a rather pinched look as did his eyes.

They asked the obligatory questions about his mother, whom Wesley assured them would be joining them shortly.

"Actually, I have a favor I would ask of you, before my mother joins us. Ask of Nell, really," he said, looking at her. "My ward is..." His lips flattened and he looked almost censorious. Not a usual expression for him. "My ward has been more of a burden on my mother than I initially realized. I don't wish to hurt my mother's feelings by insinuating to her she can't handle Cynthia on her own, but I don't think some help would go amiss. I was hoping, as someone closer to Cynthia's age..."

"I might be able to influence her behavior?" Eleanor said, a little smile twisting her lips. "Are you sure you want to ask *me* for such a thing?"

She wondered, again, how much of her transgressions her husband had shared with his friends. Surely if Wesley knew how unbecoming some of her conduct had been then he couldn't think her a proper role model for his wild ward... on the other hand, she knew he must know some of it.

"Oh, you're slowly turning into quite a presentable young lady," he teased, dark eyes glinting with appreciation for her trepidation, as if he could read her thoughts.

Eleanor stuck her tongue out at him and then immediately pulled it back in as she felt her husband step up behind her. Fortunately he hadn't been able to see her face, and she knew Wesley wouldn't tell on her. The pinched look had disappeared from his eyes, which were full of amusement as they flicked back and forth between husband and wife. One of Edwin's hands came down on her shoulder, like a gentle caress.

"She's more than presentable," Edwin said warmly. "I'm sure Nell will be happy to help with Cynthia." Eleanor twisted her neck back to look up at him, surprised by the obvious and genuine affection in his voice, but even more so by the sound of approval in his tone. Considering the reasons for why they were both in Bath, and how infuriated he'd been by some of her recent antics over the past months, she was rather shocked to hear he thought she would be a suitable influence on a wild and misbehaving young woman.

She always thought he still saw her as a wild and misbehaving young woman. And, admittedly, she had certainly acted in ways which would support that belief.

******

The beautiful blonde woman was staring up at the very handsome man behind her. Cynthia couldn't quite see his expression, unfortunately they keyhole she was peering through didn't allow that. Or see her guardian's expression.

But she rather liked the look of the woman. She was very beautiful, for one, and the way she'd stuck her tongue out at Lord Spencer indicated she wasn't overly stuffy. Actually, Cynthia was quite surprised Lord Spencer hadn't reacted with anger at such impertinence, but he hadn't. That was one moment when she truly wished she could have seen his face.

With his friends he didn't seem to be nearly as stuffy as he'd appeared to her yesterday. He was much more relaxed, even teasing and amiable as he explained he'd like Eleanor take Cynthia under her wing and befriend her. Something which Cynthia certainly had no objection to. It would be nice to have a female friend around her age.

Especially a married one, as she surmised the beautiful blonde was. Cynthia had a multitude of questions she'd like to ask her, if she was truly someone who could become a bosom bow.

"Cynthia!" The Countess' aghast voice had Cynthia bolting upright, her lips forming the word 'damn' although she didn't voice the vulgarity aloud. It wasn't worth the lecture and fainting looks which followed. Turning, she tried to look properly chastened by the time she faced the Countess.

Looking as intimidatingly regal and elegant as ever, the Countess was dressed in a gown of dark blue cambric with burgundy trimmings accentuating her statuesque bearing and excellent style. One day Cynthia hoped to be as forbidding as the Countess, she thought it would be quite a bit of fun. But she didn't wilt under the woman's hawk-like glare, her own mother had perfected that look as well, and Cynthia had become quite immune to it in her younger years. It seemed to be a side effect of indulging in "don'ts." If she'd been affected by the condemning looks and punishments she received, Cynthia wouldn't have had half as much fun as she normally did.

Behind her the door was yanked open and Cynthia could feel the dark, brooding stare of her guardian on the back of her neck and she shivered, wondering if eavesdropping would garner her another spanking.

While that had been one of her goals, because she wanted to explore the new sensations it had aroused in her, she didn't want one *yet*. Her skin was still tender after the punishment she'd received the day before.

"Mother," he said in acknowledgment, stepping past Cynthia as if she wasn't there at all. She bristled at his indifference. Wesley offered the Countess his arm before turning back, his disapproving gaze landing on Cynthia. Her bottom tingled, as if in response. "Come in with us and behave."

The Countess looked a bit startled, possibly at his invitation or possibly at his manner towards Cynthia, but she didn't gainsay her son. For once, Cynthia felt like being obedient, mostly because she needed at least another good night's sleep before she was going to risk getting another spanking. Preferably more. And also because she wanted to meet the pretty blonde woman and see her guardian acting like a something other than a stuffed shirt.

Cynthia could behave when she felt she had good reason to.

When they entered the room, both the man and the woman came forward to greet the Countess. Cynthia hung back, studying them more closely now that her vision wasn't partially blocked by the keyhole. Up close the man, Lord Hyde, was even more impressive looking, with handsome chiseled features and arresting dark eyes. His own coloring was darker than Lord Spencer's, except for his skin which was much lighter, but that just made his hair and eyes even blacker by contrast.

The woman had a warm smile, sparkling blue eyes and the most amazing porcelain complexion. For once Cynthia was a bit jealous, and more than a little aware of the golden tint to her own skin which came from spending quite a bit of time outside without the protection of a bonnet or parasol. Eleanor, as the Countess called her, must be what people called a Diamond of the First Water. Something Cynthia had never aspired to be, but then she'd never felt so awkward in another woman's presence before. Normally she felt quite assured she was the most attractive woman in the room, but next to Eleanor's angelic hues, her own coloring seemed dark and earthy by contrast.

Once they'd greeted the Countess, Eleanor turned to Cynthia, glancing at Wesley in an obvious demand to be introduced. He sighed as if it pained him and Cynthia bit her tongue to keep from saying something tart.

"Edwin, Nell, this is my ward Miss Cynthia Bryant. Cynthia, this is Lord and Lady Hyde."

"But you must call me Eleanor," said the blonde woman, stepping forward to take both of Cynthia's hands to greet her. "There's no need to be so stuffy, Wesley, I'm sure we're all going to be good friends." Those sparkling blue eyes tipped with amusement towards Lord Spencer, before settling back on Cynthia, inviting her to share in Eleanor's amusement.

Despite the insecurities this beautiful woman had roused in Cynthia, she couldn't help but respond to her open,

24

friendly gaze. It had been a long time since any of the women she'd met had looked at her with anything other than disapproval or jealousy, she realized. Not that Eleanor needed to feel threatened by her; so perhaps there was a benefit to having such a beautiful friend.

"And you must call me Cynthia. I'm delighted to meet you. My Lord," she said, directing her gaze at Lord Hyde as she bobbed a quick curtsy. He studied her, looking at her so intently with those dark, brooding eyes that she reddened. The man had the kind of look that made a woman squirm, as if he could see every naughty thing she'd done and might do in the future. How did the bright and cheerful Eleanor deal with such a man?

Then again, he seemed the perfect friend for Lord Stuffy.

Cynthia's mouth almost gaped open when Eleanor turned back towards her husband and his gaze immediately softened, making him look far more approachable and almost gentle. The last time she'd seen a man look at a woman like that... it had been her father with her mother. Certainly none of the men she ever teased or flirted with looked at her quite that way. It caused a very curious ache in her chest.

"Let's sit down and I'll ring for some tea," said the Countess, smiling broadly. "Cynthia come sit by me. And you two must tell me everything about the wedding and the honeymoon, you did honeymoon didn't you?"

"Oh yes, we spent a wonderful month in Paris," Eleanor said as she settled her skirts around her, glancing up at Lord Hyde. The little smile he gave her, along with the look of almost adoration, made the little ache Cynthia was feeling give another twinge. Although as soon as his eyes turned away from his wife, his expression hardened again.

Then she was distracted as the Earl settled himself down on her other side, rather than on the chair where she'd expected him to sit. She was now firmly wedged between the two Spencers. While she knew the Countess wanted Cynthia there so she could keep an eye on her, she didn't know why the Earl sat so close to her as well. She was hardly going to misbehave right now - she had no desire to make a complete ninny of herself in front of either Lord or Lady Hyde. For one, Cynthia rather liked Eleanor already. For two, Lord Hyde didn't look the type to allow his wife to spend time with the likes of Cynthia if she was blatantly improper in front of him.

And Cynthia did rather want a friend near her age.

Besides, as a married lady, Eleanor probably knew all sorts of things Cynthia was curious about.

The Earl's thigh pressed against hers through her skirts, distracting her, but she couldn't move away without encroaching on the Countess' space. It was only then that she realized Eleanor had asked her a question.

Blushing, she forced herself to focus, wondering why she was so off-kilter. Surely it was the presence of guests, and not the attractive and surly man beside her.

******

Seeing the amusement in Edwin's eyes, Wesley wondered again why he hadn't sat down in the chair that had been left open for him. At first he'd told himself that he'd sat beside Cynthia in order to lessen the burden of watching over her from his mother. It was a well-known fact in the Spencer household that the Countess would keep whatever child she thought was most likely to misbehave close to her side. She was adept at knowing which one was up to mischief.

But now he was sitting here, his thigh pressed against Cynthia's through her skirts, and his eyes wandering to her fantastic bosom - no matter that it was currently decently covered - he knew he'd been lying to himself.

He'd wanted to sit next to her. To discompose her the way she discomposed him.

Once he'd realized she'd been listening at the keyhole, his hand had itched to spank her again. In fact, he'd found himself becoming aroused at the thought, despite the presence of Eleanor, Edwin and, most notably, his mother. Was it the temptation of forbidden fruit? Or was it the lush curves of the young woman in question?

Either way, he knew it was a temptation he wasn't going to be giving in to. He had to get the chit married off, and quickly. Maybe he'd seduce her afterwards, he mused, once she was no longer a (possible) innocent, no longer his responsibility and had become acceptable prey for seduction. Then he wondered if the reason he insisted on casting a shadow of doubt over her innocence was for his own sordid desires.

"Wesley are you listening?"

"Ah - no, sorry Mother, I was wool gathering." Years of practice kept him from actually blushing. Nothing like plotting the possible future seduction of your ward only to be caught out by your mother. Besides which, he was going to need to convince some poor sot to marry her first. There had to be at least a few unobjectionable men who would want his favor and be willing to overlook her wild ways - unobjectionable to his mother that was. He could think of a dozen fortune hunters off hand who would be happy to take on a wife like Cynthia as long as she came with a good dowry, especially considering her looks, but his mother would never stand for it.

"I was saying there's going to be a ball at the Assembly house on Thursday. As the Earl, you should be there." The glint in his mother's eye made Wesley feel a little uneasy. He assumed she wanted him there to keep an eye on Cynthia and to assist with her chaperoning duties, but something about the way she said it made him think there was more to the matter. And that

27

whatever the "more" was, it was something she thought he wouldn't like.

"You'll be going, won't you?" he asked, turning to Edwin and Nell. Bath tended to be dull as it was, but if he had to go then perhaps his friends would indulge him as well.

Eleanor glanced at Edwin, beseechingly. Good old Nell. He could always count on her to want to get out and have some fun. Edwin's eyes rolled upwards but he nodded his head.

"Yes, I'm sure Eleanor would enjoy an evening out." He smiled indulgently at her as she beamed at him. "I know how you love to dance."

"I'll save all my waltzes for you."

The Countess shook her head and tutted. "Scandalous." But she was smiling and there was no heat to her voice.

"Yes, we caused quite a bit of talk back in London," Edwin said unrepentantly. "I am unfashionably enamored of my wife." Eleanor's cheeks turn a bright pink as he reached out and took her hand. Wes thought his mother looked a bit wistful. Glancing down at Cynthia, she was watching the couple with a strange kind of fascination. He wondered what was going through the little minx's mind.

"Well I think it's lovely," Wesley's mother said firmly. "As long as you're not completely improper about it."

Eleanor cleared her throat, still looking quite pink and pleased. "Would you and Cynthia like to come for tea tomorrow afternoon? I would love to have some company."

"I'm having tea with the Dowager Duchess of Camden," the Countess said. Wesley actually felt Cynthia wilt beside him in disappointment and he coughed to cover a snicker. The Dowager Duchess was a right old bag, he couldn't imagine she had anything approving or complimentary to say to Cynthia. "I'm sure Cynthia would love to join you, however."

"Really?!" Cynthia perked right back up before slapping her hands over her mouth, as if afraid the reprieve would be snatched away if she questioned it. Wesley didn't bother to hold back his laughter this time. When she glared at him he only laughed harder. Edwin was chuckling as well.

"I'm sure Lady Hyde will be much more... ah... convivial company for you than my own set," the Countess said, shooting a dark look at both Wesley and Edwin. He grinned at her and then winked at Cynthia, who was pretending not to notice him. But her cheeks darkened even further when he winked. There was something delightfully refreshing about her uncensored reactions; amazing she'd managed to hold onto that trait when living with his mother. It also made teasing her quite a bit more enjoyable. "And it will be good for you to have some companionship of a proper young lady."

This time, Wesley and Edwin both manfully swallowed their laughter. While her husband might be working on her behavior, Wesley doubted Eleanor would ever be completely proper.

Chapter 3

London was lonely without Hugh's friends and family. Irene was making new connections as his wife and a future Countess, but she had no idea whether or not those connections were because of her new position or because she was liked for herself. Eleanor would have been able to help her, but now she was taken away to Bath with her husband; which made Irene fret as it had been all her fault Edwin and Hugh had learned about Eleanor's plans to leave town. While Hugh assured her that Edwin would never harm Eleanor, he'd looked so black and angry when he'd left.

Irene had sent a letter to Eleanor, apologizing profusely, but it took time for the mail to be delivered. And who knew if Eleanor would write her back? Perhaps she would be too angry.

Other than Eleanor, Alex would have been someone Irene could count on to steer her in the right direction, but she didn't want to upset the wonderful new revelations between her and Hugh. After all, she'd only just barely realized her love for Hugh was very different from her love for Alex; she worried any further contact with Alex might make Hugh doubt those revelations.

She'd much rather stay in every night than go out. It was a strain to be the perfect wife in Society, to make up to Hugh for her embarrassing lack of restraint when she'd thrown herself at Alex, and all the while wondering which smiles directed her way were sincere and which were not. Staying in with her husband and his wonderfully inventive and exciting activities in their bedroom was much more preferable. Unfortunately Hugh's title and responsibilities, and effectively her own, made that an impossibility.

Standing at the front window of their house, Irene stared out onto the street, watching people passing without really seeing them. Hugh had gone out for the afternoon to his club and she'd told him she was going to visit some friends. Except she'd stayed home instead. She couldn't wait until the Season was over and they could go back out to the country, back to Westingdon. That was really where their relationship had begun, where she'd started to learn the difference between girlish love and adoration for Alex and the real love and desire which had unfolded between her and Hugh.

Two men strode into view, obviously deeply involved in conversation, and Irene blinked. Was that Hugh and Alex? What were they doing together?

She glanced at the clock. It was only half an hour till dinner, which was when Hugh had told her he'd return home.

Backing away from the window, Irene stood in the middle of the drawing room, her hands shaking, and wondered what she should do. Catching a glimpse of herself in the gilded mirror over the mantle, she could see her green eyes looked overly large in her pale face, almost frightened.

She hadn't seen Alex since the awful night when she'd thrown herself at him, desperate to prove to herself that she loved him the way she'd always thought she did, only to discover that not only was she wrong, but Alex's feelings for her didn't go beyond brotherly. Although, in retrospect, that was a good thing because he hadn't aroused a single ounce of desire in her either. Love, adoration, and warmth, but not the stronger, wilder emotions her husband inspired. But, as if that hadn't been embarrassing enough, then Hugh had spanked her in front of Alex to demonstrate how to deal with a recalcitrant wife. The entire evening had been horribly embarrassing.

Scrubbing her hands over her suddenly burning face, Irene took a deep breath. Whether or not it had been humiliating, she also realized that night had been the beginning of a turning point in her marriage. She hadn't been quite ready to admit it until then, but she'd finally seen her delusions for what they were and, because of that night, she and Hugh had admitted their emotions to each other. Now Irene was happy, at least with her marriage, and felt secure in Hugh's love for her. But it was time to face Alex as well.

After all, she did miss her friend. And hadn't she just been thinking about how bereft she was of people she truly trusted?

How like her husband to make the first steps in mending the breach. If Hugh was bringing Alex to their home at this time of night, she assumed he had asked Alex to stay for dinner.

Masculine voices rang in the entrance hall and Irene gathered her courage. Being married to Hugh had bolstered her confidence in so many ways. When she'd first married Hugh, she would have faced whatever he wanted her to because he wanted her to. Now she faced uncomfortable situations because she had learned how to have strength for herself.

******

Seeing his wife coming to greet them, Hugh had to push down the automatic rush of possessiveness which rose up inside of him. He'd run into Lord Brooke at the club and they'd sat down to have a talk over a glass of brandy. Although it was obvious Alex didn't see Irene as anything other than a well-loved younger sister, and never had, Hugh couldn't help but remember the helpless jealousy he'd experienced upon realizing that Irene's feelings had been more conflicted. They'd worked through that between the two of them, but he knew she was lonely and missed her friend. Part of him wanted the two of them to never see each other again, but he knew that was unfair and unreasonable.

Besides, even if Irene hadn't cared whether or not she ever saw Alex again, Hugh knew it would be

32

unavoidable. He'd grown up with two best friends who were still his closest friends in the world, Edwin and Wesley, and Wesley had recently become quite attached to Alex. Also, with the lands from Irene's dowry, they were now neighbors in the country. There would be no avoiding him in the future, not with those kind of connections.

And, Hugh had to admit to himself, he did enjoy the man's company. He was extremely intelligent, had a sharp wit even though he never smiled, and never sat on his laurels. Unlike many of their peers, they didn't rest on their laurels and allow others to transact all their business. It was a trait Hugh shared with his other two friends and very much appreciated in Alex.

"Hello sweetheart," Hugh said, striding forward to greet Irene and also to lend her any support she might need. He knew his wife was not always comfortable in difficult social situations. Spanking her in front of Alex might have been a mistake, but he'd been so very angry that night and he'd wanted very much to prove to her that he wasn't a monster. Punishing her with Alex as an audience had demonstrated, in a way nothing else could have, that her childhood hero wasn't going to step in and save her from richly deserved discipline. But now he didn't want a permanent wedge between her and her closest friend from childhood either. Hopefully, by having dinner together tonight, they could start a new kind of friendship between the three of them. "I've asked Lord Brooke to dine with us tonight."

Lowering his lips to Irene, he gave her a chaste but intense kiss, and when he turned back to face Alex, it was with his arm firmly wrapped around his wife's waist. He didn't look at the other man's face but watched Irene's; she was so easy to read sometimes, her emotions clearly written across her beautiful face. Hope. Desire. Fear.

"That's wonderful," she said, leaning into Hugh as she looked up at Brooke, the hopefulness in her expression was almost heart-breaking. Hugh felt his jealousy melt away a little bit, replaced by warmth at her reaction. This had been the right thing to do. A tremulous smile crossed her lips. "We're happy to have you, Lord Brooke."

For a moment, tension hung in the air and then Alex smiled back at her. Hugh was struck by the same sense of awe he always had at seeing such an expression on the man's face, but he couldn't blame him. Refusing Irene at that moment would have been akin to kicking a puppy and he didn't think Brooke had it in him, no matter how hard he usually looked.

"I do hope you haven't forgotten my name, pet," Brooke murmured as he bowed to her. Strangely the endearment didn't bother Hugh at all. It's not as if it was a particularly romantic one.

"Alex," she said, relaxing under Hugh's arm. He rather liked the way she snuggled against him even as she and her childhood friend smoothed over their current awkwardness. "It's a pleasure to have you here with us."

✳✳✳✳✳✳

Dinner wasn't nearly as tense as Irene had originally feared. Hugh and Alex seemed to have come to their own kind of truce and as long as she didn't think about the fact that Alex had seen her being soundly spanked, or what a fool she'd been when she'd thrown herself at him, then she didn't feel anxious at all. It was almost like old times. And since neither of the gentlemen would ever be so crass as to make mention of her transgression, it was surprisingly easy to pretend like it had never happened.

As the two men talked about the current horseflesh being offered up at Tattersall's, with her occasional

34

input, Irene had the opportunity to really look at them side by side. They were such a study in contrasts, despite their many similarities. While they were both able Corinthians and enjoyed the country life outdoors more than town life, Hugh's mostly easygoing nature and ready laugh was in direct contrast to Alex's much more serious mien. They weren't light and darkness in the visual sense, like Hugh and Edwin were, but Hugh seemed like sunshine and Alex more like a void sucking in light.

It hurt to see her friend brought so low. No wonder she'd gotten her emotions all confused; she absolutely cared about Alex and she'd wanted to fix what was wrong for him. She'd wanted to be *his* sunshine and bring some light to his life and she'd thought she was the right woman for the job because she loved him and she could always make him smile. Now he didn't smile as easily at her and that was all her fault too.

She didn't quite know what to do, however, as she certainly didn't want to attempt anything that could be misconstrued by her husband. Hurting Hugh again in an attempt to help Alex was absolutely not acceptable to her. Not when things were starting to be so lovely between the two of them.

Although she had to admit she was at least partially motivated by the determination not to give her husband a reason to spank her again.

"Are you alright, darling?" Hugh asked, putting his hand atop hers.

Blinking, Irene refocused on the two gentlemen who meant more to her than anything else in the world, and realized she hadn't heard a single word they'd said for at least several minutes. "Oh yes... I'm sorry. What did you say?"

"I was telling Alex that after the Season we would be heading out to the estates, although we might stop by

Bath to see Wesley, Edwin and Eleanor. Perhaps he could join us." Hugh smiled at her and then Alex, warming her insides completely. It was so wonderful how Hugh trusted her and loved her, despite feeling she didn't truly deserve it yet. She hadn't earned it.

That was one benefit to being spanked; the moment her punishment was over she'd been forgiven. Unlike when she'd lived with her mother and anything she did wrong was brought up over and over again for weeks.

"As much as I appreciate the invitation, I'm not able to make any firm plans at this time," Alex said. "I've decided to reconcile with my wife. And I have no idea how long it might take or where I'll need to be at the end of the Season." Although his expression didn't change, Irene could see the weariness in his eyes.

Anger rose up inside of her. Not that she could claim to be the best wife to Hugh, and her plans had sounded alarmingly like the way Lady Grace lived her life, but she couldn't have any sympathy for the other woman when she'd obviously hurt Alex so. Humiliated him. Whenever he walked into a ballroom, whispers tittered around the room. He was a man whose wife had left him and brazenly flaunted her affairs without ever providing him with an heir.

While Irene was well aware she had thought of doing something similar, she had never planned to be indiscreet or to hurt Hugh – even though she almost had been. Lady Grace's behavior seemed almost designed to be as painful and humiliating as possible for her husband, on purpose. Irene just couldn't countenance it, especially because Alex was such a good man. She knew he would be a wonderful husband to Lady Grace if the woman would just allow it.

"Ah... do you think she'll be amenable to that?" Hugh asked, looking rather doubtful. He would have greater insight on Lady Grace than most, Irene realized, considering his sister's close friendship with the woman.

She didn't blame Eleanor for her loyalty to a friend, even if she thought her sister-in-law could have better taste in said friends.

"Highly doubtful," Alex said, shrugging his shoulder as if it didn't matter, but Irene could see it did. Just because he didn't show his emotions very well didn't mean he was without them; Grace's desertion and actions had hurt him and Irene had always been able to see that. "I wouldn't be surprised if she makes me grovel."

"How can you even countenance that?" Irene cried out, infuriated on his behalf. "She should be grateful for another chance to be your wife and to redeem her reputation."

"Perhaps, but if I ever want an heir then I must play by her rules."

It was on the tip of Irene's tongue that he should just divorce her, but she bit down before the words could escape her mouth. After all, she certainly didn't want Hugh to think she approved of something as shockingly scandalous as ending a marriage, not when they themselves were so newly-wed and she'd almost ruined their own relationship. Besides which, the indifferent pragmatism in Alex's voice rather took her aback.

Was that how he planned to broach the subject to Lady Grace?

"I hope that's not how you plan on approaching her," Hugh said, half-choking on a laugh as he echoed Irene's thought. He looked both fascinated and slightly horrified. "I can't imagine the lady appreciating your reasoning. Grace was always ah... quite romantic. Flowers or some other gesture might work better."

For the first time, Irene felt a small spurt of sympathy for Lady Grace; she couldn't understand Alex's reasoning either. If Alex didn't care for the woman, why did he want to use her as a brood mare? Because that's all it sounded like he wanted from her, an heir. Irene couldn't believe he had started out their marriage that way; although lately she had begun to question her perceptions of Alex, she'd never thought he would value a wife for nothing other than her ability to bear him an heir.

"I've sent her quite a number of flowers over the years," Alex muttered. "It doesn't seem to have made much of a difference."

"I'm sure you'll think of something. Myself, in such situations, I prefer the stick over the carrot."

Heat rose in Irene's cheeks; it was a very oblique reference to the spanking Alex had witnessed. At the time, he'd said he was thinking about using such tactics on his own wife. It had been shocking to know Alex didn't disapprove of such discipline, but despite his words that night she still couldn't quite believe he would ever do such a thing. Even to his wayward wife.

But then again, Irene had already proven to herself that she didn't know Alex the way she thought she had. She would have never thought he'd stand mildly by while any man, even her husband, spanked her.

And when she'd first married Hugh, if someone had asked, she would have never thought him capable of such a thing either. He claimed Edwin was also a strict disciplinarian to Eleanor, who had grown up with such punishments. It was all rather bewildering sometimes. But she couldn't deny there were certainly worse things than being spanked, and she had certainly deserved some kind of retribution for her actions. Hugh was fair. She was sure Alex would be too.

"I've been thinking about it," Alex said, although the shortness of his tone indicated he didn't want the conversation to go any further down that line of thinking.

Irene knew her friend, if he was even considering it than the outcome was a foregone conclusion. Alex was very decisive over the things he absolutely would not do. She wouldn't be surprised if he tried more conventional tactics first, but if Grace proved to be as stubborn as she had been over the past years, Irene had no doubt Alex would prove a strict disciplinarian. In her youth she wouldn't have been able to imagine it; now she saw that he had hardened and grown jaded.

To her mind, Lady Grace deserved a sound punishment, even if inwardly she winced with sympathy at the thought of a spanking.

******

Alone in their bedroom, later that night, Hugh indulged in his favorite routine - brushing Irene's long, red hair. The strands gleamed in the candlelight, sliding against his palm like silk. She always sat patiently, watching him in the mirror, and allowing him to indulge for as long as he wanted. The way her eyelids would flutter, half-closed, indicated her own pleasure in the act.

"Stand up," he said suddenly, realizing he'd stopped brushing and was watching the rise and fall of her breasts under the thin, silk night rail she was wearing.

No matter she never slept in a garment, she always insisted on putting one on before bedtime. It was fast becoming one of Hugh's fantasies to have his wife walking around naked before him, covered in nothing but her shining hair, as he prepared for bed.

Her eyes fluttered all the way open in surprise, but she stood without protest, a small smile lighting up her face. Hugh loved seeing the flashes of her passionate sensuality through the modesty and propriety that had been hammered into her over the years.

Tilting her head back at him, her smile grew. "Thank you so much for bringing Alex here tonight."

While Alex was certainly not something Hugh particularly wanted to discuss right now, he did enjoy the way Irene was looking up at him. As if he'd done something noble and heroic. Which made it all worth it.

"I assumed we'd be seeing more of him in the future anyway, and I didn't want things to be awkward," he murmured as he stroked his fingers along the silk covering her shoulder, tugging it gently downward to reveal her creamy skin.

"You're an incredibly generous man," she said solemnly, placing her hands on his chest and looking up at him earnestly. Those guileless green eyes were completely open to him, something he savored as it had only happened recently, after everything had happened with Alex. Until then he hadn't realized how much Irene had kept parts of herself hidden to him; since then she'd been his, all his and he reveled in it. "I don't deserve you."

"I heartily disagree, Lady Stanley," he said, lowering his mouth to hers for a kiss.

It was evident to Hugh she still felt a great deal of guilt over her actions a few weeks past, as well as trying to run from him afterwards. While he understood she hadn't liked being spanked, at all, it had certainly brought about a pleasing change in behavior. Hugh had enjoyed spanking her much more than he thought he would, although he didn't feel a pressing need to indulge unless she truly deserved it.

Just Irene, warm and wet and eager, was all he needed to be perfectly satisfied in his marital bed.

She welcomed his tongue into her mouth, her body pressing against his so he could feel her rounded breasts flattening against his chest. Normally she wasn't quite so demonstrative right away; apparently good deeds came with rewards. Hugh wasn't going to complain.

In fact it was all he could do to keep himself from ripping off both of their clothes and having her then and there on her dressing table. But he managed the slow journey across the bedroom, leaving a trail of his clothing along the way, and allowing her to keep on her nightgown until they reached the bed. Then he stripped the garment off so he could enjoy the dancing candlelight over her body. He was quite sure Irene got a secret thrill out of being exposed by him and never knowing when he was going to undress her. Overcoming her reluctance, heating her body to the point where she stopped caring about propriety, was always a most enjoyable endeavor.

"Onto the bed," he ordered huskily, enjoying her hot blush as she scampered to the middle of the mattress, her hands hovering uncertainly above her body. Irene's first instinct once she was unclothed, unless he was touching her, was to cover herself again. Which, of course, only made him want her more. "Spread your legs."

"Oh Hugh..." she huffed, covering her face to hide her mortification as she let her legs fall open a few inches.

Laughing, Hugh grasped her by her ankles and spread them wider as she squealed in surprise. Immediately her hands came down from her face, hiding her copper-covered mound from his sight. Seeing her slim fingers laid across those coppery curls and swollen pink lips inflamed Hugh even further.

"That's it, sweetheart," he murmured, covering her hand with his own and pressing her fingers into the dewy petals of her womanhood. "I've been aching to see you touch yourself."

Unsurprisingly, Irene gasped and tried to tug her hand away, but Hugh just pressed it in more firmly, watching as he forced her to massage herself. "Hugh... stop! It's... I shouldn't... it's indecent!"

"It's delightful," he countered, feeling the wetness spread between her fingers and begin to slicken his own. The head of his cock brushed against her thigh as her legs moved fitfully, trying to close and hide her private areas from his view. Not that he was having going to allow her to get away with hiding. His body was firmly wedged in such a way she wouldn't be able to close her legs unless he allowed her - and he certainly wasn't going to do that. "You have no idea how enticing you look, with your hand between your legs, touching your quim... ."

Leaning forward, he lowered his mouth to her nipple, unrelentingly pressing her fingers into her core as he sucked the taut, pink tip into his mouth. Both rosy nips were tightly budded, indicating her increased arousal as did the flowing wetness now coating both of their fingers. Whimpering, Irene arched her back, thrusting her breasts up towards his mouth as her hips moved convulsively.

Irene groaned as the wanton desires running rampant through her body shredded away at her self-control. While she enjoyed the fact that Hugh was always willing to show her whatever she was curious about, every time she thought he had shown her everything he possibly could, he would surprise her with something new. He'd practically growled when he'd seen her hand stroking between her legs, even though she wasn't being given a choice about it.

She felt incredibly embarrassed about touching herself in such an indecent way, but she also recognized Hugh truly did enjoy seeing her do so. Although sometimes she wondered if part of his enjoyment came from her shock and initial reluctance. She had to admit, some secret part of her thrilled with excitement when her husband pushed her past the boundaries she set for herself... she especially enjoyed challenging him and making him push. His impatience with her night rails always amused her, even as it aroused her, when he would endeavor to convince her to leave any kind of garment off before bed. Still, the thought of walking before him, completely and brazenly nude, took more courage that she had.

It was easier to wear the night rail, cover herself, and have Hugh show his interest, rather than exposing herself in such a way.

The wetness at her fingertips grew as Hugh continued to lavish affection on her nipples, still forcing her to stroke her folds. When he finally shifted, pulling her hand away, her sensitive lips felt swollen and hot, ready for his cock. She gasped when he pulled her hand to his mouth, deliberately sucking each of her honey soaked fingers between his lips and cleaning them with his tongue as he stared directly into her eyes. The way his tongue traveled along her slender fingers, the insistent suckling, seemed to have a direct route to her core, which blossomed with arousal at the completely decadent act.

Releasing her fingers, damp from his ministrations, he lowered his mouth to hers and shared the taste of her sweetness, her musk. The smell of her arousal filled her nose, the taste lingered in her mouth, and she moaned at the forbidden eroticism of it.

The blunt head of Hugh's cock nudged against her and she widened her legs further, welcoming him into her body. They both groaned as he pressed and slid inwards, stretching her open. The heat of her channel seared him, pulled at him, the slick wetness allowing him to easily breach the entrance of her body and fully embed himself within her.

Claiming her lips again, their tongues danced as he flexed his spine and began to thrust, slowly and steadily, as she wrapped her legs around the backs of his thighs. As much as Irene might try to pull him into her, deeper, faster, he was far stronger and amused himself by taking his time, driving her completely, wantonly wild in his arms. Her nails dug in, body straining and arching beneath him, as she rocked upwards, seeking her culmination and unable to reach it as his weight held her down and forced her to his slower rhythm.

"Please Hugh... oh please...." Irene begged, her lips peppering kisses across his tensed lower jaw as he speared her with another controlled thrust. "I want... I need..."

"What? What do you need, darling?" he asked, his voice rough with the effort of retreating and then slowly sinking back into her while she pleaded with him. He had stripped away her manners, her propriety, and turned her into a creature of sensual desire... it was fast becoming his favorite pastime in fact. There was nothing more satisfying to him than making Irene wild with want, to hear her sweetly begging him for release.

"Harder... oh God... Hugh... faster!"

The entreaties flew from her lips, followed by cries of pleasure as she tightened around him, her tight walls spasming as her ecstasy peaked. Hugh groaned, his hips pounding furiously between her legs, relinquishing the reins on his self-control and let his body fly free. She was hot, wet, tight, and rippling around him as he plowed her, ravaged her, and she clutched at him as she shrieked with almost painful pleasure from the sudden rough stimulation.

When he buried himself inside of her completely, his cock swelling, he deliberately rubbed his groin against her sensitive folds in a circular motion, making her cry out and tighten as her swollen clit was caught between their bodies. Her pussy milked him, sucking as his cock until he burst inside of her, hot jets of seed spurting and filling her.

His breathing ragged, he slumped over her, listening to her soft moaning breaths as she quivered and stilled beneath him.

Once they had caught their breath and rearranged themselves to their usual sleeping position - Irene curled up against him, her soft bottom pressing against his groin - Hugh found his thoughts didn't want to quiet. Irene's soft, even breathing showed she'd fallen asleep easily enough, but all he could think about was his friends.

He wondered what Wesley would think of Alex's decision to reconnect with Grace. Even if it didn't happen right away, Wesley would again be the odd man out when it came to marriage. Hugh knew Wesley had felt as though he'd grown out of touch with Hugh and Edwin, especially on the advent of their weddings, and thought he had found a kindred spirit in Alex. How would Wesley feel once he finally got his ward off his hands and returned to his usual life?

Chapter 4

Cynthia gave a start of surprise when she walked into the dining room for breakfast and found Lord Spencer seated there, reading a newspaper. The Countess rarely took breakfast outside of her own room, but Cynthia hated being cooped up in one small space for any length of time, so the staff was used to serving her breakfast downstairs. What she wasn't used to, was sharing the space.

To her further surprise, as she moved towards her seat, Lord Spencer put down his paper and got to his feet, according her the respect she was due as a lady. She just hadn't really thought he saw her as such. How could he spank her, lecture her, and otherwise act as if he didn't think she was capable of propriety (although she certainly was, when she was in the mood to be), and then treat her like a lady over breakfast? Yesterday he'd treated her as more of a nuisance than anything else.

"Good morning," he said briskly, gesturing her to take the seat by his side.

It wasn't right that a man should look so good first thing in the morning. So rakish. And yet he was such a stuffy prig with her.

"Good morning," she said, determined to be amiable. It was too early to try for a spanking, even if her bottom was feeling much recovered. Besides, he might decide on some other punishment, like retracting permission to have tea with Eleanor that afternoon. And Cynthia very much wanted to have tea with the friendly woman. Especially since Eleanor seemed to know the Earl very well and he'd seemed to act quite differently around her and her husband, Lord Hyde. She found herself highly curious about the Earl, who seemed to be a mass of contradictions.

His brothers had both described him with the awe and reverence of young men looking up to an older brother of almost heroic proportions. Not only had he thwarted their father's orders, he'd made himself rich on his own merit, he was an acknowledged Corinthian, and a rakish seducer of ladies. Towards his mother he'd behaved like the perfect gentleman, as well as being almost protective. Eleanor and Edwin had brought out what seemed like a more playful side. And apparently all Cynthia engendered was stuffy disapproval.

To her annoyance, he apparently considered the morning civilities over with, and he seated himself back beside her and picked up his newspaper again, just as one of the footmen came in with her breakfast of sausages, eggs and fruit. Scowling at the black and white print, Cynthia wondered if she dared interrupt his reading.

Deciding she'd rather go to tea with Eleanor than prick Lord Stuffed-Shirt, she sat in uncharacteristic silence, picking at her food and dreaming about the upcoming Assembly on Thursday. It would be an opportunity to observe the Earl in a new setting, one with flirtatious ladies. Would he act differently there? She wondered if Mr. Carter would be there... she'd certainly enjoy learning a bit more about men and women. Perhaps, if they found a sufficiently private space, she would allow him to touch him between her legs.

Her mind drifted, fantasizing about the possibilities. Maybe not with Mr. Carter... maybe with a taller, stronger, more forceful man. What would it be like if the Earl caught her and spanked her again? And then maybe his fingers would drift down...

******

Practically cowering behind his newspaper, Wesley gritted his teeth as his ward let out a soft sigh that was completely inappropriate to the breakfast table. He hadn't been able to concentrate on the words in front of him since the moment she'd joined him. A habitually early riser, despite often staying up into the later hours of the night, he'd been warned that Miss Bryant often took her breakfast in the dining room rather than in her own room. For some reason he hadn't been able to resist the temptation of planting himself in a seat, long after he'd finished his meal.

It was almost worth it.

Cynthia was softer in the morning, her sensuality transformed from a blatant siren into something more subtle, more gently appealing. He could all too easily imagine her rising, rumpled and warm, from her sheets. Hell, he could all too easily imagine her all rumpled and warm between *his* sheets. She'd be perfect mistress material if she wasn't both an innocent and his ward.

Another soft sigh of pleasure had him gritting his teeth and he peeked over the top edge of his newspaper to find out what in the bloody hell the woman was making those sounds for.

Strawberries. She had a ripe, red strawberry pressed to her lips, staining the pink bow a darker red and making his cock quite suddenly stand to attention as her tongue flicked out to capture some of the juices spilling over her pouting lower lip. The almost dreamy look on her face, the warm flush in her cheeks, and the way her soft pink day dress clung to her ample curves only exacerbated his situation.

"What do you like to do?" he asked, putting the newspaper down almost violently on the table. Cynthia jumped, eyeing him warily as she popped the rest of the strawberry between those incredibly luscious lips.

"Excuse me?" she asked, once she had swallowed. Her amber eyes were glowing faintly in the sunlight trickling in through the windows, giving them an almost golden cast. "What do you mean?"

"What do you like to do?" he repeated, waving his hand through the air expansively. "Ride? Watercolors?

48

Gardens?" The sooner he could get her married off to an appropriate gentleman and take temptation away from under his roof, so he could return to his usual pursuits of business, his friendships and seducing socially acceptable ladies - the bored matrons of the *ton*, the better. He could find out some of Cynthia's interests, look over the field of gentleman available in Bath at the Assembly on Thursday and find her an amenable husband.

Perhaps amenable enough that once she'd popped out an heir or two, she'd be yet another bored matron he could seduce.

Strangely, the idea didn't appeal as much as it had the day before, but he attributed the restlessness he felt to impatience. After all, what man wanted to wait a few years to realize a fantasy? Even a fantasy that had been in existence for only a few days?

"I like to ride," she said, looking at him as though he was an animal at the zoo whose behavior she was trying to discern. He supposed he had spoken a little abruptly. "And I'm fond of the pianoforte. But I rather hate musicales. It's a tragedy how many of the *ton* have no talent, and most of them don't seem to realize it." He couldn't gainsay her on that, since he religiously avoided all musicales, which were little more than events designed to show off young ladies' in the Marriage Mart's musical attributes. For someone who truly appreciated music, those evenings were often torturous.

"Theater? Opera?"

"I've never been," she replied, rather wistfully.

That seemed almost a crime. A woman as stunning as Cynthia deserved to be one of the adornments in an opera box; he could imagine her in a low cut evening dress, dripping sparkling jewels - yellow topaz to bring out the gold in her eyes, breathlessly listening to a passionate aria. He'd have to see which of the men currently in Bath enjoyed such outings, there must be some, although the vast majority of that kind would be in London for the end of the current Season.

For a moment he wondered why his mother hadn't brought Cynthia to London, instead of Bath, and then he remembered the way in which he'd met Cynthia and how his mother had looked when he'd first arrived. No, Cynthia was far too wild for his mother to adequately deal with in a city like London when it was filled with all sorts of unsavory gentlemen who would be only too pleased with Cynthia's looks and lack of decorum. If she'd appeared in some ballroom, without him knowing who she was, the saints only knew what his reaction would have been.

"Very good," he said, distractedly. Cynthia gave him another confused look as he stood and left the table, but he didn't notice. He was too busy concentrating on running from temptation and the strange urge to stay and enjoy her company. It was time to retreat.

******

The house Lord and Lady Hyde in was in an equally fashionable part of Bath as the Countess' residence, although the decor showed it to be a house to let, unlike the Countess' house which was obviously a home. Still, it was quite beautiful and Cynthia found herself very quickly relaxed as she chatted with Eleanor, who seemed to be just as interested in Cynthia as Cynthia was in her. Today the blonde was dressed quite fashionably in a blue and cream damask that brought out the bright color of her eyes and enhanced the golden blonde of her hair, the stylish cut making the most of her rather striking figure.

In contrast, Cynthia was wearing a fashionably cut dark pink dress, but much less modestly than Lady Hyde's. She'd managed to get her own way on most of her dresses when she and the Countess had visited the modiste, and it wasn't until she sat next to Eleanor that she felt tawdry in comparison. But Eleanor didn't seem to think so, she barely paid attention to what Cynthia was wearing, she was much more interested in questioning her about Lord Spencer and the state of the household.

"He's not generally so stuffy," she assured Cynthia, her blue eyes sparkling with amusement. "It was quite entertaining seeing him performing as a proper gentleman yesterday. I've never seen him act quite like that before."

"I think it's me," Cynthia said truthfully. "He seemed very different from when he was speaking with just you and Lord Hyde... I mean..." Her cheeks flushed darkly to match her dress as she realized what she had just revealed. Fortunately Lady Hyde wasn't upset, she laughed in genuine amusement.

"Were you listening at the keyhole?"

"Ah... yes." Giving the other woman a sheepish look, Cynthia shrugged her shoulders. Normally she wasn't so loose-tongued, but Eleanor made her feel comfortable in a way she'd never experienced before; it was just so easy to talk to her. "I was curious about the Earl, he acts so differently around me than his brothers described."

"The Earl..." Eleanor repeated, as if tasting the words and debating whether or not she found them to her liking. "It's so hard to think of him like that... We grew up together. My brother Hugh, Edwin and Wesley. Out of all of them, Wesley's changed the least I think. At least, I thought that until I saw how stuffy he was being yesterday." She laughed again. "He was certainly playing the Earl in front of you. I wonder why."

The intelligence in those bright, searching blue eyes belied the old adage that beauty came without brains. Not that Cynthia had ever subscribed to the belief anyway, since she knew very well she was considered beautiful and she had never thought of herself as anything but rather clever.

"We ah... may not have had the best introduction." Unable to help it, Cynthia giggled conspiratorially, leaning in to tell Eleanor about running into Wesley in the street. Under the other woman's excited urgings, she even told her about Mr. Carter, at which point Eleanor's face grew more solemn.

"I've heard of him..." she murmured, sitting up straight with a rather worried expression. "He doesn't have a very good reputation."

"The Countess told me," Cynthia said with a shrug. "But he's never done more than kiss me. And a bit of... touching... above my waist," she added hastily, seeing Eleanor's shocked expression. "It's just... it's so very exciting."

"I can imagine," Eleanor said, a little smile of fellow feeling crossing her face before she turned serious again. "But, it's so much better to have that excitement with someone who truly cares about you: Someone whom you can trust."

It was true putting off Mr. Carter was sometimes tiresome, and the other gentlemen Cynthia had kissed, from further importunities. Of course, that was half the fun, letting them convince or seduce her into going just a bit farther. But so far she hadn't met any man she could truly lose her head to, not the way she read about in novels or heard whispered about from the maids. Perhaps trust was the missing ingredient? After all, if she trusted a man, then she wouldn't feel the need to constantly keep an eye on where his hands were going.

"And Lord Hyde? He cares about you? You find this... excitement with him?"

Lady Hyde blushed and hesitated.

"I'm sorry, I know it's personal..." Cynthia put on her wounded bird look. "It's just that I don't have anyone else to ask. I certainly can't ask the Countess, she'd probably faint."

The look Eleanor gave her said she didn't buy Cynthia's false despair at all, but there was no denying she couldn't ask the Countess such questions. "He does. I'm fairly certain he does." A faint flush grew in her cheeks. "And I trust him, I always have, since I was a girl. Before we married, I thought to find a man... I thought my ideal husband would be very different from him. But now I can't imagine being married to anyone else. I wouldn't want to be."

"And... and what do you do with him?" Cynthia asked, her insides curdling with excitement. She'd never spoken to anyone with the warm, wistful expression Eleanor had now. Someone who was willing to explain some of the intricacies between a man and a woman with her. All the Countess would tell her was what she shouldn't do, and while disobeying had led to some fascinating discoveries, there was quite a bit Cynthia was curious about, but which she wanted some more information on before exploring on her own. "Does he touch you on your quim? Men are always wanting to touch me there... it feels wonderful when I do it on my own, but what would I do if I got with child?"

"Good God..." Eleanor stared at her and Cynthia shrank into herself, suddenly worried she'd ruined their friendship by saying too much. What would Eleanor think of her now? Would she disapprove and pull away? Cynthia waited on tenterhooks, horribly afraid now that she'd exposed herself. She didn't think she could bear it if Eleanor rejected her now. The other woman's lips closed and then twitched in something like amusement and Cynthia found she could suddenly breathe a little easier. "This is really... these are things which should be discussed before your wedding night. And you absolutely should not let any gentlemen touch your... your quim. You've ah... you've touched it yourself?"

"Oh yes," Cynthia said cheerfully, reassured that Eleanor was not going to boot her from the drawing room. "Mother told me not to, you see. And it's quite lovely. I've thought about letting a gentleman touch me there, to see if it's different, but I don't want to get with child."

"That won't, but you shouldn't let them touch you there anyway. Once they do they might try to go further, and if they put their... um, their rod into your quim then you *will* get with child," Eleanor said rather sternly.

"Their rod?"

Eleanor blushed and gestured to her groin area. "Men have a... a rod where a woman has a quim."

"Oh, you mean a cock."

This time Eleanor burst out laughing, covering her mouth with her hands as Cynthia stared at her, slightly confused. The amusement was contagious though, and she found herself smiling. It was a rather absurd conversation, as well as wonderfully revealing. And she'd learned a new word.

"You are the most... confusing mix of innocence and too much knowledge," Eleanor said when her giggles finally subsided, although she was still smiling rather widely. "It's bound to get you into trouble. How do you know what a cock is?"

"Mr. Carter told me when I asked what was pressing against me so hard when we kissed."

"Good grief," Eleanor said, rolling her eyes. "He sounds like a complete scoundrel, he shouldn't have said that at all. The word is rather ah... crude. You really shouldn't allow him to touch you though, even if it won't get you with child. I know the Countess has asked Wesley to find you a husband, and once he has then you can explore to your heart's content."

"What about my mouth? Will that get me with child?"

"Your *mouth?*"

Cynthia found herself enjoying shocking Eleanor. There was a quality of delight, as much as some disapproval, in the other woman's reactions. And she didn't condemn Cynthia, or tell her absolutely not to do something - Eleanor was obviously intelligent enough to realize that the word 'don't' had a rather motivating effect on Cynthia, somehow "shouldn't" didn't engender quite the same response - but she explained things in such a manner to make Cynthia think more about what she was doing. It was also exciting to know she knew a few more things than a properly married lady did.

"Yes, Mr. Carter suggested I might put his co- ah... rod, into my mouth and he would find that quite pleasurable."

To her delight, Eleanor looked very much struck by the notion. "Why... I have no idea."

"Better not risk it then," Cynthia said musingly.

"Better not risk anything at all with Mr. Carter," Eleanor observed. "Unless you think you might want to marry him? Wesley absolutely won't allow you to be ruined on his watch, but Mr. Carter doesn't sound look good husband material."

"No, I suppose not." Cynthia sighed. "But he is a very good kisser."

"I'm sure if you do have a preference, Wesley would be reasonable. He was always stubborn, but very considerate."

Smiling, Cynthia allowed Eleanor to turn the subject back to the Earl of Spencer. After all, she wasn't loathe to hear more about her intriguingly confusing guardian, especially from someone who'd known him as long as Eleanor had and could provide so much insight. Besides, when it came to relations between men and

55

women, Eleanor's answers to her questions had already given her plenty to think on.

******

That evening Eleanor and Edwin dined with friends of their parents, Lord and Lady Montgomery and a small assembly of their guests. Since the Season was coming to an end in London there were some younger guests who were closer to Eleanor and Edwin's age. Eleanor had noticed that, other than Cynthia, Bath was quite bereft of anyone whom could be considered her or Edwin's "crowd." In some ways, that was a relief, because there was also less competition for her husband's attention and for hers.

She hadn't realized, until they'd left the ballrooms of London, how much of a strain it was for both of them to be constantly importuned by others. There were always women hovering around Edwin, and Eleanor realized, with his reputation, more than one of them probably had rather intimate knowledge of her husband. But by the same token, there were always men hovering around Eleanor, disappointed they hadn't seen her before Edwin had snapped her up, and now wondering if she might be amenable to some intimacies.

It had only been their stalwart attention to each other that had deflected the others, but now they could relax and enjoy themselves in this very different company. Which gave Eleanor some time to think and ponder other things, such as some of the revelations she'd had during her afternoon with Cynthia.

While Eleanor knew she'd been considered headstrong and some of her actions, especially at her coming out ball, would have been seen as brazen, she had nothing on Cynthia. It was a good thing they weren't in London or the girl's reputation would probably already be shredded. For her part, Eleanor didn't see anything particularly wrong with Cynthia wanting to know the same things Eleanor had wanted to know before she'd married Edwin. So she'd shared what she could with the young woman.

But Cynthia had had a few things to share with Eleanor too.

Such as the very astonishing idea of taking Edwin's cock into her mouth. He'd done the reverse to her, but somehow it had never occurred to her Edwin might enjoy it as well. After all, he was so very dictatorial, so very demanding in their love making, she assumed he would initiate anything he desired.

What would it be like to surprise him with something pleasurable?

She rather liked the idea.

In the past few days their relationship felt as though it had done more than relax, away from the bustle of London, it felt as though it had become something softer, sweeter. Although she didn't doubt he would still spank the dickens out of her if she were to misbehave. But honestly, Eleanor didn't feel like misbehaving as much. She was too busy trying to get her husband to admit his feelings for her, because she was becoming more and more hopeful they existed even if he didn't say so.

Perhaps surprising him with something new and different would also motivate a new verbal admission from him. At the very least, it would be fascinating to see his reaction when she wanted to take control. Would he let her?

"Nell, your mind is wandering," Edwin murmured, his finger stroking lightly down the back of her neck and making her shiver. She very nearly glared at him, right in front of Lady Montgomery, who was watching their amusement with interaction.

"I'm sorry Lady Montgomery," she said instead. "What did you say?"

"I was just declaring how glad your mother must be, having both you and Hugh make such brilliant matches. And your father as well, I know he's hated the necessity of spending so much time apart from your mother, but she really cannot tolerate London for any length of time."

"Yes, I don't believe I've ever seen her happier," said Eleanor, smiling. "Although I don't think she realized Lord Hyde would come up to scratch quite so quickly." That was a little nudge at Edwin. Even though she didn't throw any larger temper tantrums, hadn't since he'd caught her trying to leave London without him, she couldn't help but twit him a little. It was just part of her personality. And for the most part he didn't seem to mind too much. His fingers exerted just the slightest bit more pressure on the back of her neck, a warning. It made her skin tingle.

To her surprise, Lady Montgomery waved her hand dismissively. "Pish. Of course he came up to scratch immediately." The older woman smiled at both of them, her sharp eyes piercing. "It's obvious you'd be a Diamond of the First Water given a full Season, and with your antecedents and dowry, the competition would be fierce. I can't imagine an intelligent man letting any time waste, especially not one that's practically been waiting for you to step onto the Marriage Mart."

Eleanor gaped. "Waiting for me?"

Beside her, she could feel Edwin stiffen. She didn't dare look at his face.

"The two of you were inseparable as children. It was obvious to all of us who knew both of you that it was only a matter of time," Lady Montgomery said, smiling benignly.

That was a new viewpoint, one Eleanor had never considered before. She rather liked the idea of Edwin waiting for her. The only question was, was Lady Montgomery correct? Eleanor finally snuck a look at Edwin's face, but his expression was blandly impassive.

Maybe she could ask him about it later. She'd found it easier to coax tender words and memories from him while they were in bed. It was all part of her latest plan to get him to confess his feelings for her. Because she wanted a marriage based on love, and when she'd first wed Edwin she didn't know if he had those feelings for her. Indeed, she'd thought it was clear that he didn't, although she had fallen in love with him far too quickly for comfort.

While he hadn't yet said the words, many of his actions seemed to indicate something deeper than the affection of a childhood friend. But she wanted the words, the acknowledgment... the security. And she was determined to get them. In fact, the more days which passed without the declaration she so desired, the less certain she was of her perceptions.

******

Waving off his valet, Edwin finished shucking off the rest of his clothes by himself and strode into the bedroom. Eleanor had gone to bed about an hour before him, as he'd had a few matters to attend to when they'd returned home from the Montgomery's dinner. Hopefully she was still awake, not that waking her up for his amorous desires was a chore, but he always did feel a little guilty about disrupting her slumber. Even if he did enjoy it when she was all soft and languid, an entirely different Eleanor than the rest of the world ever got to see.

Fortunately, she was still awake, sitting up in bed reading a book and wearing a gossamer thin nightgown that clung to her curves. The faintest blush of her nipples was visible through the material in the flickering candlelight. Edwin grinned and strode forward, his erection hard and ready against his belly. It had been that way since he'd begun undressing, anticipating joining his wife in their bed.

Eleanor sat up, setting her book to the side as her lips curved in a small, welcoming smile. There was something to be said about a passionately inclined Eleanor, although he had to admit, he did also enjoy the chase and seduction when she was being reluctant as well. He adored Eleanor in all her moods, even the bad ones.

"Aren't you a pretty picture, waiting for me in the candlelight," he murmured, stalking closer. He could feel his blood rising as she waited patiently for him, excitement kindling on her face and in those sparkling blue eyes. Beneath the folds of her night rail, her nipples were hardening into little buds that poked out at him, begging for attention.

"Who says I was waiting for you?" she responded tartly. "Perhaps my book took my attention."

"Perhaps," he said, grinning wickedly as he reached her, knowing how she enjoyed it when he played the rake for her. "But I doubt it."

Grasping the covers, he yanked them from her body, chuckling at her outraged gasp. But she didn't fight him as he replaced the covers with himself, inserting his knee between her thighs and hovering over her with his body, his lips descending to hers and taking them with a conqueror's kiss. Her hands came up to press against his chest, fingers sliding across his skin and hair.

Then, without warning, she pushed him off to the side, taking him utterly by surprise so that he landed on his back.

"What do you think you're doing?" he asked, bemused, as she immediately followed her advantage by straddling

60

his thighs, the soft fabric of her night rail teasing his legs and groin.

"You always take the lead," she said, looking down at him in a challenging manner, her stubborn chin thrust outward. "I want to take the lead tonight."

Keen arousal, hot and needy, shot through him and he only barely resisted the urge to turn her on her back and take her immediately. It was the instinct of a man who was always in control, who had never considered relinquishing it. During his time as a rakehell, he'd occasionally come across a woman who desired to take the lead; he'd never allowed them.

But this was Eleanor. His wife.

And she wanted to take the lead.

With a supreme effort of willpower, Edwin forced himself to lay back against the pillows, dropping his hands to his side. Achingly aware of Eleanor's scrutiny as he battled with himself.

"Very well," he said shortly, uncomfortable with the idea but wanting to indulge her now that she'd made a request.

His reward was a brilliant smile that made every bit of discomfort worth it.

Leaning over him, her night rail brushing fleetingly against his body and making him ache, Eleanor pressed a kiss to his lips. Her kiss was much gentler than his, and he opened his mouth, allowing her to take the lead in this as well. The movement of her tongue was inquisitive, almost tentative, before growing in confidence and eagerness.

When she pressed her soft curves down on top of him, Edwin immediately lifted his hands to cup the ample mounds of her bottom. Immediately Eleanor pulled away.

"No... no trying to tempt me to go faster," she said fiercely, pushing his hands back down to his sides.

Edwin groaned. "I can't touch you at all?" He sounded depressingly whiny.

The teasing little smile flashing across Nell's lips wasn't the least bit reassuring. She was enjoying her newfound power over him. He hoped she got the most out of it, because this wasn't going to be on the menu on a regular basis.

"Not until I tell you that you can. I want to explore."

True to her word, she began her 'explorations.' Fingers dragged across his skin, followed by her lips, lightly at first and then harder. She constantly looked back up to his face, looking for clues about what he enjoyed and what he didn't. That was easy: he loved and hated all of it.

The light caress of her fingers, the moist kiss of her lips. When her breasts pressed against his chest and she sucked his earlobe into her mouth, dragging her teeth across the sensitive lobe, he nearly lost his control. His hips thrust upwards, his hands moving, before she pulled away, obviously delighted as his response but irritated he'd moved again.

Taking his hands, Nell shoved them up towards the rails on the headboard. "Hold onto *that* and don't let go," she admonished, her blue eyes narrowing at him.

Inwardly gritting his teeth, outwardly being as stoic as possible, Edwin obeyed. It was not in his nature to acquiesce easily to something like this. Eleanor sat back, studying him, and a little smile went across her face.

"I have an idea," she said. Her weight left him and Edwin let out a long breath, taking the opportunity to marshal his willpower back underneath his control.

Eleanor seemed bent on testing it, and while part of him enjoyed her brazenness, he was also not entirely comfortable with it. But she was pleased, and that counted for something.

When she came back, one of his cravats hanging from her hand, Edwin scowled darkly at her. "Absolutely not. You are not tying my hands."

The look Nell gave him was reminiscent of when they were younger and he'd said something she considered stupid.

"No, I didn't think you'd let me do that." It was reassuring to know she had some measure of what kind of man he was, at least. He was *allowing* her to be in control, and he could take back her lead anytime it pleased him. Even restraining his wrists wouldn't help her. Truthfully, it would probably only make him more likely to take it back sooner rather than later.

What Eleanor wanted quickly became evident as she placed the cravat over his eyes. Edwin groaned. He'd liked watching her even if he couldn't touch her, and he knew her touch was going to become much more intense now. Although he'd never let another woman blindfold him, since their marriage he and Eleanor had made love in complete darkness several times. He'd found the experience achingly erotic, being able to feel but not see her.

But he allowed her to tie the cravat around his head, before dropping his head back to the pillow beneath it. His fingers gripped the rail he was holding so hard that the bed creaked.

******

Utterly delicious.

If Eleanor was asked to describe how her husband looked at this moment, those were the words that came

63

to mind. His hard body was tense, stretched out before, a veritable banquet for her eyes. In fact, that was part of why she'd wanted to blindfold him, so she could look her fill without feeling awkward, as he could no longer watch her look at him.

Trailing a finger down the center of his chest, all the way to his belly button, she watched in fascination as his muscles tensed and quivered. Out of the corner of her eye, she could see his fingers re-wrap around the rail of the headboard, as if he was reminding himself not to let go. Licking her lips, she lowered her mouth to his chest, kissing one brown flat nipple.

His cock jerked and he sucked in air in response. From the way his jaw tightened, he liked it nearly as much as she enjoyed having him play with her nipples. When her teeth nipped at the tiny bud, he growled under his breath and Eleanor giggled.

"You'd better not be laughing at me," he said darkly, his head swinging towards her. She could just imagine the glare she was receiving beneath his cravat.

Instead of answering, she just lowered her mouth to his other nipple, her hand on his stomach tracing lower to brush against the silken shaft of his cock. Edwin moaned. A rush of heady power went through her. Was this what he felt like when he had her tied down and at his mercy?

No, of course not. He'd inevitably feel more. Because when she was tied down, she was truly at his mercy, whereas she was all too aware that at any moment he could decide he was tired of indulging her and she'd find herself on her back with him between her thighs in a heartbeat. The thought of him turning the tables on her made her heart beat faster, but that wasn't the point of tonight.

She wanted to explore. To see if she could pleasure him the way he pleasured her. To know more about his body.

Lifting her head from his nipples, she brushed her fingers over his cock, watching as it strained and jerked at her touch. It was an angry, reddish looking color, and the tip was weeping a whitish creamy substance - his seed. Fascinated, Eleanor rubbed her finger through it and Edwin groaned again, his big body shifting towards her.

"You like that?" she asked, rubbing her finger over the tip of his cock again, collecting the wetness and spreading it over the bulbous head of his shaft.

"Yes, I like it," he replied through gritted teeth.

It was all Eleanor could do not to giggle again. Shifting herself down the bed, she pressed her lips against his hip, her face very close to his straining cock as she worked up the courage to actually put the turgid organ in her mouth. How would Edwin react?

He seemed to like her lips against his hip, especially when she nibbled gently on the jutting bone. Letting her fingers play over the length of his cock, she worked her way down to the heavy sack beneath. It was wrinkled, soft, and Edwin's grunt of surprise followed by his low moan when her fingers gently rolled the swellings within it told her it was also very sensitive.

"You like this too."

"Yes." His voice was short, almost angry. The bed creaked again.

Eleanor realized she had better get to the main event soon or she might not get her chance. Gathering her nerve, she gripped his cock at its base. It was hot and hard in her hand, and Edwin's breathing began to quicken as her fingers wrapped around the shaft.

For a moment she hesitated, and then she leaned forward, taking the entire head into her mouth. It was soft against her tongue, textured, and his seed tasted slightly bitter and slightly sweet at the same time. She wasn't sure if she liked it. But she did like the taste underneath, a kind of musky, hot male flavor that made her want more.

Edwin gasped, his hips rising, trying to push more of himself between her lips, and she was so surprised that she let him. Yes, he liked this *very* much. As some of her saliva began to gather at her mouth, she sucked to keep from actually drooling down his cock, eliciting another moan and jerk of the hips from her husband. Oh... he liked that too. Experimentally she sucked again, moving her head up and down a little bit, the way he thrust into her body when they were making love.

Quite suddenly her mouth was empty again, the flavor lingering on her tongue, and her head was pulled back so she faced the furious, glittering dark eyes of her husband.

"Where did you learn to do that?"

Chapter 5

Possessive fury had a hold of Edwin like nothing ever before. At first he'd been enjoying Eleanor's tentative explorations, frustrating though they were. He'd been able to feel her hesitations, her delight, and so he'd persevered and relaxed enough to lose himself in the sensation. After all, the whole point of removing them from London had been to take the time to reconnect and woo his wife, prove he wasn't taking her for granted. Allowing her to take the lead, to blindfold him no less, was part of that.

He'd been enjoying her ministrations so much that when her hot mouth first clamped around the head of his cock, all rational thought had flown from his brain. Only the slightest vestiges of good intentions had kept his fingers wrapped around the rail of the headboard, rather than flying down to press her mouth more firmly on him. Then she'd sucked, her tongue flicking against him, her mouth sliding further down his cock and back up, and he'd had the sudden, horrifying realization that Eleanor had quite a bit of knowledge she shouldn't.

Throughout their marriage so far, she'd experienced quite a few things he was sure most wives in their social set hadn't. In part thanks to the wedding present Wesley had given him, as well as his own particular tastes, but not this. It just hadn't been on the top of his list, not the least because it meant trusting Eleanor to be on her very best behavior as he would be putting his most tender parts in her care.

And while she was no longer the unmanageable brat he'd married - indeed, she'd become quite the proper lady in public, for the most part - he hadn't been sure whether or not to introduce this particular act into their lovemaking yet.

While he could see Eleanor might think of kissing his cock, even licking it - after all, that was what he did to her pussy on a regular basis as he loved the sweet taste of her honey and watching her writhe as he pleasured her - he couldn't quite countenance that she would think to take him within her mouth and *suck.* Ergo, someone else had introduced the idea into her head.

Which was when he'd ripped the cravat from his eyes and grabbed her by the base of her hair, pulling her off of his cock, unable to even enjoy the sight of her kneeling over him in her gauzy night rail, her lips wrapped around his shaft.

Sitting up as he was, he was big enough that he still had to tilt her head back to see her eyes, gleaming sapphires of shock as she stared up at him. Edwin's hand tightened on her hair when she didn't answer him.

"Nell," he growled. "Where the bloody hell did you learn to do that?"

Perhaps it could be considered his just desserts if some other man had coaxed his wife into some kind of intimacies, considering what a rakehell Edwin had been before he married. But the pain lancing through his chest said his heart didn't care for such equality, and the utter rage engulfing him indicated his temper didn't either. He'd thrash whatever man had dared touch Eleanor in such a way. And once he got himself under control, he would blister her bottom like never before for allowing it.

"Cyn- Cynthia," Eleanor whispered, looking almost frightened. "Did I... Did I do it wrong?"

The answer was so unexpected that Edwin literally felt dizzy, as if his world had just shifted on its axis. Relief, so sweet it was almost painful, swamped him. Every muscle in his body relaxed and he loosened his hold on her hair. She wasn't lying, she was too surprised, too shocked by his reaction to think of a lie like that. Besides, her answer was so ridiculous it had to be the truth.

"*Cynthia?* How did she know?" he asked. Not particularly because he wanted to know the answer, but because he couldn't think of anything else to say. Of course he knew the Countess had told Wesley that Cynthia had been throwing herself at various gentlemen, and Wesley himself had said the chit was brazen, but Edwin certainly hadn't expected *this*.

"She said a gentleman had asked her to do it..." Eleanor said hesitantly, reaching up to rub the back of her head. Immediately Edwin let go of her hair completely, smoothing the hair with his fingers, a look of contriteness on his face.

"I'm sorry, sweet, I didn't mean to hurt you," he said. "I was just so surprised... I..." He hesitated, scrambling for words as he reached out for her.

And Eleanor realized exactly what had happened. Whereas Edwin's fury had obviously abated, hers now sprung up to take its place. She glared at him.

"You thought another man had...! You thought I did... I did *that* with another man!" She pointed her finger at him accusingly, absolutely furious. "You... You utter *slow top!*" Didn't he realize she had no interest in any other man but him? It's not like she was the one who was backward in showing affection. In her anger, she conveniently forgot she originally also spent just as much time giving him the cold shoulder in her efforts to spur him into declaring his feelings.

"I'm sorry, Nell," he said, grabbing her hand with the pointing finger and trying to kiss it. She yanked it away, still utterly enraged. "I just knew that I hadn't shown you... well... anything like that. You're a very passionate innocent, for all I knew some bloody scoundrel had tricked you into doing something like that." The dark look crossing his face at the very thought was heartening, but it didn't do anything to relieve her frustration and fury.

"Get out. I don't want you anywhere near me you... you... blackguard!"

The contrite expression on Edwin's face - or, as close to contrite as the expression on his face every became - subsided under a much sterner mien. "I apologized Nell, I know I hurt your feelings but I won't tolerate insults."

"Like the way you just insulted me?" she spat at him, not at all mollified. "Get out. If you think I could do that with another man... well... maybe I should! That would show you, you bloody bounder!"

With a growl, Edwin grabbed hold of her wrist again and yanked. Eleanor shrieked as she was pulled forward, and then yelled out in fury as she realized he'd pulled her over his lap. Ignoring her screeching, Edwin ripped the gossamer gown from her body, leaving her gasping as he rent the fabric up the center and bared her. Not that it would have been any protection anyway.

Shifting himself so his legs were off the bed and Eleanor was hanging over them, Edwin sighed. He did feel a bit guilty about what he'd suspected of his wife, not to mention the fact that he *had* insulted her, but his insult had been in all innocence whereas she was deliberately being as outrageous as possible. Not to mention the cursing. Her threat to find another man to be intimate with had his blood boiling, even though deep down he knew she didn't really mean it. At least he hoped she didn't.

But either way, such a threat was not to be tolerated.

"If this is what comes of allowing you to take the lead, you won't be allowed such a privilege again," he growled, landing a hard blow to the center of her bottom without any preamble or warm-up. Eleanor shrieked and kicked, forcing him to shift the position of his arm slightly to make sure she didn't slide right off his lap.

SMACK! SMACK! SMACK!

70

"I apologized. I explained."

SMACK! SMACK! SMACK!

"You didn't have to accept the apology if you were still angry, but continued insults will not be tolerated."

SMACK! SMACK! SMACK!

"And do not *ever* try to order me from our bed again. It will not work and you'll get this and worse."

SMACK! SMACK! SMACK!

Eleanor was howling now, her bottom turning a bright, roasted red as Edwin's voice calmly intoned over her furious yells. Tears dripped down her face and onto the floor as she wore herself out struggling, to no avail. Hanging limply over his lap, she wished she could shut her ears to his lectures about proper conduct and threats to lock her in their bedroom morning, noon and night if she even *thought* about intimacies with another man, all the while Edwin continued to pepper her burning bottom with further chastisement.

It was the longest spanking she'd ever endured, her legs kicking long after she'd thought her muscles had turned to water as occasional strokes landed sharply against the tender crease between her cheeks, her wrinkled bottom hole, or the plump swell of her pussy lips. That last elicited particularly pained cries from her, something Edwin noted because the contact from his palm increased immediately.

He spanked her entire bottom, from the upper curve down to her sit spot and then continued down to mid-thigh, with occasional hits in between on her tender quim. She was burnt up, seared, all over her bottom and in between. And yet she knew every time his hand connected with the plump lips of her womanhood, he could feel the wetness trickling out there. Shame, which she never became accustomed to, welled up inside of her and just made her wetter.

Finally he pulled her back up and cuddled her on his lap, letting her weep onto his shoulder as he used the cravat she'd blindfolded him with to wipe her face clean. The press of his hard thighs against her bottom was painful, but the comfort and warmth of his arms was too much to resist.

"I'm sorry," she said, weeping more tears as he gentled her. "I was just so incensed you would think... I didn't want to listen to your apology. I just wanted to hurt you."

"And you did, brat, but not because you called me names. I hurt because I hurt you."

It was the sweetest thing he'd ever said, the most revealing of what might be his true feelings for her, and it nearly took Eleanor's breath away.

"Now then," Edwin continued, his hand wandering down to the hot red flesh of her poor bottom as he looked at her tear streaked cheeks. His cock was rock hard, pressing against her hip, although she hadn't been paying attention to it a moment before. The look in his dark eyes was intensely aroused and she realized her punishment had had its usual effect on him. Indeed, it was a wonder he'd stayed his desires in order to comfort her. "It's been far too long since I've properly spanked you wife and I think I will mount you from behind so I might best enjoy my handiwork."

Eleanor's face flamed. "Oh Edwin...."

"Oh Eleanor," he murmured back, stealing a kiss from her swollen lips as he caressed her breast with one hand, squeezing her bottom, and enjoying her small cry and wince, with the other. While he could not explain his obsession with a well punished bottom, the fact was, a woman's erotic pain incited the most incredible lust in

72

him without fail. Even when he would have killed any other man who caused her the slightest hurt in any way.

When he placed her on the bed, the rounded cheeks of her bottom high in the air, Eleanor didn't protest. The cool air felt good against her hot cheeks and thighs, and especially across the swollen, wet flesh of her pussy. Fingers trailed over her sensitized skin and she shivered, knowing Edwin was looking his fill at the aftereffects of her punishment. What she didn't understand was why it excited her so, both the discipline and his scrutiny.

With his wife bent over so submissively, so easily, Edwin couldn't help but reflect upon how far they'd come since the first days of their marriage. Back then she would still be fighting him at this juncture, and he doubted she would have accepted the cuddling, although he rather enjoyed it. Still, he appreciated her submissive posture even more.

Nell would always have a fiery spirit, but he wanted that. Perhaps, in some ways, she'd felt the need for a harsher spanking tonight.

Sliding his fingers up her sides, he fitted his body over hers, groaning with pleasure as her hot arse and thighs pressed against the front of his body, his cock nestling easily between those rounded cheeks as he squeezed her breasts. Beneath him, Eleanor gasped and bucked slightly as he pinched her nipples, whimpering with the need he had built inside of her. His cock slid between her hot cheeks as her hips moved, making her squirm even more as her sensitive skin rasped against the rough hair of his body.

Pressing her face firmly into the sheets, Eleanor moaned, long and loud, as her fingers dug into the mattress beneath her. Curled over her knees as she was, with Edwin's weight on top of her, she couldn't move an inch even though she wanted to try and flatten herself on the bed. Edwin's fingers plucked and twisted her nipples as the pleasure and pain mingled in her center; his body felt like sandpaper against the flaming skin of her bottom and yet it did nothing to dwindle the flames heating her insides. With each tug of her nipples, she felt her need grow stronger, higher, and she bit her lip to keep from begging.

It didn't shame her when Edwin gave her a pleasurable spanking, but she could not understand her body's reaction to being disciplined by her husband. At the very least, she didn't want him to know exactly how aroused being punished by him made her - it's not as if the man needed any encouragement.

When she thought she might actually start begging if he didn't fill her emptiness soon, Edwin finally shifted, drawing his hips and body back. She sighed with relief and then pleasure as the cool air trickled back across her poor bottom and then the hard tip of Edwin's cock nudged against the entrance to her pussy. When he pushed into her, hard and fast, stretching her so quickly over his thick cock, she cried out. His body slapped against hers, stinging her red cheeks and thighs and she gasped and wriggled, her walls tightening instinctively around him as the pleasure and pain zinged through her.

"Damnation Nell... you're so tight and hot... hot all over," Edwin said, groaning appreciatively as he pulled back his hands and body, allowing him to lift her lower body further upwards. The sight of his cream coated cock slamming into her hot red quim, surrounded by the jiggling red flesh of her ass and thighs, was the stuff dreams were made of. Every inch of her had been spanked and he could hear Nell's panted breathing as she squirmed and adjusted to the hard fucking from behind, her pussy tightening with pleasure despite the sting.

With her legs pressed together, she was even tighter than usual, gripping his cock with her vaginal walls so

74

the friction was almost painful even for him. He could feel the heat emanating off her backside even when he pulled away before thrusting forward again. Fingers digging into her hips, he smoothly pulled her back onto his cock every time he thrust forward, increasing the force of his movements.

From the soft, muffled moans and the way her pussy convulsed around him, he knew she was enjoying it more than she'd ever admit.

But there was one more topic he wanted to address while he was deep inside of her, claiming her, taking her in the way only he had a right to.

"Nell..." he said, between thrusts as he grit his teeth to keep from spewing too soon, like an immature youth - but that was how much she aroused him, so it was difficult. "If you ever again threaten betray me with another man... I will do things to you that you can't even imagine."

And as he said that, he popped his thumb in his mouth for just a moment and then lay his hand on her red bottom, the heat searing his palm as he placed his wetted digit against the crinkled hole of her anus and pressed. Although he'd never intended to use the dilators Wesley had provided him with in their wedding gift, if using Eleanor in such a base and dark way was what would get her attention, then he wouldn't hesitate. And Edwin knew from his school days and the canings he'd received just how humiliating and painful certain items inserted into that orifice could be.

His cock hardened even further at Nell's outraged cry as his thumb burrowed deep into her forbidden hole; it was hot and tight and dry, clasping him so tightly he thought it might cut off the blood flow to his thumb. Before he could remove it, Eleanor screamed her ecstasy and, as the velvet grip of her pussy rippled around him, he realized the introduction of his thumb into her virgin anus had caused her to climax. Or had she climaxed despite it?

Either way, the sound of her culmination during such a lewd act, as he fucked her soundly from behind, was Edwin's undoing. Crying out her name, he thrust hard into her grasping cunt, allowing her body to milk him of every last spurt of his seed.

******

Later, Eleanor woke in the middle of the night with a pressing need to use the chamber pot. She'd fallen asleep almost immediately after Edwin had laid down beside her, pulling her into his arms and sleepily kissing her. When she returned to the bed, she whimpered as she rolled onto her stomach. Almost immediately, Edwin reached out and pulled her into his body, nestling her sore bottom against his groin in his sleep.

She wriggled for a moment and then settled, trapped by his arms even if she had wanted to get away. But she didn't.

Thinking over his reactions tonight, she felt more sure than ever that he must have feelings for her beyond mere affection. That she meant more to him than just being an extension of Hugh, more than a playmate whom he thought he could rub along well enough with in marriage. And hadn't Lady Montgomery said Edwin had been waiting for her to grow up? Perhaps she could trust her ladyship's perceptions, if she couldn't trust her own.

Maybe she could be content with this. Maybe she didn't need a verbal declaration.

Shoving aside the little pit of doubt in her stomach, the whispering worry that his attentions wouldn't last forever, Eleanor clutched his arms closer to her body and fell back asleep.

Chapter 6

Steadily working through his correspondence, Wesley spent Thursday morning shut up in the study of his mother's house. The sounds of servants, his mother, and his ward were pushed away and put out of mind while he attended to his responsibilities. When Cynthia poked in her head to request permission to visit the nearby shops, he grunted an affirmative, not paying much attention and just wanting her away so he could concentrate. The steward for his estates needed his time, his partner in shipping needed his time, as did his allies in Parliament who were writing to him about the latest bills.

So when he finally reached the short note which had arrived from Edwin that morning, warning him about the rogues who had been importuning Cynthia for intimacies that, while they wouldn't get her with child, would absolutely ruin her for any kind of respectful marriage - and the impertinent chit had been brazen enough to suggest Eleanor pleasure Edwin with her mouth, Wesley was in no mood for it. He would have gone roaring through the house looking for his ward, and had been standing to do just that, when he remembered she'd gone off to the shops. Sitting back down, he thought darkly about what he was going to do to her bottom when she and his mother returned.

How could his mother be so lax in her chaperonage? Or perhaps the problem wasn't that his mother was lax, perhaps it was just she couldn't anticipate Cynthia. After all, she'd never had to watch over a young lady before, particularly as difficult a one as Cynthia was turning out to be.

On one hand, Wesley couldn't entirely blame the men of Bath. With the Season going on in London, Cynthia must be the most enticing young miss in the entire area. And she didn't at all dress or behave like a proper young lady. She was temptation incarnate, with those firm curves and her pouting mouth. Hell, what he wouldn't do to have her use his mouth on *him*.

Wesley groaned as he realized that thoughts of his ward had given him yet another impressive cockstand; an occurrence which happened far too often for his peace of mind. He absolutely needed to find a willing woman, perhaps tonight at the Assembly after he looked over the field of possible husbands for Cynthia. Strangely, he didn't particularly enjoy the idea of another man sampling her charms first... but it's not as if he was going to marry her, so if he wanted her then he would have to wait. While she certainly was a funny little thing and he enjoyed her intelligence and personality as much as her sensuality and attractive exterior, when he did finally marry it was going to be to a woman who enjoyed the same proclivities as he did.

Although... perhaps she did? The thought inserted itself into his mind as if it had been hovering there all along, just waiting for the right time to make an appearance. She certainly hadn't reacted to the spanking the way he'd expected. Just a bare hour later she'd behaved as if nothing had happened. Not at all what he'd anticipated.

A short rap on the door broke through his thoughts and he sat back up straight in his chair, scowling down at the bulge in his trousers before he looked back up.

"Come in."

"Actually, I was hoping you would come out," his mother said as she opened the door wide. "You've been shut up in here all morning."

"Ah. If I had realized you were back I would have come out already. Where's Cynthia? I need to speak with her."

His mother blinked at him. "She's at the shops, she said you gave her permission to go."

Now it was Wesley's turn to stare back at his mother, completely flummoxed. "I thought she meant to go with you."

"I wasn't feeling up to a trip out."

"Then who did she go with?" He could feel his temper rising and reminded himself that he shouldn't become angry with his mother; somehow he was quite sure she didn't have half the idea of what Cynthia got up to. If she did, she would have probably had vapors on a daily basis.

"Her maid, of course."

Which would cover the bounds of propriety, but Wesley was absolutely certain Cynthia would easily run right over any maid. His temper snapped.

"Dammit Mother, she's not allowed to leave the house unless accompanied by you or me or... or... Lord or Lady Hyde. Otherwise, the damned chit's confined!"

"Wesley!"

Ignoring his mother's outraged gasp at his language and intemperate tone, Wesley stalked right past her and out into the hall. He felt a bit bad about snapping at her, but really! After all the complaints she'd sent him over Cynthia's behavior and she didn't keep a closer eye on her? Intellectually he understood propriety was met since she'd taken her maid, and his mother wouldn't look beyond that - she would trust the usual measures would suffice. But Cynthia wasn't a usual young women.

No, she was a brazen hoyden, a sensual temptation, and soon she was going to be a very sorry young woman with a very red bottom. And to make his temper even worse, his damn cock twitched again at the thought.

******

79

It hadn't taken very long for Cynthia to realize which shops the maids found interesting and which they didn't. She picked up some ribbons first thing, lingering there long enough over the colors she was sure even the maid was losing interest, before moving on to search out a new bonnet, new gloves, and see the new fabrics at the *modiste's*. Only after that did she finally make her way to the bookstore, where there was a very convenient bench outside. By now they'd been about for several hours, and she knew the maid would have no interest in going into a bookstore.

Which was good because Cynthia didn't want her there.

"Good afternoon, Mr. Worthing," she said as she swanned into the shop after giving her maid permission to sit on the bench and enjoy watching the people who were passing on the street.

"Good afternoon, Miss Bryant," the shop owner said with a little leer. She gave him a dazzling smile in return. As a much older man with a portly belly, he didn't seem to need more than a smile or two and a flash of her ankles and calves on occasion to keep him satisfied. And in return, he let her have free run of his shop.

Cynthia wasn't interested in most books, it was true; she certainly wasn't a bluestocking. Romances interested her only so much, and only on rainy days when she couldn't go outside anyway. Anything which required her to sit for any length of time - other than playing the pianoforte - wasn't high on her list of enjoyable activities.

But Mr. Worthing had a collection of quite interesting books on a high shelf in the very back of his store. She didn't think he realized that she knew they were there, as she'd found them completely by accident and had hurriedly pretended to be engrossed in something else when she'd heard him approaching. Since then she'd come back on several occasions, hoping to get another glimpse at the interesting pictures she'd barely seen.

Maybe even read some of the passages. So far she hadn't been able to, as there were usually other people in the store, but she never lost hope.

"Miss Bryant," she heard someone say as she passed by one of the rows of books. Turning back, she peeked her head around the corner and saw Mr. Brandon, second son of the Duke of Manning, one of the men who liked to flirt with her and steal a kiss. Not husband material; the Countess had told her he was only in Bath because he was outrunning creditors as his father had declined to bail him out yet again, but he was very handsome and also a very good kisser.

"Mr. Brandon," she said, smiling back and raising her hand for him to kiss.

Today, however, he looked somehow *less* than normal. Smaller, less interesting, less attractive. It took her a moment before she realized it was because she was comparing him to the Earl. Who was not only taller and broader of shoulder, but also had much more of a presence about him. Perhaps because he was an established Earl, rather than a second son, even a second son of a Duke.

"I had no idea, when I stepped out this morning, that I might be so fortunate as to come across you. You look..." His eyes swept over her dress, which was one of her more modest pieces. "Enchanting." Putting his finger on her shoulder, he trailed it down along her neckline, causing Cynthia to catch her breath. Even if he wasn't as intriguing as the Earl, the sensation made her skin tingle. "Teasing my senses by covering what I long to see... to touch..."

His mouth was coming closer and closer to hers and she tilted her head back, eyelashes fluttering as she readied herself for the kiss.

"Get your damn hands off my ward."

Cynthia gasped as Mr. Brandon was wrenched away, the stentorian tones of her guardian cutting through whatever pleasure she'd felt a moment before. Dread and excitement clashed in her stomach, curdling like a bad mixture of milk and hot water, as she opened her eyes to see the Earl bodily hauling Mr. Brandon out of the aisle.

"Unless you want a dawn appointment with me, you will not approach her again and I will not hear a word about this from anyone," the Earl hissed, just barely loud enough for her to hear. Oh goodness... a duel?!

Before she could react, Mr. Brandon stumbled away, babbling reassurances in a frightened manner that made her sigh. Whatever attractiveness he'd had, he'd just completely lost. How disappointing.

Then the Earl turned back to her, his hazel eyes dark and hard.

"Ah..." she said with a weak smile, trying to think quickly. With the Countess it wasn't nearly so hard to come up with something to say. "Good afternoon, my Lord."

Well apparently that wasn't the right thing to say at all. Growling under his breath, the Earl reached out and grabbed her arm, hauling her back towards the front of the store. Cynthia dug in her heels, not particularly wanting to be a spectacle.

"My Lord," she hissed, pulling at his fingers on her upper arm, "you're going to attract attention!"

******

The reminder stopped Wesley in his tracks. No, he hadn't just demanded that the scoundrel who had just been about to kiss her - in the middle of a bookstore! - would keep quiet, only to alert everyone himself. In sleepy Bath, bodily dragging his ward down the middle of the street would do more than cause comment, it could cause scandal as people speculated over *why* he might be doing such a thing. And then his mother really would have vapors.

Growling, he slowed his pace, taking her hand and firmly wrapping it around his arm before covering it with his own so she couldn't get away. While such a stance might seem a bit overly familiar, considering she was his ward and not a lady he was wooing, it would cause far less comment than his previous hold. To his intense annoyance, she not only gave him a brilliant smile of approval, she then transferred her smile to the owner of the bookstore.

"Thank you Mr. Worthing, I'll see you another day," she said with a cheery little wave.

Wesley forebear to tell her that she absolutely would not be seeing the smarmy man another day; he doubted his mother would be agreeable to coming to this dusty hole in the wall and neither would he. Especially with a man like that, who eyed Cynthia far too speculatively as he responded in kind.

As they walked down the street, Wesley's temper wound tighter and tighter with every step. The chit didn't act as if she'd been caught doing something wrong, unlike the blaggard he'd caught her with, she was just as cheerful and chattery as ever. It was enough to drive a man to drink. He stepped quickly, mindful of not making a scene, but knowing the sooner he got her to the house the better.

Cynthia nodded to and greeted several people, although Wesley kept her moving, giving them nothing but a quick nod. He'd probably get an earful later from his mother about his short demeanor, but he wasn't going to allow Cynthia to slow him. The second they got back to the house he was going to give her as red a bottom as ever.

Kissing a man! In a bookstore! Where anyone could have come across them!

Growing grimmer by the minute, he darkly wondered how often she met men in bookstores – and elsewhere. What she might be doing with them. Although Edwin's letter had indicated that so far she hadn't completely ruined herself (according to what she'd told Nell) as she was being careful not to end up with an unwanted pregnancy, but that didn't mean she could act however she wanted. If anyone other than himself had seen her and that rogue, it would have been all over town in minutes. And then his mother's reputation and social standing would have been affected as well.

At least, that's what he attributed his dark rage to. It definitely couldn't have anything to do with how she'd been about to kiss another man, had her pink lips turned up to accept his, her body leaning towards him... after all, Wesley was planning on marrying her off to some poor sod who would get to sample her delights on a daily basis. Why would he feel anything akin to jealousy just because she was about to kiss another man?

Growling under his breath, Wesley picked up his pace again as they drew closer to the street where his mother's house was. The sooner he could get her inside and vent his feelings on her upturned arse, the better.

******

The look on the Earl's face was not at all helping matters, Cynthia thought with some exasperation. She'd been doing her best to avoid attention by acting normally, but he'd looked as grim as the reaper while he'd been "escorting" her home.

Truth be told, she *might* have been overplaying her hand a little. After all, it hadn't been strictly necessary to greet every single person she saw on the street. But it was strangely fun to tweak at the Earl's nerves, especially when he was in a temper. She was feeling rather breathless as how easily he manhandled her, the strength she could feel in his arm.

And she had wanted another spanking after all. If this didn't earn her one from him, then what would? She couldn't have planned it better if she'd tried.

Although his silence and glares made her feel more nervous than she would have expected; she covered up her anxiety with a cheerful bravado that seemed to grate on him. Which, in turn, amused her, and she was quite sure he could tell she was amused and it incensed him even further.

Her bottom tingled underneath the swishing skirts of her day dress and she could feel the wetness gathering between her legs. The Earl might be a bit of a prig and a stuffed shirt, at least where she was concerned, but there was just something so delicious about a truly masterful man. None of her other suitors had ever affected her quite like he did, which was really too bad because she couldn't seem to influence him the way she did them.

Then again, perhaps it was her inability to sway him that she found so attractive. It wasn't often she came across a man such as him, one who was wholly desirable and yet seemed completely indifferent to her, one who managed to both intimidate and attract her, and one whom was completely oblivious to her manipulations. Even when she poked at him, metaphorically speaking, he didn't stop in his track, he just bulled right through and continued towards his own goal.

As soon as he got her in the house, he picked up his pace again, dragging her towards his study.

Sheer perversity made her dig in her heels this time. "My lord, can't you slow down?"

Instead of responding, the Earl halted completely, turning on her with such a burning glow in his hazel eyes that she nearly stepped back. Then he tugged her towards him, swooping low, and the next thing she knew Cynthia was upended over his shoulder, all the air knocked from her lungs.

My goodness.

That was... impressive.

She was very aware of the searing heat of his body, the ripple of his back muscles beneath her hands, and the hot clamp of his palm over the back of her thigh. For once, she decided to be meek. After all, she wanted him to spank her, not throttle her, and she instinctively recognized his temper was probably nearing the throttling point. Besides, if she struggled, he might just "accidentally" drop her - and she really wouldn't be able to blame him.

If he found anything suspicious in her sudden passivity, he didn't voice it.

By the time he reached his study, setting her down so suddenly that she stumbled backwards - her knees hitting something and causing her to tumble down into the sturdy chair behind her, she was feeling a bit dizzy from being upside down for so long. It wasn't necessarily a bad sensation, combined with the tingling of her body which came from being in such close contact with him. Excitement fizzed and popped inside of her, making her feel quite bubbly and chipper.

Which she did her best to hide, but from the way he was looking at her with narrowed, eyes, she had a feeling it was leaking through. Attempting to put a proper look of contriteness on her face, she folded her hands in her lap and looked up at him through her lashes.

"Explain yourself," he said, glaring down at her and crossing his arms over his chest.

Back to this again. Cynthia sighed. "You gave me permission to go shopping."

"I was under the impression you were going to do so with my mother."

"I never said that."

"Noted. However, in the future, you will not leave this house unaccompanied by either myself or my mother. Or Lady Hyde if she desires your company."

Cynthia brightened at the thought of more time with Eleanor and then she subsided again under the Earl's gimlet eye. "Very well. If you insist." At least she wasn't being confined. And if she really wanted to get out on her own, she absolutely trusted her own ingenuity to see her way.

"I do. Now. Explain what you were doing in the back of the bookstore with that... that..."

"Gentleman?"

"Not the word I was looking for."

But apparently it would do, because the Earl didn't offer another one. He just glared down at her, one long finger tapping against his bicep expectantly.

"I just wanted to visit the bookstore," Cynthia said, smiling brightly. Quite aware her attitude was grating on him. "Mr. Brandon found me there and we exchanged some pleasantries."

"And some kisses."

"No." Well that was the truth. While she did want a spanking, just to see if it caused her to get all wet and hot again, she found it was just as enjoyable to verbally poke at the bear.

"But you would have, if I hadn't come along then," he said grimly, the tempo of tapping from one long finger increasing as he spoke. "Right in the middle of a bookstore where anyone could have come along and seen you. And your maid was *outside* where she wouldn't have been any use as a chaperone."

"She's not in trouble is she?" Cynthia asked, suddenly worried. After all, she didn't mean to get someone else into trouble with her antics. And, while the Earl couldn't get rid of her as his ward, it was definitely within his power to dismiss the poor maid. "I quite exhausted her with our shopping, she just wanted to sit and rest."

"I'm aware she's not up to your weight," the Earl said. "And I have no desire to punish her for something so completely out of her control. But rest assured, you will not be given such an opportunity again." The concern for her maid did her credit, he had to admit to himself, even if she was driving him into a frustrated fury.

He'd truly thought spanking her on the day of his arrival had signaled to her that things would be different now the head of house had arrived. Instead she seemed completely unaffected. Well... perhaps not entirely unaffected. She'd become immediately docile once she'd realized how very serious he was, and she had kept him from dragging her through the streets, which would have cause quite a bit of gossip. But he wasn't going to tolerate this kind of behavior from her.

Abruptly deciding he wasn't going to mention any of the information from Edwin's letter, because if he did then Cynthia might not let anything more useful drop to Eleanor, Wesley uncrossed his arms and stepped back. His ward had given him plenty of reason to punish her without bringing that up; and he and his mother would be keeping a very close watch now so she wouldn't have any opportunity to sneak off and meet with any of the bastards.

"Stand up."

Looking at him almost curiously, a gratifying hint of wariness entered her movements as she stood. At least he knew his looming intimidation wasn't entirely ineffective. With any other young woman, he'd admire the brazen spirit and her obvious sense of humor; he was much less enamored of it in a young woman whose reputation and future was his responsibility.

"Bend over the arm of the chair and lift your skirts."

Even though she knew he was about to spank her, discipline her, a trembling excitement went through her limbs. Feeling rather breathless, Cynthia turned and placed her upper body over the wide arm of the chair. The leather padding cradled her hips, pushing her bottom high into the air, while her upper body rested on the wide chair. She could feel her nipples hardening as she reached back to grab her skirts and pull them upwards. It wasn't the most efficient position to do so, but catching a glimpse of the Earl's face, it was obvious he was rather enjoying the slow bunching of her skirts around her hips and the way her long legs were revealed to him inch by inch.

She realized he was looking at him as a man looks at a woman, the way most men looked at her. Was that how he'd looked the last time he'd spanked her?

And this position was so much more revealing than being over his lap. Cynthia's breath came in short pants as she realized how much of her lower body, her secret areas were exposed to his gaze by this position. With her legs spread to maintain her balance, she could feel the cool air coming in through her split drawers and wafting across the heated inner lips of her womanhood. It was quite exciting to be so exposed to her trenchant guardian's eyes, to watch his face and see his gaze so intent upon the upturned curve of her buttocks and the pink flesh between them.

A surprising amount of apprehension settled in her belly, despite the fact that she wanted this. Now that she was in position, offering up her buttocks for his chastisement, memories of how very much her first spanking had *hurt* were suddenly bubbling up. Somehow she hadn't thought about that part of it when she'd been remembering; she'd just thought about the incredibly intense pleasure which had followed when she'd rubbed herself.

The sudden touch of his hand brushing against her flesh, just barely skimming it as he parted the split in her drawers and drew them to each side, brought her back to the present. Biting her lower lip against the anxiety coiling inside of her, Cynthia tried not to squirm.

Seeing the creamy expanse of skin and the pouting pink lips of her pussy, lined with darling dark curls of hair, Wesley's cock came to immediate attention. Somehow, up until then, his anger had overridden his desires and he'd managed to keep his physical response in check; but having her so submissively, vulnerably proffered up to him was his undoing. Fortunately, as she was already bent over with her face firmly pressed against the leather seat of the chair, there was no way she could know of his response.

"You will not leave the house again without one of the chaperones I've described."

Smack! Smack!

Cynthia gasped at the sudden assault, her creamy skin immediately showing pink and then fading as his hand landed and retreated. The way her flesh jiggled was more than a little enticing.

"You will not meet with any gentleman in private."

Smack! Smack!

The next blows landed below the first, one to each cheek. He had started at the very top curve of her sweet cheeks and he was going to make his way down to the bottom of each mound before coming back up again. At least.

Smack! Smack!

"If a man attempts to speak with you in private you will immediately search out your chaperone."

Just thinking about the bloody bastard in the shop, leaning in, ready to kiss her, had Wesley's ire jumping again.

SMACK! SMACK!

The blows he landed on the under curve of her buttocks were swiftly followed by two slaps directly on her sit spots. Cynthia cried out, her bottom wagging up and down as she danced to avoid the burn.

"Stand still," he ordered, smacking the insides of her thighs as her legs began to come together. Immediately she planted her heels back on the ground.

SMACK! SMACK! SMACK! SMACK!

Pinkened flesh jiggled as he worked his way back up those ample hillocks again, his cock throbbing as he watched every ripple of her body; he spanked her hard enough to leave an imprint of his hand on her soft flesh and make it jig and bounce. The first row of slaps down her buttocks had been a warm-up, to pink her skin and make her ready for the real spanking.

He hadn't started out with a certain amount in mind, he was quite ready to continue until her bottom was burning a bright cherry red. She certainly wouldn't be sitting comfortably in Bath's Assembly rooms tonight. There was no point in forbidding the outing, as he, his mother, as well as Edwin and Eleanor would be there to watch over her; besides, he needed to inspect the field of suitors for a husband for her. But he was determined she wouldn't be able to sit without remembering his warnings and why she *must* be on her best behavior.

It appeared the previous spanking hadn't made quite the impression he'd thought. He was determined this one would.

Cynthia's tears were falling quite freely now as she struggled to maintain her pose, her fingers clutching at the edges of the seat padding to keep from reaching back and covering her bottom. Glory be, it hurt so much more than she'd remembered! And yet with every whack of the Earl's palm against her flesh, her insides clenched and quivered and she could feel the front of her woman's mound pressing against the arm of the chair and making her tingle.

Obviously there was something very wrong with her body that it could become so horribly confused.

"I'm sorry, I'm sorry," she cried out, finding the words that had ended the spanking last time. "I won't do it again!"

"Correct, this time I will make absolutely sure you won't."

SMACK! SMACK! SMACK! SMACK!

Squealing, Cynthia tried to rear up as the Earl's hand came down even harder. To her horror, his free hand immediately pressed down on the small of her back, easily holding her pinned like a bug as he continued the assault on her bottom. It was *burning*, and every stinging swat bit into her deeper as he continued spanking her.

When she tried to reach back, to stop him, he just grasped her wrists in his long fingers and used her own hands to help hold her down! Sobbing, Cynthia kicked out uselessly, not caring anymore what the Earl might think. But there was no stopping his assault on her flaming posterior; the spanks came swift and sure, peppering her bottom even further now that he sensed his point was truly being made.

She'd never felt so completely helpless, so incredibly out of control in her life. It sparked something deep inside her, some craving, that had never been awoken or fulfilled. There was no stopping the man, not with words or by struggling; she was pinned and bared to him in the most primal way. If he wanted to, he could touch every inch of her woman parts, he could spank her bottom raw, he could do whatever he wanted to her.

It was intensely arousing, even as the awful burn of the spanking flayed her. Somehow she hadn't expected this. Last time, he hadn't been nearly this brutal even though he'd turned her bottom bright red; this time he was pushing her far beyond that point, to where her garbled promises and pleas actually felt sincere. She would agree to anything just to make him *stop*.

Looking down at the cherry red, dancing bottom in front of him, Wesley felt his cock throb in response. He'd already known it had been too long since he'd had a woman, but it had particularly been too long since he'd been with a woman who enjoyed the same exotic inclinations he preferred. The ladies of the *ton* were willing to be seduced, but most were not very inventive and most were unwilling to try anything new.

Turning his ward's bottom from a lovely cream to this flaming red was the closest he'd come to satisfying his more improper desires. If he could keep her bent over and use the slick oils he'd brought back from India to lubricate the winking little pink hole between those swollen, red cheeks and then shove his cock it, taking her in the most base and perverted way possible, then his desires would be completely satisfied. Unfortunately, so far he hadn't found a woman in England who was willing to go beyond a certain point with him.

Hell, if he could find an accommodating widow, he'd probably marry her on the spot. Eventually, he'd probably marry some young miss who was more enamored of his title than his person, beget an heir and a spare on her, and have a mistress for his... games. Since it was doubtful any sweet young miss would be willing to even try the decadent perversions he favored.

With an inward sigh, Wesley landed two more hard smacks on Cynthia's sit-spots, startling himself when his fingertips came away wet. Stepping back, he brought his fingers to his nose, wondering if he had pushed her too far, if she had wet herself... but the musky scent of aroused woman filled his nostrils. Just like the time before, only this spanking had been much more thorough and he truly hadn't expected her to have this kind of response today.

Shocked to his core, he didn't say anything as Cynthia stood, her skirts rustling back down to the floor, and turned and fled. He caught a glimpse of her face, streaked with tears, eyes glazed with shock. There was a moment when she glared at him before fleeing the room.

And he was so busy smelling her scent on his fingers that he didn't stop her.

Leaning back against the desk, his mind ran over the possible ramifications of his discovery... and what he was going to do about it.

******

Locking the door behind her, Cynthia heaved a few more sobs. She was still surprised the Earl had let her go without a further lecture, but she hadn't been about to stay and allow him to whack on her poor bottom some more. Last time hadn't been nearly as painful!

Hustling over to the mirror, she yanked up her skirts to her hips and sucked in a shocked breath. Her bottom was so red it was nearly glowing, and when she reached around to press cool finger tips to its agonized surface, she could actually feel the heat emanating from her skin.

"Bloody hell..." she murmured, almost in awe. The rounded mounds actually looked rather swollen.

If it wasn't for the stinging, burning, throbbing, she would have been utterly fascinated by its appearance. Stroking her fingers over the sensitive surface, she shuddered. Even the softest touch caused an increase in the stinging.

It wasn't until she noticed how she was squeezing her thighs together that she realized the delicious feeling of needy pleasure had built up in her quim. Cynthia groaned. How was that possible? She hadn't understood it the first time either, but this was beyond the pale.

Gently rolling herself onto her bed, she hissed in pain when her weight pressed down on her bottom. Lifting her skirts up to her hips, she planted her feet on the bed to help relieve the pressure on her sore buttocks, just as she had the last time. When her fingers pressed down into the folds of her womanhood, the slick wetness was more than it had ever been before and her little pleasure nub was hard and aching.

Cynthia moaned as she began to rub herself, her free hand reaching into the top of her dress to pinch and play with her nipples. Somehow being rougher than usual with the hard little tips of her breasts balanced out the throbbing flames of her bottom. Gasping, shocked at how quickly she was reaching her pleasure, Cynthia rubbed her little pleasure nub harder and harder, squealing a bit as her bottom began to move up and down, bouncing off the bed.

The flashes of stinging pain that flared every time her bottom bounced intensified the exquisite ache between her legs, a repercussion she was becoming familiar with. She clenched her teeth over a scream as the most delicious ecstasy ripped through her, her arm becoming sore as she rubbed and rubbed and rubbed, riding out every last exquisite ripple of pleasure.

Gasping, completely out of air, she rolled onto her side. Her bottom throbbed. Between her legs pulsed. And this climax had been even more intense than the last one after she'd been spanked.

Was there some connection between how hard the Earl spanked her and how high her pleasure went?

Yet, there was a warm ache between her legs which still wasn't satisfied. Moaning, Cynthia gently rubbed little circles over her wet flesh until the insistent need began to build again and then she rubbed, rubbed, rubbed, until she was thrashing and gasping again with ecstasy.

After three intense orgasms, the poor girl was utterly wrung out. Her bottom was on fire, the ache between her legs had subsided but still felt like something was missing, and she was completely exhausted. After all, it had been a long morning and afternoon, followed by the spanking and then more rubbing and ecstasy than she'd ever experienced before. It was a wonder she hadn't rubbed her little nubbin off.

Hazy, mostly sated, Cynthia rolled onto her stomach and fell asleep with her dress still on and hiked up around her hips.

Chapter 7

When the maid knocked on her door, awakening her, Cynthia forgot herself so far as to roll onto her back and sit up. Yelping, she jolted off the bed, whimpering a bit as her flesh jiggled. Her bottom was still incredibly sore, although it hadn't stopped her from her exhausted sleep.

"Miss? Are you awake?" The maid's voice was accompanied by the rattling of the doorknob. "It's time to dress for dinner."

"Yes, yes, I'm awake, just a moment," Cynthia said, rushing over to the mirror.

Shockingly, the skin of her bottom was only pink rather than red now, although the deep ache from her punishment lingered. Her bottom was still sensitive to the touch, with a feeling of almost bruising underneath even though it barely *showed* any ill effects. Somehow the lack of evidence seemed monumentally unfair, as if she'd been denied a badge of honor to wear for having endured the punishment.

Another knock on the door reminded her the maid was waiting. Cynthia sighed and let her skirts drop back down again.

******

The composed debutante who was shown into the drawing room didn't at all resemble the sobbing, red-eyed young lady that Wesley had punished. He couldn't keep too close an eye on her, however, or Eleanor and Edwin would notice. Or maybe they wouldn't; the two love birds seemed rather wrapped up in each other, although he had noticed Eleanor was sitting rather gingerly.

He deduced Cynthia wasn't the only young woman to be disciplined in the past twenty-four hours.

The Countess looked up and smiled approvingly at her ward's appearance. The rose pink damask set off her sensual good looks, bringing a bright pink to her cheeks and lips and setting off the rich brown of her hair and eyes. He wondered if it was anything close to the current color of her bottom, and when she glanced at him with a challengingly mischievous look in her eyes, he wondered if she'd purposefully dressed to remind him of her spanking. The little minx. Although they didn't know each other very well yet, he wouldn't put it past her. The part of him that didn't want to think of her as his responsibility thoroughly approved.

Blast.

But she *was* his responsibility and he'd resolved to forget the moment of... contemplation he'd had earlier in the day. He didn't want to get married yet. Especially not to a brazen, bold little hoyden who would keep him hopping with her antics. And Cynthia needed to be married off quickly – not just for his mother's sake, but now for her own. Before he ruined her utterly.

Of course, then he'd be honor bound to marry her...

Stop it you bloody fool.

Pasting a smile on his face, he watched as his mother's escort for the evening, the elderly Viscount Vernier, bowed over Cynthia's hand, complimenting her on her delightful appearance. Following Vernier, Wesley bowed over his ward's hand as well, murmuring his own compliments.

He watched as she greeted Edwin and Eleanor, the latter with every evidence of delight. Yes, he'd been right not to inform her that Eleanor had shared some of her confidences; the women were well on their way to a true friendship – and knowing Edwin, he was fairly sure Eleanor hadn't meant to betray Cynthia's confessions. As long as the chit knew not to attempt any of those intimacies until after she was married, he'd stay content. And keep a weather eye out.

"What has she done now?" Edwin asked in a low voice, sidling up to Wesley as Eleanor, the Countess and Cynthia began to chat, while Vernier listened with an indulgent smile on his face. Wesley wondered if the older man was hard of hearing, as a discussion about the shops of Bath could hardly be stimulating to him.

"What do you mean?"

"You look like you want to throttle her."

"I do not," Wesley said gruffly, trying to compose his features. It was harder than he'd expected because he was already trying to cover his initial reaction to Cynthia's presence and his thoughts about what color her bottom might be. He noticed that when she settled on the couch next to the Countess she did so very, very carefully and she didn't glance in his direction the entire time. Knowing her bottom was still aching did nothing for the state of his breeches and he blessed the fact that he'd worn a looser fitting pair than usual.

Still, he didn't want anyone to know his ward was getting under his skin. So he forced a smile and turned away from her so he could stop focusing on all the soft, white skin revealed by her low neckline and watching her shift back and forth as if trying to find a comfortable way to sit on a very sore bottom.

"I may need to enlist you and Eleanor to help my mother and I keep an eye on her this evening," Wesley said in a low voice. He hadn't told his mother that Cynthia bore stricter watching, mostly because then he would have to explain *why*. And if Eleanor and Edwin were going to be there, then he could rely on them. Well, on Edwin, certainly. Nell might help out, but she was also just as likely to take Cynthia's side, as far as she thought Cynthia could be trusted. Wesley had a feeling Nell's definition of how far Cynthia could be trusted differed greatly from his own.

Edwin raised one dark eyebrow. "Never thought I'd see the day when you admitted to a woman being too much for you to handle."

Scowling, Wesley waved his hand, as if to wave Edwin's words away. They needled, particularly because there was just the smallest grain of truth to them. "I've never met one that was so bent on her own destruction."

Laughing, Edwin clapped him on the shoulder, giving him a nod that was both apologetic and accepting of the request as the ladies looked up at them, obviously distracted from their own conversation. Interestingly, when Cynthia met Wesley's eyes for the first time that evening, she blushed.

Then he saw the way her lips parted before she looked away and he realized she hadn't been blushing. She'd been aroused. Was she thinking about her spanking? As his breeches tightened uncomfortably, Wesley realized he was contemplating his ward in a way he'd firmly decided *not* to.

Damnation. He needed to find her a husband and quickly, and he needed to find himself a feminine distraction even more quickly. He would definitely use the Assembly tonight to achieve both goals.

******

If Wesley had thought the evening was going to be easy, his first glimpse of Cynthia in a ball gown rudely disabused him of the notion. She was temptation incarnate; if they'd been in London men would have been throwing themselves at her feet with the more dangerous rakes and roués circling like the hungry wolves they were. The low dip of her neckline revealed what seemed a scandalous amount of the upper curves of her breasts, all her gleaming white flesh an invitation for lips and trailing fingers. One brunette curl rested on

100

her shoulder, showing off how pale and creamy her skin truly was; the rest was wound about in an elaborate coiffure with a silver ribbon that matched the gauzy netting over a dress of aquamarine.

The entire ensemble made her look both older and more tempting than ever, with those wide, laughing hazel eyes and curved, smiling lips. This was no hoyden, this was a sensual siren, elegantly draped and expertly presented to the entice the male senses. He was so intent on controlling his inevitable reaction to the way the gown clung to her ample curves that he didn't even notice the flash of feminine awareness and satisfaction in her eyes upon seeing his reaction. Cynthia was not the usual young miss; she was quite aware of her effect on men and she was finally observing the same symptoms in the Earl.

It was immensely satisfying.

When he raised her hand to his lips, meeting her eyes, his gaze suddenly shuttered as Wesley realized he'd been thrown enough by her appearance to show his true reaction. He actually had to remind himself that he wasn't going to marry the chit just because he ached to bed her.

The lazy smile that slid across his face was a mask, but it was also a smile designed to set women's heart's fluttering. A smile that had actually caused a debutante to swoon earlier in the Season when he'd favored her with it - not that he expected Cynthia to behave in the same manner as that silly chit, but he knew it should at the least make her uneasy.

"You look... absolutely divine tonight, Miss Bryant. I'm sure even in sleepy Bath the gentlemen will be clamoring for your attention. Just remember not to give any of them too much of it."

Cynthia felt rather breathless. When she'd dressed for this evening she'd wanted to stun the Earl, to show him she could do the pretty and play the part of a proper lady, just to get a rise out of him. Certainly not because her bottom was still aching and she was worried about being on the receiving end of another spanking - surely the Countess wouldn't allow any disruptions to their planned evening.

The rakish grin on his face had set her heart pounding; it was a smile many men had given her, but none quite so effectively. Perhaps because this was the first time the Earl had looked at her like *that*? Or perhaps because he was the only male to have ever seen her private areas? So far she'd always kept the men who kissed her from taking matters beyond a certain point, and that point was any parts underneath her clothing, but the Earl's spankings didn't afford her any such protection. Which might possibly be why they excited her so.

Still, she didn't appreciate the reminder that he didn't have any faith in her ability to behave. She could when she chose to.

Tilting her head haughtily up, she snapped at his bicep with her fan, trying to ignore just how impressive a bicep it was. No padded shoulders needed for the Earl. The look of surprise at her retaliation almost made her break character and giggle.

"I'm sure I don't know what you mean," she said coolly, in her best impression of the Countess' quelling tones. The edges of her lips curved upwards, as they always did when she was about to utter something purposefully outrageous. "I always bestow my attentions to the gentlemen *equally*."

The Earl's hazel eyes narrowed, the smile slipping from his face and it really was all Cynthia could do not to laugh out loud at him. Despite how much her bottom hurt - and it truly did, although much less when she was standing rather than sitting - she just could not keep from prodding at him. The implication that she allowed quite a few gentlemen some... ah... liberties was not lost on him and he obviously didn't like.

With something approaching a growl, his hand tightened on hers as his eyes flashed rather dangerously and Cynthia suddenly realized she was baiting a tiger with a very short stick. An *uncaged* tiger.

"Oh Wesley, couldn't you do something about your hair?" The Countess' dismayed tones preceded her down the stairs and Cynthia breathed a sigh of relief as the Earl straightened, his grip on her fingers loosening slightly. She yanked her hand back as the Earl looked past her up and his mother, and used the opportunity to slide sideways and away from him.

"My hair is fine, Mother," he said, obviously somewhat exasperated and yet his tone with her was as respectful and gentle as always. He bowed as she reached them. "You look lovely tonight."

The older woman's face lit up at the compliment from her eldest son. Not that his words were anything but the truth; she was garbed in a dark burgundy gown with a black netted over gown, both trimmed with silver, and she looked the epitome of a fashionable matron of the *ton.* The garnets shining around her neck and at her ears emphasized her position and status, as if her regal bearing wasn't enough. It was at times like this Cynthia found the Countess most intimidating.

Fortunately the Countess looked at her with every evidence of approval as she thanked her son. "Cynthia, you look *parfait!* That dress is exquisite, Madame Bissette truly outdid herself."

Cynthia beamed at the Countess, bobbing a small curtsy which caused her breasts to look particularly precariously confined to the dress and Wesley caught his breath. In London he'd seen plenty of fashions with lower necklines, but somehow with Cynthia's ample curves even a neckline this low seemed too much. Not that his mother noticed, but the other gentlemen at the Assembly tonight certainly would.

And probably not the ones he would approve of as a husband for Cynthia.

Grimly foreseeing a rather frustrating evening ahead, Wesley ushered his mother and Cynthia out to the waiting carriage.

******

Edwin and Wesley stood at the edges of the room, watching Miss Bryant and Eleanor as they passed through the steps of a quadrille with their respective partners.   Surprisingly, for once, there seemed to be more gentlemen willing to dance then there were women to dance with – Wesley supposed it was the fact that most eligible young ladies were currently in London for the end of the Season, hanging onto the hope they might make a match of it before the Season ended – so he and Edwin didn't have to stand up for every set.   If there had been young ladies sitting out, the Countess would have expected both of them to step up and do their duty, as she saw it.

Watching Eleanor laugh up into her partner's face, Edwin had to struggle only slightly with the jealousy that clawed its way up his chest.   Since their arrival in Bath his and Eleanor's relationship seemed to have taken another turn.   A much gentler one – other than the spanking she'd earned for her attitude.   He knew, on some level, her body enjoyed receiving discipline as much as he enjoyed meting it out, but she wasn't willing to admit that and she always was on her best behavior after a punishment.

A slow smile spread across his face as he remembered this morning, when he gave her the opportunity to explore his body again and she'd taken full advantage of it.   This time she hadn't relented with her mouth until he'd spurted his seed, and she'd swallowed every drop of it.   The many blessings of a passionate and curious wife.   Afterwards, he'd tied her wrists to the bed and made his own leisurely exploration of her body, ending

104

with his mouth on her clit and his fingers stroking the insides of her heated quim. By the time she climaxed for him, he was already hard and aching again and he'd taken the opportunity to bury himself inside of her while she was still limp and quivering from her climax.

They hadn't left their bed till well past noon.

Now, as he watched her dancing with other men, he could still feel the jealousy rising up inside him every time she smiled or laughed, but it was accompanied by a kind of warm security. He'd been wooing her, not just while they were in bed, but with long talks and gifts and a showering of affection. His wife was a wonderfully tactile creature, and he'd found she rather enjoyed snuggling up under his arm while they were reading together in the afternoons. The sensation of having her there was a bit distracting, but he enjoyed it nevertheless. And it seemed as though the more innocent caresses and embraces they shared, the warmer and more open she became towards him.

Not once, since they'd come to Bath, had she reverted to the cold ice queen she had occasionally inflicted on him while they were in London. He still didn't know exactly what had made her run hot and cold towards him, but he hoped her current behavior was an indication that his tactics and affections would mean her attitude towards him would continue to be more stable.

Next to him, Wesley growled under his breath, and Edwin turned his attention towards his friend. Wesley's attitude towards his ward was providing both Eleanor and Edwin with a great amount of entertainment, especially this evening when he was watching over her like a hawk.

"Is something wrong?" Edwin queried, his tone entirely innocent as he covered up his amusement. Wesley just continued scowling in the direction of the dance floor and Edwin had to cough to cover a laugh. "You could always dance with her again, if it bothers you so much."

"What?" Wesley whipped his head around, looking at Edwin suspiciously. But Edwin had seen the way Wesley watched his ward.

"It'd be totally acceptable, as her guardian, to secure a second dance with her," Edwin said blandly. Unusual, but acceptable. They'd already done the pretty once, while Edwin danced with Eleanor, but as Wesley had danced with the Countess and Eleanor, Edwin had seen where his friend's eyes had been watching. And since they'd retired from the dance floor, Wesley hadn't looked anywhere else.

Even his mother was eying him speculatively, not that he seemed to notice. And Wesley always noticed.

Now he seemed to be thinking over Edwin's words and giving them serious merit. Then he shook his head and Edwin had to hide another grin. "No. I can watch her just as easily from here."

While Edwin had happily stepped into marriage in order to secure Eleanor, and Hugh hadn't fought the steps leading to his marriage with Irene, it appeared Wesley wasn't going to go quietly. In fact, his reaction was that of a man who was going to fight his emotions to the bitter end. But Edwin didn't doubt Wesley was attracted to Miss Bryant, even if she was a bigger handful then Nell. Privately he thought that might not be a bad thing; he wanted his friend to find the same happiness in marriage he had, and he didn't think that would be possible if Wesley married one of the proper debutantes and kept a mistress on the side. A wilder and less proper wife like Miss Bryant would keep Wesley quite occupied.

The dance ended and gentlemen very properly escorted Eleanor and Miss Bryant back to him and Wesley. There were several obvious rakes in attendance, but so far they'd held back from approaching either of the ladies as they were well guarded by Wesley and Edwin.

Eleanor and Miss Bryant immediately began chatting, both flush from their exertions. Resting a gentle hand on his wife's back, Edwin enjoyed the way she immediately leaned towards him, as orientated towards him as he was to her. To his amusement, both Wesley and Miss Bryant were doing something similar, although of course Wesley didn't touch her. But there was something in both of their stances which made it clear, to him, that they were both very aware of each other. The little sidelong looks Miss Bryant was giving her guardian, as well as Wesley's blatantly intentional way of *not* looking at her, now that she was off the dance floor, said volumes.

"Is it like this in London?" Miss Bryant asked Eleanor, giving Wesley another little look from beneath her eyelashes. For all intents and purposes, his focus seemed to be on the other side of the room, but Edwin could see the way Wesley's eyes drifted back towards Miss Bryant before he jerked back to the direction he was facing. "The Countess says this is tame compared to the entertainments there."

"This is more enjoyable than London, in many ways," Eleanor said, laughing. She tipped her head back up to share an intimate look with Edwin and he couldn't help but grin back at her; she was so alight with happiness. He, too, preferred Bath at the moment. "I much prefer the room to dance – and plenty of gentlemen to dance with – than some of the crushes we attended during the Season."

Undaunted by her reference to the many gentlemen, Edwin just slid his hand to her hip and tightened his fingers a bit. "I prefer the gentlemen here as well."

Eleanor laughed, tapping her fan against his chest in teasing reproof, as Wesley chuckled. Miss Bryant looked confused, but of course she wouldn't understand that the London ballrooms were filled with the kind of gentlemen Edwin would prefer to keep away from his wife. He was sure he was fulfilling Eleanor's needs, she would never become one of the bored matrons of the *ton* if he had anything to say about it, but he still preferred to keep her away from the rakes and *roués* who were always looking for a bored matron and a complacent husband.

Most of the gentlemen here were either younger men who had fled the capital and the matchmaking mamas as soon as it was permissible or older men who didn't have wives to insist they finish out the very end of the Season. The older gentlemen were the ones who would be looking at Miss Bryant as a bride, the younger men were practicing their flirts with her, but the truly dangerous gentlemen who were present took one look at Wesley and moved on to easier game. Although, Edwin had seen more than one of them acknowledge her; apparently before Wesley's arrival Miss Bryant had made the acquaintance of every single rakehell currently in Bath.

One of the older gentlemen, Mr. Bright, came up to claim Miss Bryant's hand for the next dance. Perfectly eligible, cousin to a Marquess, and obviously on the lookout for a wife, and yet Wesley gave the man a suspicious look anyway. This time even Eleanor caught his obvious reluctance to let Miss Bryant off his arm. Edwin saw the surprise on her face before Mr. Marks came to claim her for the next dance. She shot a glance at Edwin, her sapphire eyes sparkling with amusement at Wesley's behavior.

Just then, the Countess appeared at Wesley's side, a pretty but very young lady at her side. Actually beaming at her son, she pushed the young miss forward.

"Wesley, this is Miss Whyte. She'll be making her debut next Season in London but her mother wanted her to experience some of the social life here in Bath before that. Miss Whyte, this is my son, the Earl of Spencer."

"Oh!" Miss Whyte said, fluttering her eyelashes up at him as if his title was news to her. Which was ridiculous considering the Countess must have already told her. If she hadn't even come out yet then she must still be technically in the schoolroom. Dressed in a charming pastel pink dress which was the height of fashion, and nevertheless made her look rather washed out with her pale hair and eyes, she was the epitome of everything Wesley avoided while in London. She dropped to a curtsy, fluttering her eyelashes. "It's an honor to meet you my Lord."

She simpered up at him and Edwin barely smothered his laugh as Wesley stared at her, then his mother, in complete horror. It was only as the breathless miss looked up to meet his eyes again that he blanked the expression from his face.

"Miss Whyte," he said, bowing over her hand. "May I also introduce my friend, Lord Hyde."

"My lord," Miss Whyte said in acknowledgment, but without the simper. It was obvious the Countess had informed her that Edwin was ineligible as future husband material. Which was a relief; he only had to deal with the bored matrons Wesley normally preferred, who were looking for a sensual distraction from their husbands. Debs no longer had any interest in him whatsoever.

"Miss Whyte was just telling me how much she loves to dance," the Countess said, absolutely irrepressible, despite the glare her son was giving her over the young lady's head. Ignoring him completely, she gave the young miss an encouraging smile, before turning it onto Wesley himself. "My son is a wonderful dancer."

"Yes, but as you see I can't desert Lord Hyde and leave him bereft of all company."

"Oh, I can certainly keep Edwin company," the Countess said, her gaze sharpening. "I had something I particularly wanted to speak of with him."

There was nothing Wesley could do at that point; his mother had neatly trapped him into a position where his options were either to be unconscionably rude or to ask the young lady to dance. And Wesley always did what was proper, especially in front of his mother.

Covering up his chagrin with a bow, Wesley held out his hand to Miss Whyte. "Well then. Miss Whyte, may I have the pleasure of this dance?"

"Oh yes, my Lord," she said breathlessly, eyes shining with anticipatory pleasure it bordered on being predatory, despite the fact that she couldn't have missed his reluctance. It was this kind of behavior which made Edwin eternally grateful he had Eleanor; even when she had first been presented, he couldn't imagine Nell behaving like that.

The set had just started, so they'd barely missed a step, and Wesley led the young woman out onto the floor to join the other couples.

"There was something you wished to speak of with me?" Edwin asked, rather curious now. He couldn't think of anything the Countess might wish to say to him that she couldn't say in front of others.

"No of course not, don't be dense. I just needed Wesley to dance with Miss Whyte."

Edwin laughed at the Countess' high handed ways. "Why? You can't imagine he would seriously consider a schoolroom miss like her, not even next Season when she's out."

The Countess shook her head. "Really Edwin, your lack of experience in the marriage mart is appalling. My son is bound and determined to marry a proper young chit, at some point in the future, but he'd be absolutely miserable with the kind of milk and water miss he'd undoubtedly pick out for himself. And no matter what he thinks, having a mistress, or even several, on the side can't make up for that. Once he's been forced to interact with a few of them, he'll realize his intolerance for them and my Cynthia will look even better by comparison."

"Your Cynthia?" Edwin asked; he'd been following the Countess' logic up to a certain point but she'd just lost him completely. "What does she have to do with it?"

"Why, she's perfect for him, of course!" The Countess waved her hand at the dance floor where it was perfectly obvious to Edwin, knowing his friend as he did, that Wesley's attention was focused far more on his ward than on the chattering Miss Whyte. "She's clever, she's lively, she's far more interesting than any of the usual misses - Nell excluded of course, and he's already interested in her but he's resisting. The twit." She snorted. "I drag him all the way out of London to Bath so he could see her before any other real competition engages her attention and he can't see what's in front of his face."

"I thought you were despairing of her," Edwin said, thoroughly startled and slightly in awe. He hadn't realized how devious the Countess was.

"Well I was, a bit," she admitted, continuing to watch the couples whirl around the floor, looking rather calculating. "She's a handful, but that's what makes her perfect for Wesley. He'd never be happy with a woman who didn't have a sense of adventure and the gumption to indulge in it. Cynthia has a bit of maturing to do, but I'll be here to guide her, and Wesley needs to snap her up before some other, more discerning and ready to act, gentleman realizes what a treasure she is. Of course, the more young misses I can push at him who drive him batty, the more he'll appreciate Cynthia." That last was said rather contemplatively, her eyes already roving around the room as if looking for her next decoy.

"My god..." Edwin stared at her in complete wonder. Thank goodness he'd had the sense to shackle himself to Nell immediately, and he was even more grateful his own mother preferred to stay out of London. Although, he didn't mind giving up his bachelorhood and rakehell days for his wife, so perhaps his mother wouldn't have resorted to such straights.

Although, he could see Eleanor's mother doing so if she thought he was blind to Nell's charms. After all, her own father had been the one to approach him. Obviously no one felt he needed as delicate a hand as they thought Wesley did.

The Countess smiled as she watched the couples on the dance floor. This particular set required some switching of partners throughout the dance, and Wesley had masterfully maneuvered himself and Miss Whyte so they would be trading with Mr. Bright and Cynthia.

"Watch. A few more dances with empty headed misses and a few quiet spinsters, and Wesley will realize a young lady like Cynthia is exactly to his temperament." And with that, the Countess swanned off again as the last notes of music were played, presumably to find Wesley another partner before the next dance started.

******

It was utterly demoralizing to realize being an Earl still meant trotting at the behest of one's mother, Wesley decided, four interminable dances later. She'd practically thrown Miss Whyte at him, followed by Miss Lovelace, Miss Smith and Miss Prentice. Although Miss Prentice wasn't so bad compared to the other three; she was on the shelf at eight and twenty, but he still thought she'd make some other chap an admirable wife. At least she had a brain in her head which was more than could be said for his previous dance partners, even if she was too quiet and retiring for him to find her intriguing.

Taking the initiative, he secured his mother's hand for the next dance, rather than waiting for her to foist the young lady at her side on him. With every evidence of delight, she followed him out onto the floor.

"Madame, just what do you think you are doing?" he asked, finally showing some of the pent up aggravation which had been building all evening. Even before his mother started lobbing young misses at his head, if he was to be honest about it. Trying to look out for a suitable husband for Cynthia was turning out to be harder than he'd expected. And finding a distraction for himself, even more so. The fashionable, bored matrons of the *ton* were apparently all seeing out the end of the Season in London, not Bath, and there wasn't even an attractive young widow around. Not a likely prospect in sight, and so he'd had nothing more to do than watch as Cynthia danced with gentleman after gentleman, none of them quite right for her. "When you threatened to descend upon London to find me a bride if I didn't make my way to Bath, I presumed that meant my presence in Bath would stay such attempts."

"Oh, I'm not serious about any of these young ladies," his mother said, her light laughter not at all reassuring. "Although after Miss Whyte is presented, you might think of taking another look at her, I'm sure she'll have matured by the next Season. I'm just getting my hand in, ensuring I'm up to snuff for next Season."

"Next Season?"

"Well of course. I fully expect Cynthia to make a match before then, which means I'll be free next Season to concentrate entirely on you." She beamed at him, as if her words weren't the foretelling of doom to come. "After all, you are the Earl now and there is the succession to consider."

Good Lord, he could actually feel the walls closing in about him. "There's no need to concern yourself with the succession just yet, Mother, I have plenty of time. There's Mathew and Vincent after all."

"Your brothers don't want to be the Earl," she said with a sniff. "Even if either of them were suited to it. No, Matthew's army mad and Vincent's obsessed with art and living abroad. They'll be reassured to hear of your marriage and subsequent heir."

There really wasn't an argument against her statement, as she was completely right. Wesley cast about for some other excuse.

"I'm sure I can manage the business on my own, Mama, as much as I appreciate your intentions."

"Not from what I hear about your acquaintances," she said, her tone making it clear the gossip of his various female acquaintances - none of which could be considered marriageable - had definitely reached his mother. "You'll need me to help you make the right sort of connections for that. But don't worry, I'm going to spend the next year gathering as much information as I can so we can go into next Season quite prepared!"

Feeling as though the floor was decidedly tilted, Wesley stumbled through the last few steps of the dance, earning a reproving look from the Countess as he tripped over his feet. Although it was quite a bit of time away, next Season suddenly seemed to loom far too closely. He couldn't even quit London and retreat to his estates to avoid his mother and her schemes; there were too many of his responsibilities now tied up there and he would need to be present for Parliament regardless, not to mention he didn't doubt his mother would find some way to coerce his presence even if he balked.

Unable to stomach dancing with another empty headed chit after his mother's pronouncement, he stole Eleanor for the next dance and then managed to procure another dance with Cynthia. At least he could talk to them. By the time his dance with Eleanor finished he was feeling a bit more like himself although she was looking at him a bit curiously.

Cynthia, on the other hand, didn't seem to have any hesitations about questioning him.

"Are you feeling alright?" she asked, peering at him as if she didn't recognize him. Actually, he was feeling much better now that he was dancing with her, having successfully avoided his mother again, but he wasn't going to tell her so.

"Quite."

"You don't look as though you are. Although you're decidedly less pale than when you were dancing with your mother," Cynthia said. Wesley had to laugh. When it came to polite conversation his ward was abysmal, but she was entertaining. Then again, he found it rather refreshing that she didn't languish behind miss-ish airs, and most other gentleman probably did too.

"My mother... my mother..."

"Is making you dance."

"Yes."

"Don't you like dancing?"

"It depends upon the partner."

She seemed to think that over for the next few steps as they went apart and then came back together.

"Do you like dancing with me, or did you only ask me because I'm not as bad as the young ladies your mother is choosing for you?"

Wesley had to laugh. Brazen, that's what she was. A young lady should never ask such a direct question. "Dancing with you is utterly preferable to dancing with them."

"That's an evasion, not an answer," she said, frowning up at him.

"Clever baggage."

"Well fine then, I don't want to talk to you either." And with that, she put her nose in the air, barely looking at him as she gracefully made her way through the steps.

Which only made Wesley want to make her talk again.

"What kind of man do you want to marry?"

Silence.

"Cynthia."

She looked at him in a rather significant way and he sighed.

"I asked you to dance both because I didn't want to dance with another one of those useless chits and also because I like dancing with you. You're quite graceful you know."

The brilliant smile he received in return made something inside his chest do a strange flip even as his breeches tightened in front.

"I'd like to marry a man who doesn't bore me."

"Is such a man hard to find?"

"Yes and no. I've met quite a few men who don't bore me, but none of them seem interested in marriage."

This time Wesley growled in response to her smile. She didn't even seem upset at the idea of attracting men who wouldn't make her a respectable offer. Just amused and possibly slightly interested. Well she would have to wait to accept carte blanche from any of them until after he found her a husband. Although if he found her one who didn't *bore* her, then perhaps she wouldn't even be inclined to.

"Aggravating baggage," he said, although his tone wasn't severe at all. Cynthia just smiled brightly at him again, her cheeks flush with happiness.

******

Later that night, in his study, Wesley studied the glass of brandy in his hand rather than sipping from it. He'd poured himself the alcohol, but had yet to drink a single drop, although the current subject of his thoughts certainly merited it.

Marriage.

And it looked as if he was to have any choice in his bride, he must do so before next Season. Who knew what young ladies his mother might consider appropriate for the position of his Countess if tonight was anything to go by. The Miss Whyte's of the world drove him batty, it was part of the reason he'd assiduously avoided the marriage mart at all costs while in London. Even though he was newly an Earl, it seemed the *ton* had understood he wouldn't be looking for a bride during his first Season back from India.

Next Season, with his mother in town, it would be completely different. Young ladies would be loath to pass up the opportunity to be a Countess, especially to an Earl who didn't need their dowry as an influx of cash. And his mother's presence, and encouragement, would only exacerbate matters. It wouldn't just be his mother's machinations he would have to be wary of, but all the matrons and young ladies of the *ton*.

Did his mother really think he'd be happy settling down with one of those bird brained, conniving, marriage hungry misses? He adroitly dismissed the fact that he'd been thinking along those lines originally, because he'd been thinking about marriage in the far distant future.

But now he was realizing he might need to move sooner rather than later, he couldn't quite reconcile himself to the idea.

Especially when Cynthia kept popping up into his mind. Cynthia and the slick, musky wetness her body had produced despite - or perhaps because of? - her spanking. Just thinking about it caused his cock to swell. She didn't want a husband who bored her... well, that was as good a criteria to go on as any. Wesley knew he wouldn't bore her. And he didn't think she would bore him.

Hell, just this morning he'd been considering something along those lines, based on nothing more than his attraction to her and the wetness of her quim after being punished. And he'd decided against it, but that was before he'd known his mother's plans.

If he had to choose a bride, and soon, he could do worse than a chit who, at least, entertained him. Made him laugh. And it was damned hard to keep his hands off her anyway.

The notion merited serious contemplation. Wesley swirled the contents of his brandy glass around, watching the amber depths as they sloshed back and forth. Edwin had married for love, Hugh had married for land - although it had obviously turned into something more, so he would marry for... what? Lust?

Maybe. Perhaps he could convince his mother to set aside her plans for at least another year, take some time to think.

Although, by that time Cynthia would be married off if his mother had anything to say about it. Wesley brought the snifter up to his mouth and drained it.

Chapter 8

Irene was so glad the Season was coming to a close. She was looking forward to returning to the countryside with Hugh. The Duchess of Richmond's ball was everything she disliked about London society - it was an absolute crush, too loud, too packed and the odor left a great deal to be desired - but it was one of those events everyone must attend. Which accounted for the great number of people sipping tepid, watered down lemonade and eating stale pastries as the night wore on.

Even worse were the number of alluring, sophisticated and flirtatious ladies who filled the capital. While her mother had impressed upon Irene that it was commonplace among the *ton* for a man and wife to have relations with others outside of their marriages, she hadn't realized how much it would directly affect her. At the time she'd thought it was something to be desired, because she thought she and Alex would finally be able to be together in some manner.

Now she realized she loved Alex in a completely different manner than she loved her husband, the idea of Hugh enjoying intimacies with a woman outside of their marriage was terrifying and painful. At first she hadn't even realized it might be a possibility, but it seemed there were far too many married ladies who would be happy to pry Hugh away from the side of his delicate wife. Many of them had bought the story of her fainting in the gardens (thankfully not realizing the truth of the matter), and they assumed Hugh would want to enjoy relations with a woman who was more robust. More sensual.

Several rakes had looked her way as well, but somehow Hugh had managed to make it clear he was not going to be a complacent husband and those men had taken their attentions elsewhere. From what she understood from Hugh's mutterings, they thought she was with child and so would be safe to dally with. Another repercussion of her "faint" in the gardens. However, he was showing himself to be protective enough over her that they were more interested in easier game.

Irene didn't mind that, of course. She certainly hadn't known how to deal with the flirtations of the Earl of Sunderland or Viscount Bowlen. But she did mind the women who were proving to be remarkably tenacious in their pursuit of Hugh. Every time Irene was separated by her husband at an event, when they found each other again he always had managed to attach some harpy to his person. It was enough to make Irene want to tear out their elaborately coiffed hair.

But tonight she hadn't been able to avoid a visit to the retiring room. The lemonade might be tepid and watered down, but she'd been thirsty enough to drink it anyway. And Hugh had said they couldn't quit for the evening yet; apparently one must always stay a certain amount of time at the more important events, which this was.

Not for the first time, she desperately wished she had never planned to run away with Eleanor and that her sister-in-law was still in London.

Catching sight of her husband's golden head of hair through the crowd, Irene breathed a sigh of relief and began making her way over to him. At least Hugh was tall enough she could usually find him fairly easily, even in a crush like this.

It wasn't until she was closer that she saw the dark head of a lady with her head tilted back, simpering up at him. Irene's breath caught in her throat, nearly strangling her. This was so, so much worse than any of the random ladies whom Irene merely had a passing acquaintance with; this particular lady had just cause to want to do Irene as much harm as possible.

When Lady Grace had pulled her aside and quietly set her down for her behavior with Alex, Irene had haughtily told the new wife that she and Alex were long-time friends, there were more feelings between them than Lady Grace would understand, and she certainly would not change the way she acted towards Alex just because he was married. Now, as a wife herself and with her new understanding of what it was like to be married to a man who was much sought after by other ladies, Irene realized she felt guilty about the way she'd behaved. No wonder Lady Grace hadn't liked her after that. Irene certainly hadn't given her any cause to.

Although it still didn't excuse Lady Grace's awful behavior towards Alex, mere days later, and the way she'd betrayed her marriage vows. The way she gallivanted throughout the *ton*, causing scandal along the way and humiliating Alex. He deserved better than Lady Grace; Irene's viewpoint on that certainly hadn't changed. But it didn't seem to affect the guilt now sweeping through her either.

Irene had never expected to see the lady here, at the Duchess of Richmond's ball, flirting with her own husband. Beautiful, accomplished Lady Grace, who, despite the scandal, was one of the most sophisticated and sought after ladies of the *ton*. Who had already stolen one man away from Irene - even if now she knew she didn't really want him. Irene absolutely did want Hugh and she was perfectly willing to fight for him.

"There you are," Hugh said, smiling as Irene hurried up to them, out of breath from practically running headlong through the crowd. "I was just telling Grace you were here, somewhere."

She bristled at Hugh's easy use of Lady Grace's given name, even knowing his sister was a longtime friend. "How nice to see you, Lady Grace," Irene lied, her voice cold.

"Viscountess," Lady Grace said, her stunning blue eyes glinting with a cruel light. The intonation she gave the title only emphasized the fact that Irene never, ever, called her Lady Brooke. Tilting her head back towards

121

Hugh, she shared a decidedly intimate look with him. "I've just been having the most... delightful chat with Hugh." The sensual purr she used to say Hugh's name had Irene's hackles climbing.

Either her husband didn't notice anything or he didn't care, because he just smiled back at the horrible woman.

"How nice of you to keep him company while I was away," Irene said, her tone implying that now she was there, Lady Grace need not continue to do so.

"Oh but of course, I'm always happy to have a talk with one of my *oldest friends*," Lady Grace said, laughing merrily. She'd stressed the last two words, making it clear to Irene that this closeness to Hugh, this relationship with him, was giving her great vindication for Irene's treatment of her when she'd married one Irene's oldest friends. A reiteration of Irene's words that marriage was not going to change the way she treated Alex. The irony was not lost on Irene, although she didn't have any idea what to do about it.

Anger, true anger like she'd never felt before, was building up in her breast, making her feel flushed all over. Even the guilt was feeding into her anger, because she didn't want to feel it and she didn't want to feel any sympathy for Lady Grace.

"It's always nice to see you as well, Grace," Hugh said amiably, smiling down at her. Irene was going to claw those sapphire eyes out, she really was. And tear out all her long, luxuriant dark hair. Lady Grace had the kind of effortless, stunning beauty Irene had always envied. Just another reason to dislike the woman. "I know Nell will be gladdened to hear you were here tonight."

Lady Grace's smile turned a little brittle before she returned it to its usual sparkle. "I do miss Nell so. I may visit her once the Season is over." Which, of course, would deprive Irene of her sister-in-law's

122

company. Leaning in towards Hugh, Lady Grace leaned forward in a manner which nearly completely exposed her bosom; Irene couldn't even imagine how much of a view her tall husband was getting of the woman's well-rounded breasts. "Will you be spending any time with Eleanor and Lord Hyde in the coming months? If so, I'll have to ensure our visit coincides."

The little look she flashed Irene's way made it clear this was for her benefit. All of it.

Something hot and awful flashed through Irene, and she found herself lunging at Grace before she even realized what she was doing. Her fingers caught up in the other woman's dress, hooking into the fabric, before Hugh's arms were suddenly around her, yanking her away. The sudden ripping sound of Grace's dress left them all gaping. There was a large hole in the lace over gown, right at the waistline, where Irene's fingers had managed to find purchase.

"What is wrong with you?! You... you..."

Oh no... Hugh's arms tightened Irene as if he was afraid she might launch herself at Lady Grace again, but she'd already regained control over her impulses. Enough so to be mortified as people around them began to turn, staring at the wreck Irene had made of Lady Grace's skirt and the mottled red of her face as she glared furiously at Irene.

"Grace!"

Alex suddenly shoved his way through the crowd of on-lookers, causing more than one lady to gasp and begin to fan herself in anticipation of this latest *on dit*. They might not be sure exactly how Lady Brooke's dress had become torn, but it was common knowledge that Lord and Lady Brooke hadn't exchanged a single word in years, despite recently making appearances at the same events.

At nearly the exact same time, Lord Conyngham, rumored to be Grace's current lover, pushed through the crowd across from Alex, ending up next to Grace. The lady took one, wild, look at her husband and immediately turned to the arms of her lover, who turned her around so their backs were to Lord Brooke and Conyngham began to push his way back through the crowd.

"Excuse us," Irene could hear Lord Conyngham saying. "Lady Brooke needs to use the retiring room." And then they were gone, disappeared into the crowd, leaving Alex looking after them and everyone else looking at him.

It was moments like that which should have made Irene feel justified in her past words to Lady Grace. Seeing the utter blankness on Alex's face, she knew he was covering some kind of very deep emotion as he watched his wife walk away in the arms of another man. She should have wanted to say something even worse to the woman. But having seen Lady Grace so blatantly flirting with Hugh and then paling at the sight of her own husband, to the point where she'd looked like a ghost, Irene suddenly felt cast adrift.

What if, with her confused feelings for her husband, their positions had been reversed and she'd had words about Lady Grace's friendship with Hugh and Grace had responded the same way Irene had? What must that have been like for Lady Grace, as a new bride? And now, to be attacking Grace – despite any real provocation, just the anger Irene hadn't been able to control… She might not approve of the Lady's behavior with Alex, but regret and shame washed over Irene for her own.

"Alex, I was thinking of going to White's after dropping Irene off at home. She's got a bit of a megrim." Hugh's hand tightened on Irene's arm, as if warning her not to contradict him. Not that such a gesture was necessary; it was as if he'd read her mind. She truly didn't want to be here and her head actually was starting to pound a bit. "Would you like to join me?"

For a long moment, Alex just stood there, staring blankly at Hugh, and then he shook himself. "Yes. Thank you. The Duchess surely won't miss us, it's such a crush here."

Hardly satisfied with the lack of dramatic revelations or declarations, the lords and ladies around them turned away, realizing they weren't going to get anymore meat for gossip fodder. Although what they'd witnessed would cause enough of a stir. Irene just prayed no one had seen exactly how Lady Grace's dress had been torn.

Once again, as if sensing her thoughts, Hugh leaned in to whisper in her ear. "Lady Wife, I will deal with you tomorrow. Tonight you will think about what you've done and why you've earned yourself a punishment."

Irene just nodded, wilting a bit against him. She didn't argue, because, after all, what could she truly say in her defense?

✶✶✶✶✶✶

Climbing the stairs to his bedroom, Hugh sighed. It had been a long night. At the club, after they'd left the Duchess of Richmond's ball, Alex had quietly gotten very, very drunk until Hugh eventually poured him back into the carriage and took him home. Then Alex's butler had taken over responsibility for him. Hugh highly doubted the man would remember much of the evening, after the instigating incident.

Hugh didn't dislike Grace, although he sometimes found her to be rather sharp and self-centered, but he didn't at all like what she did to Alex. It hadn't even occurred to him that her behavior might grate on Irene, although Edwin had said something about the two ladies not getting along. After so many years of spending time with Grace and Eleanor, he hadn't even thought about

Grace's normal flirtatiousness until Irene had actually lunged at her.

A little smile played on his face before it slipped away. As gratifying as his wife's jealousy might be, considering that just a few weeks ago she'd thrown herself at Alex, he couldn't allow her behavior to go unpunished. It seemed his love's impulses were bound to continue to get her into trouble.

If he hadn't caught her up, who knew what she might have done to Grace in the middle of the most socially important ball of the Season? The resulting scandal would have been almost impossible to recover from, for both of them.

But at least he wouldn't have to punish her this evening. He was too tired. Even if the idea did makes his groin stir with interest. And it would give her time to think through her actions; and stopping to think was definitely something his wife needed to work on. While she wasn't quite the calm, sedate bride he'd initially thought he was marrying, he did love his wife, but he was learning more and more that she was ruled by her impulses when her emotions ran high. Emotions she had learned to pent up under the disapproval of her mother; and while he was happy she didn't feel the same need to hide them from him, she obviously had very little practice controlling them without the inhibiting presence of her mother. That may be fine in the country, but not here in town where the wrong move could end up having repercussions which spanned far beyond one person.

Cutler helped him undress before he donned his dressing gown and went into the darkened bedroom. There was a single candle lit next to the bed, on his side, casting only the dimmest light throughout the room. Irene's red hair glinted in the candlelight, spread out across the pillow, and despite his exhaustion, Hugh felt his groin stir with interest again. Coming closer, he could see her fist balled up under her chin and the slight

126

puffiness to her eyes that told him she'd been crying before she'd fallen asleep.

He hated to know she'd been weeping, but he also hoped it had taught her a lesson.

Ignoring the hardening state of his cock, Hugh let his dressing gown fall to the floor and crawled in beside his wife. As usual, she was wearing her night rail. Sighing, he tugged it up to her hips so he could cradle the length of his cock between her bottom cheeks, pulling her tightly against his groin. It was one of his favorite ways to sleep. She only stirred slightly as he turned back to blow out the candle, before wrapping her in his arms. Despite his aching arousal, he fell asleep almost immediately.

******

Surely this was torture.

Sitting across the breakfast table from her husband, Irene couldn't concentrate at all. She'd been picking at the plate of fruit, which was all she'd thought she could stomach, while Hugh read the newspaper and drank his coffee. Their normal everyday routine, but today wasn't a normal day was it? No, she knew she was getting a spanking today.

And making her wait for it was just cruel.

She'd woken late and alone, although it had been obvious from the impression on the pillow beside hers and the rumpling of the sheets that Hugh had crawled into bed with her at some point during the night. That he'd had left without waking her wasn't, by itself, unusual but it still caused her stomach to stir with anxiety. When she'd come down to the breakfast table, she'd found him already there and waiting for her, as he always did when she didn't wake up next to him.

But she found her appetite had deserted her, wondering whether or not he was going to spank her immediately after breakfast. If he was going to tell her when he was going to do it. She didn't think she could wait until this evening, before bed. Dragging out the torment throughout the entire day would just be too much.

Looking over at the doorway, where a footman was posted, Irene gave him a discreet little wave of dismissal. Surprised, but obviously not going to argue, the man exited the room. Hearing the door close, Hugh looked up from his paper.

"Hugh," she said, as he sat up straight, frowning at the door the footman had just disappeared through.

"Yes sweetheart?"

Irene took a deep breath, gathering her courage. It was better to ask and find out now than to sit in worried anxiety. The words came out in a rush. "When are you going to spank me?"

Well that got his attention. Hugh's head whipped around to face her, his blue eyes boring into hers. When he looked like that she couldn't help but feel even more nervous; he was normally so cheerful, always smiling with his eyes if not his mouth, but right now he looked every inch the disciplinarian. She squirmed under his focused attention, even though she tried to keep still.

Folding the newspaper, Hugh put it down next to his coffee as he considered her words.

"Do you want me to spank you?"

"No... I mean... no... but if you're going to I want to know when you're going to do it." Irene wrung her hands in her lap. For a moment she'd actually thought she was going to say 'yes,' just because she was overwhelmed by guilt over her behavior last night. Even though she didn't want the spanking, she somehow thought she'd feel better for being punished. Transgression, punishment, and then everything was forgiven. So much less demoralizing then the way her mother would pick at her for weeks on end when she'd done something wrong.

"Oh, I'm absolutely going to spank you, Irene. I realized, looking back, that Grace can be overly familiar with me on occasion and how it may have looked to you. But that doesn't excuse your own behavior. No matter the provocation, attacking her was absolutely unwarranted."

Irene hung her head, feeling absolutely abysmal. "I know Hugh. I'm sorry."

"I'm aware there is some tension between the two of you, but you're going to have to learn how to deal civilly with her. She's one of Eleanor's best friends as well as being a friend of the family, even if my parents are disappointed in her current behavior. And if Alex reconciles with her, you're going to be seeing her even more often. The two of you need to at least be able to have a conversation together, and that relies as much on you as it does on her."

As galling as it was to admit it, Irene knew that was true. She didn't have to let Lady Grace get under her skin. Before finally falling asleep last night, she'd thought of a hundred different ways she could have handled herself. All of which would have made her look better and Lady Grace look worse.

Instead, she'd just reacted without thinking and had made herself look very bad indeed. She really hadn't meant to tear Lady Grace's dress. And she'd also realized that, in some ways, her past behavior had set her up for the way Lady Grace had flirted with Hugh last night. After all, Irene had done the exact same thing to Alex – even if he hadn't noticed – and then scoffed when Lady Grace had done the right thing and quietly pulled her aside, in private where she wouldn't be embarrassed, to request she desist. If Irene had handled her own situation with half the same amount of decorum she wouldn't be in the spot she was in now.

She could feel her husband's eyes on her studying her. "Alright Irene. I think you'll feel better if we get it over with sooner rather than later. Let's go to my study."

Following Hugh along the halls of their home, to his private area, Irene was surprised at the cessation of anxiety she felt. She was still nervous, it was true, but there was something reassuring about her husband's authoritative demeanor and care of her. This might not be the most convenient time for Hugh to punish her, but he'd seen how much the anticipation was upsetting her and he was going to take care of it. Of course, she'd rather not be punished at all... but was that true either? Did she want to walk around with this sick feeling in the pit of her stomach whenever she thought about her behavior and the possible ramifications?

When they reached his study, Hugh stepped around behind his desk to a large cabinet he kept back there, while Irene waited nervously on the other side, wringing her hands in front of her. She eyed the chair she'd been bent over the last time, knowing she was going to be in the exact same position in just a moment. But for some reason, now that she was here, all she wanted to do was put off the punishment for as long as possible.

Would her emotions ever cease to contradict each other?

Hugh pulled something from the cabinet and shut it, turning so she could see what he had in his hands. It was a long, stiffened piece of leather, almost two feet long and Irene paled as she looked at it.

"This is called a tawse, sweetheart. It's going to sting, but it's not going to mark you up or seriously harm you. I think what you've done merits more than just a regular spanking. And I want *you* to start thinking before you act. It seems to be an ongoing problem for you."

"Yes Hugh," she whispered, staring at the instrument of torture. Remembering Flora had said a caning was the worst punishment, worse than any of the others. Awful that her maid had known such things, but now Irene was grateful to know Hugh wasn't using the worst of such instruments on her. And she was especially grateful Flora was no longer in her mother's house where such punishments were apparently commonplace.

Something in Hugh's face softened as he looked at her trembling form, although he still looked very severe. "It will hurt sweetheart, and you won't like it, but I promise it won't truly harm you."

Irene nodded, unable to voice anything further. It felt like her throat was closing up. And at the same time, she wasn't truly afraid Hugh would hurt her, it was just the fear of the unknown. What would it feel like? How much would it hurt in comparison to a spanking?

"Bend over the chair and pull up your skirts," Hugh said, nodding at the chair in question. Not that she needed it; Irene remembered her last encounter with the chair quite vividly. At least this time there was no one around to witness her punishment.

Her heart was racing as she gathered her skirts, pulling them up to her waist and bending over the chair. Automatically she spread her legs for balance, feeling the split in her drawers opening slightly as she did so. Even though the current fashion was for closed drawers, all of Irene's were done in the split style. The ones she'd originally brought with her had all been remade by Flora, for exactly this reason.

Hugh moved behind her, pulling the fabric to either side of her body, making the soft white drawers framed the creamy cheeks of her bottom. His wife looked absolutely delicious like this, trembling slightly, her bottom well rounded, legs spread so he could see those adorable copper curls framing the pink slash of her quim. The bunched skirts obscured most of her upper body but he could see she'd rested her head on her folded arms and was biting her lower lip as she waited. Looking at her, his cock began stirring immediately. While he didn't completely understand why punishing his wife had such an effect on him, he was growing used to it.

"I'm going to give you twenty, Irene. The next time you act without thinking, it will be forty with the tawse."

A tremor went through her body and Hugh reached out to rub her bottom comfortingly. The rounded cheeks were satiny and firm beneath his palm, and he felt, more than heard, the sigh that went through her. Rubbing her soft skin, Hugh squeezed a bit, enjoying the feel of her flesh beneath his fingers. It pinked the skin of her bottom, but he didn't necessarily think that was a bad thing; the rubbing would warm her skin a bit so the bite of the tawse wasn't quite a total shock to her system.

After a few minutes of rubbing and squeezing those rounded globes, Hugh stepped back. Irene tensed again, waiting as he raised the tawse. He waited until her muscles trembled and then relaxed, unable to hold their tension for such a length of time, before bringing the leather down across her rear.

WHAP!

Irene shrieked, her hands immediately coming back to cover the thick red line which had appeared across the creamy surface of her skin. It did more than sting or burn, although it did both, but the pain also went deeper into her flesh, as if the tawse had actually sunk into her body.

"Move your hands, Irene."

"Please Hugh... it's too much," she begged, looking over her shoulder at him with tears in her eyes. But he just looked back at her calmly and shook his head.

"No it's not, sweetheart. Now move your hands back or I will tie them in place for you."

Whimpering, Irene put her hands back down on the cushion of the chair, burrowing her head in her arms. The throbbing ache in her bottom was already starting to subside, but she knew it would return. And she was expected to take nineteen more?

WHAP!

Somehow this one wasn't quite as bad, maybe because now she knew what to expect, but Irene still cried out as the throbbing pain spread deep into her. Somehow the tawse made it feel as though it was striking a much larger area than it actually was; as if there were waves of torment spreading across her skin in the aftermath of a strike.

WHAP!

This one caught her lower on her bottom, near her thighs, and Irene's body bounced up and down, as if her flaming cheeks were truly on fire and she was trying to use the air to cool them.

By the time Hugh had reached ten strokes across her chastised rear, Irene had lost count and was sobbing into the cushion, her fingers digging into the leather to keep herself from reaching back and covering her scalded skin. Heat and pain flared and barely subsided as the tawse slapped against her over and over again. Whenever she began to dance too much, her feet jigging her body up and down, Hugh's hand would come down on the top of her bottom, holding her in place until she regained control over herself.

The sorry state of his wife's bottom, by the time the twentieth stroke had been applied, should have made Hugh feel sorry for her or perhaps satisfied with a job well done. Instead, his overwhelming emotion was pure lust. The glowing red cheeks seemed to be emanating heat, they looked swollen and hot, as if the skin had been tautly drawn across them. Reaching out, Hugh rubbed the flaming surface, much the same as he had before he'd punished her, and felt the blaze searing his hand.

Unable to contain himself, he tossed the tawse onto his desk and reached for the front of his trousers, unlacing them and pulling his cock free. Hard as a rock, throbbing with need, a few drops of fluid were already decorating the tip. Fisting it in one hand, he rubbed his fingers along Irene's slit with his other.

She moaned, her hips moving up and down again, and he felt the moisture begin to seep from her body. It didn't matter that her bottom was a scalding torment, her pussy eagerly began to cream as he played with the soft folds. The soft moans reaching his ears sounded like a cross between pleasure and pain, making his own need surge higher.

Pressing his cock to her opening, he couldn't help shuddering with anticipation at the sight of his large rod pressing into her, between her well-roasted cheeks. Her bottom was even redder than her hair. Pushing in, both of them moaned as her wet sheath parted for him, and he gripped her hips and shoved hard into her. The heat from her bottom pressed against his groin as he filled her completely, her walls clenching around him as she let out a little cry.

"Oh sweetheart..." Hugh murmured. "You took your punishment very well, now let me make you feel good."

Irene truly wished it didn't feel good. It seemed so wrong she could find any pleasure at all when just moments ago she'd been sobbing her heart out from the scorching agony the tawse had ignited in her bottom. But just the touch of Hugh's fingers against her most sensitive folds and she'd felt her arousal surge with a shocking intensity. Then he'd pushed into her, and the sensual thrill had begun to throb along with the pain in her bottom.

She moaned as he pulled away and then thrust deep again, his stroke long and firm but gentle enough his body didn't slap too painfully against her bottom. Of course, she knew that would change eventually, but for now he began taking deep, sure strokes, kindling a new kind of flame deep within her. With every thrust she could feel the head of his manhood rubbing against a spot deep inside of her that made her gasp and spasm; every time he pressed home, the hanging sack would slap pleasurably against her splayed folds and little pleasure nub.

Excitement built within her, even as his strokes came faster, harder. Her body thrilled to the connection of their bodies, even as her bottom began to burn again whenever his thrusts rocked against it.

Pushing back against him, Irene could feel her body tightening around his rampant cock, her breathing coming fast and hot as the chaotic mix of pain and pleasure began to build up towards ecstasy. She moaned, loudly, gasping Hugh's name as his thrusts became rougher, wilder. It was exactly what she needed to take her over the edge.

The rapture bubbled upwards and over, peaking in a glorious burst of light and tingling satisfaction that spread throughout her entire body. It blossomed and rebounded, like a wave sloshing against sides of a bowl and she was the bowl. Nearly mindless with the astonishing climax, Irene vented her overstimulated nerves with a scream into the cushion in front of her, spasming as Hugh roughly thrust hard and deep and his cock surged inside of her.

The hot clasp of Irene's rippling cunt, the fiery skin of her bottom pressed against his groin, contributed to what was possibly one of the most intense orgasms of Hugh's life. It felt like his cock was bursting, swollen to the point of being almost painful, until the pleasure splintered and he flooded his wife's womb with his seed. Her pussy sucked and squeezed, he was only dimly aware of her screams of pleasure as he struggled to remain upright behind her while the pleasure drained him.

"Bloody hell..." he grunted, his body bowing forward. Planting his hands on the opposite arm rest, he arched over Irene.

The red puffy eyes and tear tracks down her face didn't detract from the glowing, satiated expression and satisfied smile curving her lips.

Reality slowly brought itself back together as he softened inside of her body, reluctant to leave the welcoming confines of her quim. Hugh stayed over her, panting as he got his breath back and just enjoyed feeling her body against his. Especially her hot little bottom. With a groan, he forced himself back upright and disengaged.

Between her pale thighs, her pussy was swollen pink and very wet, just beginning to seep the white cream of his seed. Hugh twitched her drawers shut and pulled her skirts down before lifting her into his arms. She seemed to be almost dreamy as he settled them both down on the chair, cradling her in his lap with his arms tightly around her and her head pillowed on his shoulder.

Long moments passed as they just sat there, contentedly soaking in the other's warmth and company. Irene shifted occasionally, easing the pressure on her sore bottom against Hugh's hard thighs as he stroked her shoulders, back and neck with light fingers.

"You know," she murmured eventually, "I don't enjoy the punishment, but I have no complaints about the aftermath."

Hugh chuckled, the vibrations traveling through his chest and rumbling against her cheek.

"And I don't enjoy the necessity of punishing you, but I'm rather fond of the aftermath myself."

"Just don't think to punish me when I don't deserve it just because you like what comes next," Irene warned, although she couldn't quite manage to sound severe. She poked him in the chest with her finger, but kept her cheek pressed against his shoulder so he couldn't glare at her. "I don't care what my response is afterwards, I do *not* enjoy being spanked."

"You're not supposed to, sweet."

There was another long moment of silence. Despite the throbbing ache lingering in her bottom, Irene felt strangely content. Almost kittenish; she rather thought she could purr and rub herself all over her husband and be very happy. The soreness between her legs was a good kind of soreness and it helped to ease the worst of the pain leftover from the tawse.

"I'll be civil with Lady Grace, but I won't tolerate her flirting with you. I don't care how she used to treat you, you're married to me now."

Her husband chuckled again, tightening his arms around her. Lips pressed against her forehead, which was all he could reach with the way she was cuddled against him. "You have no need to feel jealous, wife. I have no eyes for any woman but you."

Tears sparked in her own green eyes as she snuggled closer to him. "I do love you, so very much, Hugh."

"And I you."

Chapter 9

Watching over his ward with an eye towards marrying her himself, rather than marrying her off to someone else, felt very strange. And, at the same time, Wesley was fending off his mother's attempts at "practicing" finding him a suitable wife. Although, of course, he didn't tell her the direction of his thoughts; he had no idea how she would feel about Cynthia as a daughter-in-law when she'd been having such trouble with the young woman, but if she did approve then he'd find himself leg-shackled by his next breath.

His physical attraction to Cynthia aside, he began to mentally list the reasons she might make a suitable wife. For one, she could behave when she felt like it. Perhaps it was all the time spent with his mother, but when she was quite adept at being haughtily proper when the situation called for it. For another, she was already learning the responsibilities of the post since she was spending most of her time at his mother's side. She was smart, she didn't hesitate to speak her mind when they were in private, and she could make him laugh.

A few days after the Assembly he'd attended with her and his mother, he'd happened upon her while she was practicing the pianoforte. Well, he'd heard the haunting sounds trickling down the hall and he'd followed them, completely entranced by the beauty of the sound. She wasn't just technically good, she played with emotion, imbuing her playing with a quality that went far beyond enjoyable. He didn't know how long he'd stood in the doorway, not wanting to enter and break the spell of her music.

Sitting upright on the bench with her back to him, she'd gently swayed back and forth as her fingers danced over the keys. It had surprised him that she was playing a rather melancholy piece, when she was so very often the very picture of amiable cheerfulness. But it was incredibly beautiful and he'd become as lost in the music as she obviously was.

Eventually he realized he'd been standing there for far too long and he'd crept away, back the way he'd come. If he did marry the chit, he'd make it his business to take her to the opera. And the theater.

He also realized that playing the pianoforte was one of the few things Cynthia was willing to do which involved sitting down and staying still. Any other time she was required to do so, she quickly became rather squirmy. When he asked his mother about it, she said Cynthia did much better out on the estates where she could ride and walk about outside rather than have to concentrate on things like embroidery.

And, of course, the overwhelming reason he might marry her was her response to discipline. Add that to her natural sensuality, and she might just be able to satisfy him on all fronts. He realized, with some chagrin, that even when he thought about other women, none of them held the temptations Cynthia did. Sure, there were women in London he could return to, sate his appetite with, but he'd rather be here torturing himself with a young miss that was out of bounds for seduction. It was as appalling as it was entertaining.

It was a rainy Tuesday when he'd realized just how much she hated being cooped up indoors. He was sitting in the library, reading through some of his letters, when she came wandering in. When he looked up, they nodded acknowledgement at each other and then he went back to his letters while Cynthia wandered around the room.

And wandered.

And wandered.

"I know this library isn't as big as the one on the estate, but it has plenty of books to choose from," he said finally, without looking up. "Surely there must be one who catches your eye."

Cynthia sighed and he heard her wandering back in his direction. A moment later she was plopping down in the seat across from him, slumping back into the cushy chair. Hardly proper for a young lady. She'd looked more like a sulky school girl, if it wasn't for her luscious curves which were snugly cupped by the dark green fabric of her day dress.

"I've read all the ones I'm interested in."

Wesley raised his eyebrow. "There can't be very many you were interested in then."

"There aren't."

He laughed and looked up to see her smiling at him, eyes twinkling merrily. "Then why did you come in here?"

"There wasn't anything else to do. I played the piano for hours this morning and then your mother tried to make me practice embroidering. She's in bed now with a megrim, by the way," Cynthia said, waving her hand with exasperation. The Countess was probably laid low just from the effort of dealing with a bored Cynthia. Although Wesley was starting to worry about his mother's megrims; she had them quite often and he wondered if they were occurring even more often than she admitted. It seemed as though she only relinquished her watch over Cynthia when she was sure Wesley was there to take over. "There's nothing to do in the house and no one to leave the house with me." She smiled brightly at him. "Unless you'd like to?"

"No thank you." Wesley had absolutely no desire to take a bored Cynthia out in a closed carriage in the rain. He wasn't such a fool as to enclose the two of them in such a situation when he had enough trouble keeping his hands off of her while there were witnesses around.

"Blast."

She slumped again as Wesley looked up, glaring at her. "Watch your language."

For a moment he thought she was going to argue or say something else, and his pulse began to pick up at the thought of having an excuse to punish her - what better way to spend a rainy afternoon? - but then she subsided again. He went back to his letters.

Scrape.

Scrape.

Scrape.

Wesley looked up. She was sitting back far enough in the chair that she could swing her feet, but her shoes were scraping over the carpet as she did so. With her head tilted back to stare up at the ceiling, she couldn't be very comfortable. She would stop soon.

At least, that's what he told himself.

Scrape.

Scrape.

Scrape.

Scrape.

"Isn't there another room you could go to?"

"There's no one in the other rooms to entertain me."

"No one's entertaining you here." Although he could think of several ways he'd like to entertain her. But not with his mother and the upright Manfred lurking the halls, not to mention the various maids and footmen who would all report him to the Countess if they caught him doing... well, what he'd like to be doing. He might be the Earl but he had no illusions about where the household staff's loyalties lay. Not that he blamed them; hell, he'd be tempted to tell on himself. Even if he hadn't definitively decided to marry the chit yet.

"But you're here so there's at least the possibility of entertainment."

Scrape.

Wesley put his letters down, feeling quite in sympathy with his mother and her megrims. "Fine. What do you want to do?"

"I want to go out."

"Not going to happen." Wesley looked over her impassively, trying not to let his gaze linger on the hint of cleavage at the neckline of her dress or the way it clung to her curves. "We could play cards."

"Oh yes please!" Cynthia came abruptly upright. "I'm completely out of practice. Do you know how to play poker?"

"Do *you* know how to play poker?" Wesley asked, staring at her. The game had become quite popular with gentlemen, but it was not at all a proper game for ladies to play. Especially not young, unmarried ladies.

"Oh yes."

"I should spank you just for that," he muttered under his breath. Standing, he offered his hand to Cynthia and she placed hers in his as he helped her up from the chair.

✶✶✶✶✶✶

Her guardian was watching her with a gimlet eye as he dealt out the cards, so Cynthia smiled back at him as sunnily as she knew how. Over the past week she'd learned that the Earl's stern mien often covered his true emotions; she enjoyed surprising a smile from his mobile lips and occasionally even startling a burst of laughter from him. When Lord and Lady Hyde came to visit he would unwind even more. It was only when they were alone that he would take on the persona of a hidebound bore. And sometimes she could tease him out of his persona and into acting more naturally with her.

Why it mattered so much to her she wasn't quite sure. Perhaps because he constituted something most men didn't: a challenge.

Besides which, she often found herself drawn to him. Like today, for instance. If she'd truly set her mind to it, she probably could have found some activity to entertain herself. But she hadn't wanted to; she'd wanted his specific company. And so she'd sought it out.

It was also risky, seeking the Earl's company. A hint of danger for her own person, a way of tempting herself. She wanted another spanking and yet she didn't. Sometimes she just wondered if she wanted him to touch her. He had very big hands and she was quite certain they would fit perfectly over certain parts of her anatomy. Such long fingers... much longer and thicker than her own.

Shaking her head, Cynthia concentrated on her cards. They were playing for pennies, of course.

"So who taught you how to play poker?" the Earl asked, discarding two of his cards.

"Your footmen on the estate," she said, sliding one card out of her hand to be replaced. "And some of the gentlemen here in Bath have been willing to play with me on occasion."

The Earl started. "My mother allowed that?"

143

"I didn't say your mother knew."

Those expressive lips tightened, his eyes darkening as he glared at her across the table. Silence reigned for the rest of the hand, which he won. Shuffling the cards, he gave her a long look.

"Have you been losing your pin money to these men?"

"Of course not," Cynthia said calmly, picking up the cards he'd laid down for her. She smiled brightly at him. "This is the first time I've played for money."

"What did you play for before?"

"Matchsticks with your footmen while they were teaching me. And the gentlemen of Bath seem to prefer kisses."

The slamming of his palm down on the table made Cynthia jump. "You will not be playing Poker outside of this house again."

"There seems to be a lot I can't do outside of this house," she said, rather crossly, glaring at him.

"Count your blessings I don't blister your bottom for playing poker with rogues and... wagering... kisses."

Cynthia snorted. "You can't spank me for something I did in the past."

"I can spank you for whatever I want and you'd do well to remember that, baggage." Something about the way he said it made her look at him suspiciously; his mood had suddenly changed to almost cheery again.

"But you won't?" Blast, she sounded almost wistful. She didn't truly want him to spank her again. They were rather enjoying themselves right now.

The little look he gave her made her blush hotly and she looked down at her cards again to avoid his gaze. What was it about him that set her so off kilter? With other men it was easy to be flirtatious, to tease and tempt; with him, it seemed that things she wasn't sure she wanted to show always leaked through.

"Not this time."

Ominous enough to make her shiver. Cynthia changed the subject to the awful weather, putting on her protective social mask and taking refuge in the conversational subjects deemed acceptable for a young lady and a man. This seemed to amuse the Earl, but he followed her line.

As they played, she started to wonder if she was avoiding a spanking because she truly didn't want to be spanked, or because she was beginning to worry about her reactions to the Earl. Her emotions seemed to get rather tangled around him. Although he was sometimes stiff and starchy, at other times he was the most exciting man she'd ever met. But he was also trying to marry her off to someone else, and so she shouldn't be thinking of his hands or his fingers or lips. She would eventually explore all the pleasures and forbidden things she wanted to, but not with him.

The amount of disappointment she had at the thought only confirmed to her that she needed to stop titillating herself with the Earl. Which meant no more spankings. Because eventually she'd be someone else's wife and he would never be hers.

Even though she suddenly felt like crying, Cynthia covered it with a bright smile. And then she took him for all the pennies he was worth.

******

Over the next few days, Wesley noted a change in Cynthia's behavior. Perhaps it was because the weather had returned to normal, but he found himself unusually disgruntled by the fact that she was rarely to be found on her own. Even in the house, she was most often found with his mother.

He found himself missing her company; her conversation, her quick mind, and especially her outrageous little comments. Most especially, he missed being able to look at her as much as he wanted to without his sharp-eyed mother there. The only time he saw her on her own was when he heard the playing of the pianoforte, and he would often sneak in the room to watch and listen, but he never interrupted. It would break the spell.

Besides, he didn't think being completely alone with her was a very good idea. He still hadn't decided whether or not he wanted to marry her. Although he was having the devil of a time learning more about her when he couldn't spend any actual time with her.

They were on their way to attend another Assembly, Cynthia and his mother chattering as if nothing was odd about the fact that his ward wouldn't look at him. Not the easiest thing to do when he was sitting across from her in a closed carriage. When he helped her out, she caught his eye, blushed, and looked away again. So at least he knew he still had some effect on her. He wondered what was going through the chit's mind, that she had so suddenly absented herself from his presence, almost immediately after telling him that she preferred company to entertain her.

Dressed in a pale turquoise gown with gold edging which picked up the golden tints in her hair and dipped even lower than the pink dress she'd worn to the last Assembly, Cynthia was absolutely resplendent. Wesley had been surprised his mother hadn't insisted on a fichu to cover up all her creamy breast flesh - she was nearly bare to the nipple! - but the Countess hadn't even looked twice. While it was the current fashion for certain ladies in the capital, Wesley certainly hadn't noticed any young misses dressed like that. Although, he also had to admit, he didn't often look at the young misses.

Still, he couldn't stop himself from looming over Cynthia as he led both her and his mother into the room, one on each arm, and glaring at one of the young gentlemen who nearly stumbled over his own feet when he caught sight of Cynthia. The brazen chit just smiled and waved her fan, gently stirring the brunette curls resting on her shoulder. Wesley had to resist the temptation to reach out and wind a curl about his finger. He counted his blessings that at least Cynthia wasn't allowed to waltz, and wouldn't be unless she was taken to London.

Not that he would have allowed anyone other than himself to waltz with her, not dressed as she was this evening. It would be too much temptation for any man.

"Miss Bryant!" An eager young buck, whose name escaped Wesley, came bounding up to grasp her hand. Annoyance flashed through him as Cynthia giggled and accepted the overly flourished bow her young courtier made. It was a poor imitation of a true rake's elegance. "I was hoping you'd attend this evening. May I claim the first dance?"

"Her first dance is mine," Wesley said sharply, gaining a look from his mother. To his surprise she didn't say anything, just raised her eyebrow at him before turning and walking towards the corner where her contemporaries and Lord Vernier were sitting. Cynthia looked up at him, obviously surprised and a little wary of his tone.

The idiot in front of them wasn't at all perturbed. "The second then, Miss Bryant?"

"Of course, Harry," she said with a smile and Wesley nearly snarled at her use of the twit's given name. The young man brightened even further at the intimacy and bowed; after taking a second glance at Wesley he scampered.

147

Cynthia poked him in the side with her fan.

"Ow. Gently there, baggage." He rubbed the spot where she'd poked him, even though it hadn't been particularly hard, hoping to make her laugh. Instead she frowned up at him.

"Why were you so mean to poor Harry?" she chided him.

"Poor Harry's an idiot and a coward."

"Running away from you when you're scowling like *that* is a sign of intelligence, not cowardice," she countered. "In fact, I think I'll follow his example."

As she moved to pull away from him, Wesley grabbed at the hand which had been resting on his arm and yanked her back against him. "I claimed the first dance and the musicians are about to start."

She scowled up at him; unlike 'poor Harry,' she didn't look the least bit intimidated by his dark glare. Of course, that was one of the things he liked best about her, even if it would occasionally be more convenient if she was. Still, he wouldn't want a wife who always turned and ran the moment he glared. He needed a wife, like Cynthia, who was made of sterner stuff.

"I don't want to dance with you."

"Too bad."

Feeling unaccountably cheerful all of the sudden, Wesley pulled her towards the dance floor.

******

Avoiding her guardian was proving to be more difficult than Cynthia had anticipated. Not only did he have an eagle eye, but all of the gentlemen who danced attendance on her seemed to have some kind of understanding with him which included returning her to his presence at the end of every dance. Normally she

148

would have been returned to the Countess, as her chaperone, but everyone seemed to understand the Earl was standing in for the Countess this evening. She didn't know where or how anyone had received the impression, but every single gentleman had somehow received the unspoken message. The worst part was the dances themselves had ceased to be interesting, whereas standing on the Earl of Spencer's arm made her tingle all over. Which was exactly the kind of situation she wanted to avoid.

His over-protectiveness aside, his indifference to her was as rampant as ever. The low neckline she was wearing had gotten a glance of disapproval rather than interest, unlike at the last Assembly. And now he was scowling practically every time she looked at him, other than the first dance when he'd taken great joy in forcing her to dance with him after he'd been so rude to poor Harry. Then he'd been remarkably cheerful, as if pleased with himself for thwarting her. The only reason she hadn't snubbed him was she hadn't wanted to make a scene. She realized he probably didn't like her using Harry's given name, but the young man was harmless and it made him so happy when she did even if it wasn't entirely proper.

From the impatient shifting of the Earl's feet whenever she was on his arm, she deduced he'd rather be anywhere else. Although at least his mother wasn't throwing overly young beauties at his head at the moment. Perhaps that was why he was being so overbearing with Cynthia; if he was performing his duties as her guardian, his mother would leave him alone.

Either way, she didn't appreciate his looming presence. Half of the fun of Assemblies had been sneaking off and enjoying some illicit kisses with some undeserving gentleman. But with her guardian watching over her so closely, it was proving to be impossible. Besides which, his mere presence had apparently scared off the usual rogues who would tempt her.

149

He was the biggest, most powerful, most authoritative male in the room and not afraid to use his heft to achieve what he wanted. And damned if that didn't make her body feel warm and excited all over.

"Blast," she muttered under her breath as her current dancing partner led her right back to where her guardian was standing next to Lord Hyde. Unfortunately there was no escape for her, Eleanor hadn't been feeling well and so hadn't come tonight. Lord Hyde was only here to back up Lord Spencer. As the center of both their attention, she felt hemmed in and trapped. It wasn't at all pleasant.

With barely a glance at her, the Earl took her back on his arm and settled her at his side, while he and Lord Hyde continued their conversation. Her presence encouraged several other men to join them, but none of them were very interesting; just the kind of staid, boring young men whom the Earl probably thought she should marry. But next to him they all looked unrefined, unexciting and thoroughly unbearable. At least if he asked, she could tell him that all of them bored her beyond belief. Then again, since meeting him, it seemed as if every man was becoming boring.

Cynthia tried to tug her hand away and the Earl turned his head to frown at her. She smiled sweetly, insincerely, up at him. "Excuse me please, I need to visit the lady's retiring room."

He hesitated and then nodded, releasing her. "Come right back."

Inwardly fuming, Cynthia didn't bother to respond, she just walked away as quickly as she could without looking like she was running. The smile she pasted on her face seemed to fool the young gallants around her, who all allowed her to pass on her way to the retiring room. At least there she could have a moment to herself, no need to deal with aggravating men!

There were several other young ladies in there, tittering and gossiping. Not surprisingly they were all in alt over the presence of the handsome Earl of Spencer. Cynthia recognized Miss Whyte, who was embellishing greatly on the Earl's interest in her and his promise to seek her out next Season.

"Spencer's the most *divine* dancer," Miss Whyte was gushing to her friend, fanning herself delicately. "And so very handsome. I do believe his mother prefers me over any of the other young ladies here... she *specifically* told me she would look for me next Season."

Blech. If the Earl actually married that simpering ninny... What was the Countess thinking?!

Well it wasn't Cynthia's business anyway.

Feeling even more sour, Cynthia splashed some water on her face and tidied her hair before sighing and stepping back out into the social whirl. At least she had the most interesting dress of all the young ladies present, although she did have to watch out deeply she breathed. Ninnies in the retiring room, an overbearing stuffed shirt in the ball room... where could a girl go to have some peace of mind around here?

Looking around the room for her guardian, Cynthia saw to her surprise that he was out on the dance floor again, his mother watching smugly from the sidelines. Well that was something, anyway, although dancing would keep him from hovering over her between sets. She also didn't like the little pit in her stomach that seemed to grow as she watched him dancing with yet another beautiful young lady. This time next year would she be in London, married to someone who wasn't nearly as exciting or interesting, and forced to watch the Earl's courtship of some simpering debutante? It seemed likely. It also seemed like a scenario that would motivate her to tear her hair out.

"Cynthia..." A male voice whispered to her side. "Cynthia..." She looked over to see Mr. Carter standing by one of the columns, obscured from view of the dance floor. *Probably hiding from the Earl*, she thought with some despair. Still handsome, but his appeal had definitely lessened since the last time she'd seen him.

Still, at least he was fun, and she did like the way he kissed. Besides, flirting with him would mean she could distract herself from watching the Earl dance with young misses and dwelling on her future. Smiling brightly at him, she glided over to where he was standing, enjoying the way his eyes traveled over her gown and lingered on her nearly exposed breasts. "Hello Mr. Carter."

"Your new guardian must be very strict, poppet," he said, putting his fingers beneath her chin to tilt her head up. Cynthia's breath caught in her throat; he wouldn't really kiss her here, would he? Where anyone could see? Although that was part of the excitement of Mr. Carter, he was so often doing exactly what he was not supposed to. "I haven't seen you in an age."

"He is quite a nuisance," she said with a little sigh, fluttering her eyelashes up at him. Nuisance wasn't quite the word for it, but it was true in many ways. Mr. Carter smiled, the rakish grin which used to set her pulse pounding. Now she felt a small tingle of excitement, but compared to the Earl's occasional smile, Mr. Carter's no longer seemed so special.

"Would you like to take a walk outside?" he asked, releasing her chin and offering his arm. "There are some lovely flowers out on the terrace we might... admire."

Cynthia glanced at the dance floor where it appeared her guardian was fully occupied with the young blonde woman who was simpering up at him. Giving Mr. Carter her brightest smile, she wrapped her hand around his elbow. "I would love to."

******

"My Mama told me Spencer House is one of the most beautiful on the coast, with a lovely little folly done in the Grecian style, and acres and acres of land as well as being so close to the sea you can go bathing on a daily basis! Not that I would ever do such a thing," she said, tittering in a manner which made Wesley's ears hurt.

Despite the fact that Miss Durand was speaking of his own estates, Wesley hadn't been able to get a word in edgewise since they'd started dancing. Instead, he just listened as the chit described every bit of his own lands to him, in the excitable terms of her youth and her mother's ambitions. Recently arrived in Bath, Miss Durand and her parents had been forced to shorten her first Season due to Mrs. Durand's health. The matron had been ecstatic to discover an eligible nobleman in Bath and he'd overheard her telling the Countess perhaps it was fate, rather than her health, which had forced them to quit the capital a week early.

As a gentleman, Wesley just gritted his teeth and danced with the chit, counting down the measures of music until he could escape.

Out of the corner of his eye he saw the dark hair of his ward exiting the retiring room and stopping to speak with someone he couldn't quite see. For the most part she'd been remarkably well behaved during the evening, although he knew she was chafing under his close watch. But he'd found himself feeling remarkably possessive.

That feeling of possessiveness, combined with his short-patience for seeing her dancing with other men, and his even shorter patience for young ladies like Miss Durand, had pretty well convinced him he should have Cynthia as his bride. Even if it meant giving up his bachelorhood before he'd originally planned. At least he wouldn't have to spend torturous Seasons in the capital while his mother threw all sorts of empty-headed and title-hungry young harpies at his head. And he could satisfy his lust for Cynthia.

Tomorrow he would speak to his mother and then he'd propose. Well. First thing he'd visit the shops and buy a ring, then he'd speak to his mother and then he'd propose. Ladies expected a betrothal ring. Just thinking about it made the unstoppable flood of Miss Durand's words more bearable; he just let them wash right over him while he planned.

He didn't expect Cynthia to balk. And if she did, well she was obviously ripe for seduction, he would have no trouble bringing her around. The frisson of attraction between them was mutual; it shouldn't be any hardship to convince her around to his way of thinking. In fact, part of him almost hoped she needed some persuading. Even if she didn't, then they could certainly do some celebrating and he could discover whether her lips were as sweet as they looked.

Glancing over her way again, every muscle in his body tensed as he saw her walking towards the doors on the arm of the man she'd been speaking with. Wesley didn't recognize him, but he knew the type immediately. After all, like recognized like. It was impossible to mistake that elegant walk, the confident swagger, and the impeccable dress with just the hint of dissipation as belonging to anything other than a true rake. And, like a true rogue, he'd waited until the opportune moment while the guardian was involved in a situation he couldn't extricate himself from and the young lady was unchaperoned.

Looking around the room frantically, Wesley couldn't locate Edwin either.

"My Lord? Is everything alright?" Miss Durand looked legitimately concerned. Probably because he was swinging his head back and forth in a panic and his dance steps had slowed almost to a complete halt.

"Ah yes, sorry my dear," he said, giving her a tight smile. "I just saw someone I need to speak with as soon as possible."

"Oh." Miss Durand thought about this and then pouted up at him, in a way she probably thought was attractive but made her look a bit like a fish. "I was so hoping you might come and speak with my Mama and I. I'm sure she'd love to hear more about you."

Apparently Mrs. Durand knew more about him and his estates than he did, going by the information she'd imparted to her daughter. Not that he'd have accepted such an invitation even if she hadn't.

"Perhaps some other time," he said shortly.

To his relief, his obvious distraction contributed to Miss Durand's pouting silence for the rest of the dance. He practically scooped her up off the dance floor and deposited her back with her doting Mama before dashing off towards the door he'd seen Cynthia go out of.

✳✳✳✳✳✳

"Find a way to come out tomorrow and meet me," Mr. Carter whispered in Cynthia's ear, his hands sliding up and down her sides in a way she found quite exciting as his palms brushed her breasts. Lips moved down her neck and she let her head fall back as she sighed with pleasure. The way he was touching her was almost enough to make her forget the Earl. "I'll make it worth your while."

"Perhaps. If I can manage it," Cynthia whispered back, her hands tightening on his coat as his palms cupped her breasts and squeezed. Some of his fingers were touching her bare flesh because her dress was cut so low and the sensation of skin against skin thrilled her. If he just dipped his fingers into the neckline then he'd be able to touch her bare nipple. It would be the most she'd ever allowed him, but she was feeling reckless and wild tonight, willing to tempt ruination.

Mr. Carter had her backed up against one of the outdoor columns, in the shadows and partly concealed by a large rhododendron. And if he wasn't as exciting as the Earl and didn't make her heart race as fast as the Earl did, he was still a very good kisser and right now she felt all swollen and tender in her breasts and between her legs. He was very good at making *her* feel very good. Perhaps she should risk a punishment to go meet him tomorrow... now that she knew it wouldn't get her with child, she was even more wildly curious about what it would be like to see his cock and even take it in her mouth.

Right now that portion of his body was firmly pressed against her lower stomach, a throbbing ridge which made her feel even more excited when she rubbed herself against it.

When he brought his mouth back to hers, Cynthia parted her lips eagerly, moaning a little as he squeezed her breasts tightly in his hands. His tongue explored her mouth eagerly, his fingers stroking along her bare skin and she was sure that at any moment he was going to slide his fingers into the top of her dress and touch one of her swollen nipples. The little buds were aching for attention.

Suddenly Mr. Carter was gone and Cynthia found herself nearly falling over as half of her support disappeared. Clutching at the column behind her, she stifled a shriek as she looked up to see the Earl, face red with fury, punch Mr. Carter. The gentlemen stumbled back and landed on his arse, holding one hand up to his injured face. Mr. Carter stared up at his assailant and Cynthia's heart pounded, wondering what was going to happen. Would they fight? Would the Earl demand Mr. Carter marry her?

This was the first time she'd been caught in such a situation and she had no idea what to expect. And, she suddenly realized, she didn't want to be married to Mr. Cater, even if the Earl did force him to offer. Having the two men in front of her, it was obvious which one she truly responded to, which one her emotions were tangled up in, and for a moment she utterly despaired.

The Earl moved so he was standing between them, his back to her, but she could see his anger in every line of his body and his clenched fists. She thought she actually might faint from the sheer build-up of anxiety in her burdened lungs.

"Get out. And stay away from her." The Earl's voice was low, soft, and murderous. In fact, she'd never heard him sound so dangerous, so threatening, even when shed been discovered with Mr. Brandon in the bookshop. For once, she truly did feel a bit frightened of him.

"She was willing," Mr. Carter said, getting to his feet and still holding his hand over his eye. His dark blonde hair was slightly rumpled, as were his clothes, but he would still have been handsome if it wasn't for the ugly expression across his face. Cynthia hadn't expected him to offer to make things right, but still! His ungentlemanly verbal retreat sincerely made her hope the Earl didn't push the point.

She *truly* did not want to marry Mr. Carter.

"She won't be anymore," the Earl said shortly. "Now get out."

The stood there for a moment, staring each other down, and then Mr. Carter gave a sharp nod and turned and left.

Clinging to the column, Cynthia realized she was trembling all over. She was in so much trouble. More trouble than she'd ever been in her life. All the air seemed to vacate her body as she sighed out, thankful the Earl had let Mr. Carter go. Although she did wonder why he wasn't threatening pistols at dawn this time. Unless, of course, he was placing equal blame on her as he was on Mr. Carter.

She felt rather ashamed of herself, for the first time.

When the Earl turned around, his face was harder than she'd ever seen it, but his eyes were burning with a fury she could see even in the dim lighting. She stared up at him, her mind blank, her body still tingling slightly from Mr. Carter's attentions. And she couldn't think of a single thing to say.

Chapter 10

With Cynthia's disheveled state and his own towering rage, there was no way he could take her back through the Assembly rooms, so instead he took her through one of the side exits and they traveled the back halls to get to the front. There was no one there, thankfully, except a few servants who looked at them and then looked away. His ward was flushed, her lips swollen from kisses, her hair mussed, and the neckline of her gown slightly ripped, which told him exactly where the other man's hand had been. Who knew what the blaggard might have done if Wesley hadn't gotten there just then.

Strangely, having caught Cynthia with another man didn't make him any less eager to marry her. If anything, he was more determined than ever to lay his own claim to her. With his own rampant libido and penchant for all things sexual, he wasn't the least bit concerned with keeping her satisfied. Hell, he'd love to satisfy her. And if he had to keep her chained to his bed to ensure her faithfulness, he didn't have a problem with that either.

The front hall was deserted as well, everyone was already in the Assembly rooms and he could hear the buzz of conversation and music coming from behind the doors. Thankfully they were closed so there was no one of importance to notice their sudden appearance. Keeping a firm grip on her bicep - not that she was struggling, she seemed too shocked and overwhelmed by his appearance and reaction to try and resist - Wesley motioned over one of the footmen.

"I need you to find my mother, the Countess of Spencer, and inform her my ward has a megrim and needs to return home."

The man nodded, barely glancing at Cynthia, and disappeared into the Assembly rooms to find the Countess. Trying not to tap his foot impatiently, Wesley occupied his time by sending another footman to have the carriage brought round and then silently trying to get his temper under control. By the time the carriage was waiting for them, the footman he'd sent to find his mother was returning, unaccompanied.

"My lord, the Countess has decided to stay and has accepted the offer of a ride home from Lord Vernier."

"Very well," Wesley growled, trying not to take his temper out on the poor footman. It wasn't his fault the Countess wanted to stay and be social and didn't realize what a situation she was putting Wesley in. He realized this might be for the best; if his mother saw Cynthia right now she would have some idea of what the chit had been up to and who knew what her reaction might be.

Dragging his ward behind him down the street, Wesley practically tossed her up into the closed carriage before climbing in after her. With the curtains drawn and only letting in the dimmest amount of light, they were, quite suddenly, alone. He rapped on the top of the carriage to let the coachman know they were settled and the carriage immediately began to move, rocking forward.

Sitting across from her, Wesley crossed his arms over his chest to ensure he would keep his hands to himself.

"Alright miss. You may now explain yourself."

There was a sigh from the other side of the carriage. Unfortunately he couldn't see her expression so he couldn't tell if it was a contrite sigh or an impatient one. "I should rather think the... situation you found me in was self-explanatory."

"What I don't understand is *why* I found you in it. Are you trying to shame me? My mother? Do you realize what could have happened?"

"Of course I do," she replied, sounding rather cross at his questions. Wesley could see her leaning back and crossing her own arms beneath her chest, tossing her head rather haughtily. At least he could see what she was doing even if he couldn't make out her expression, although her intransigence just made his temper climb even higher. "But everyone was inside, we were in no danger of being caught out."

"You're lucky I caught you out. If anyone else had then you'd be ruined right now," he growled, tightening his arms against the urge to reach out and position her over his knee. "Do you *want* to be ruined?"

"No, of course not."

Exasperated, Wesley tossed his hands up in the air, nearly overbalancing as the carriage rocked at the exact same time - which didn't help his temper at all. She sounded absolutely sincere, which made even less sense to him given her behavior. "Then why do you keep putting yourself in situations where you might be ruined?"

"It's exciting. And I've never been caught before."

Completely fed up, Wesley grabbed the infuriating chit and pulled her across the carriage, upending her over his knee. She shrieked, kicking and wriggling to get away, but once he had her voluminous skirts flipped up it was even easier to hold her still because the skirts were covering her upper body and making it harder for her to move. Underneath her petticoats she wasn't wearing any drawers and the pale cheeks of her bottom glowed faintly in the dim light of the moon coming through the window.

Well they wouldn't be pale much longer.

SMACK!

A muffled howl and she kicked out, connecting only with the walls of the carriage. There wasn't much room for her to maneuver, which was all to his advantage especially as he'd gotten a firm hold round her waist.

SMACK! SMACK! SMACK!

The soft flesh of her bottom jiggled and gave under his hand, he was spanking her with all the considerable force he could muster given the somewhat limited swing the carriage required. It was also a bit harder to keep her on his lap in the moving conveyance, even though she'd stopped squirming. He could still hear her muffled cries with every slap of his hand against her bottom and his cock throbbed in response.

SMACK! SMACK! SMACK!

He spanked her until his hand was beginning to smart and he could see her cheeks had turned bright red under the assault. Heat was emanating off the glowing surface and her body was limp over his lap, her pleading sobs still muffled by all the skirts. Grimly he kept spanking, determined to implant this lesson in her mind. If he'd had something to spank her with, he would have.

Suddenly Wesley realized the carriage had stopped; they were home. He ceased spanking her, listening to her sobs as he breathed heavily in the warmth of the carriage, his hand resting on her hot bottom. For a moment he hesitated, but he knew the coachman would realize not to interrupt. And he had to know.

He let his hand slide down between her legs.

******

If she'd thought her prior spankings were bad, this one had been even worse. The Earl was merciless, ignoring her pleas, her apologies, and every smack was as hard or even harder than the last. The entire surface of her bottom felt like it was on fire, her lower body an inferno that blazed with agony, and yet the slaps just kept raining down anyway.

162

The skirts around her head caught her tears, her hands braced as best they could against the floorboards of the rocking carriage. She'd been rather frightened of being thrown against the opposite seat, until the pain of the spanking had completely overwhelmed her and she couldn't think of anything else except begging the Earl to stop. When he didn't, she just sobbed into her skirts, clutching at the floor and kicking her legs in pained response.

When the assault suddenly ceased, she almost didn't notice. Her bottom was throbbing so badly it felt like the slaps were continuing; it was more the cessation of sound that caught her attention. Tears continued to fall as she cried, almost dizzy from the pain and her upturned position.

Then the Earl's large hand rested on her bottom, much cooler than that glowing surface, and she shuddered all over at the intimate touch. To her shock, his hand began to slide downwards, his fingers moving inwards towards the crease of her bottom, and then touching the swollen folds of her quim. As soon as he did so, she realized she'd had her usual reaction to being spanked, as inexplicable as it was.

And a man was touching her for the first time. Not just any man, but *him*.

Cynthia moaned as the Earl's fingers slipped easily between her folds, torn between humiliation at his discovery, extreme arousal, and shock he was touching her in this way. Her hands batted at her skirts as she tried to squirm away, but he secured his tight hold on her body and the layers of fabric effectively trapped her so she couldn't even attempt to push his hand away. And that just made her even wetter.

Touching herself and having someone else touch her was completely different. She couldn't control or even anticipate where the Earl's fingers might go, and the uncertainty seemed to make the sensations even more intense as he stroked her. Cynthia gasped as the inquisitive fingers stroked up and down her slit, all the way up to the little pearl at the apex which was surely swollen beyond anything she'd ever felt before. Her wetness had completely soaked her pussy lips and, as the Earl continued to caress the sensitive folds, was even now spreading to the tops of her thighs as she became more and more excited.

Very dimly, she heard the Earl chuckle and murmur something. She couldn't make out what he said, but he sounded pleased. Normally she would have been infuriated by his amusement when she was in such a position, but right now she didn't care what he did as long as he didn't stop touching her! The need growing inside of her core was more intense, more demanding than she'd ever felt before.

His other hand curved over her bottom and she groaned as he squeezed the tortured flesh, igniting the sharp bite of pain again... it mingled strangely with the pleasure that his stroking fingers were creating in her pussy. Enhanced it even, the way eating something bitter made sugar taste all the more sweet.

Then one of his fingers pressed to her opening and slid inside of her. Cynthia cried out, her hips wagging up and down at the shockingly delightful sensation. His finger was much longer and thicker than her own, moving back and forth, deeper and deeper as the rest of his fingers continued to play with and stroke her folds. He began squeezing her reddened bottom in time with his finger thrusts, causing the burn and ecstasy to collide deep inside of her until she couldn't tell which was which.

"Oooooh..." she cried out.

This was wicked. Sinful even. Far worse than any of the other rules of propriety she'd ever broken, and yet she had no control over it – which was a heady sensation. Cynthia had always been in control of what rules she broke and how she broke them; suddenly having it taken away from her was beyond exciting.

A second finger joined the first and she gasped at the stretch of her inner muscles, of the probing invasion of a man's fingers. Something pressed against her clitoris and she bucked and heaved as the Earl's hand squeezed and his fingers stroked. The shocking rapture blossomed outward unexpectedly, her first climax at the hands of someone other than herself and all the more intense and surprising because of that.

The pain from the spanking and the incredible ecstasy from her climax was almost too much. She cried out, gasping for air, fighting back blackness that edged in around her vision; the feeling she was going to faint grew stronger as the Earl's fingers continued to stroke, wringing every last ripple of pleasure from her squirming body. He pushed her far beyond the edges of pleasure that she found for herself, leaving her sobbing at the strength of her orgasm.

Finally the movement stopped and Cynthia slumped over his lap, shuddering as his fingers slid from her quivering pussy.

******

Beautiful.

That was Wesley's first thought. Cynthia's bright, glowing bottom was a thing of absolutely beauty, the wet swollen folds beneath it only adding to the attraction. His cock surged, but he beat back the impulse to lay her against the opposite seat in the carriage and take his pleasure. Still...

Leaning back, Wesley shifted Cynthia just enough to allow him to unlace his breeches, freeing his cockstem from the tight confines of fabric. With a groan, he fisted the hard rod in his hand and pumped, several times. It was all he needed for great white streams of cum to spray across the flaming surface of her bottom, making it look even redder than before in contrast. The pleasure of release left him groaning in satisfaction, more satisfaction than he'd had ever since he'd arrived in Bath.

Panting, he took his sore hand – sore from spanking her bottom, so he could only imagine how said bottom felt at the moment – and rubbed the white rivulets of seed into her red skin. The friction of his hand against her sensitive cheeks made Cynthia whimper, a sound he could barely hear through her skirts.

With another groan, Wesley secured his breeches and then brought Cynthia up to a sitting position, seating her back on the bench she'd started out on. She was sniffling, her nose red, her eyes pink and wide with shock. The expression on her face was rather dazed as she stared across at him. Her breasts had come out of her low cut dress and Wesley reached forward, cupping them in his hands and pinching the hard little nipples as he stared into her eyes.

Cynthia shivered and moaned, rocking slightly on the seat, which was surely very uncomfortable right now. Hearing movement outside, Wesley tamped down on his desires to continue playing with her and he drew her dress back up over her breasts. The image remained seared in his mind, however, and he looked forward to being able to enjoy those luscious mounds with a more thorough examination later.

Opening the carriage door, he gave a nod to the coachman who was obviously pretending momentary deafness. Good man. Taking Cynthia by the hand, he pulled her out of her seat and gathered her up in his arms, ignoring her muffled protest as he cradled her body against his. With one arm behind her back and the other tucked under her knees, there really wasn't any way for her to resist him even if she hadn't been so dazed. She was a nice, soft armful; she felt right snuggled up against him.

"Thank you, Lordan," he said to the coachman, before swinging his ward around and heading for the front steps. He made a mental note to ensure the man received a bonus tomorrow. There was nothing like cold, hard cash to help ensure silence. Even if he planned to marry her, he didn't want his Countess to have a sullied reputation or for anyone to think he was marrying her because he *had* to.

There was no one on the street; it was too early for most of the fashionable of Bath to be returning home, which was good since there would be no one to gossip. And he trusted his mother's staff to keep their lips sealed, especially once the betrothal was announced. The only person they would tell was his mother herself, and he intended on speaking with her first thing tomorrow.

Cynthia murmured and wriggled a bit as he went up the stairs, obviously beginning to come out of her pleasure induced stupor.

"Stay still so I don't drop you," he said, rather lightly as Manfred opened the door. The lines of disapproval in the old man's face were deeply drawn. There was definitely one servant who wouldn't hesitate to tell the Countess everything, but Wesley knew he'd be forgiven once he explained. And there was every chance Manfred would wait till tomorrow to inform the Countess anyway. Telling her tonight would only disturb her sleep, and Manfred wouldn't do that. So all Wesley had to do to evade a scene was ensure he reached his mother before Manfred tomorrow morning.

Murmuring something again, her words too indistinct for Wesley to make out, Cynthia snaked her arm around his neck to further secure herself in his arms as he made his way for the stairs. Grinning, he could nearly feel Manfred's eyes boring into the back of his head. He knew exactly what kind of picture he and Cynthia made. Manfred obviously thought Wesley rather thoroughly ruined his ward, in the carriage, right in front of his mother's house.

Well, that wasn't too far from the truth. He had certainly ruined her although not as thoroughly as he might have liked. And considering no one but the servants knew, it's not as if she was truly ruined anyway. But enough that he would have been forced to make a proper woman out of her, if he hadn't planned to already.

Having maneuvered his way up the stairs, Wesley headed towards Cynthia's room. She was snuggled into him now, her head resting on his shoulder, her fingertips lightly playing with the hair on the back of his neck. As long as she knew it was him carrying her and she wasn't thinking of some other man, then he certainly didn't mind. And his desire was already rising again as the back of his neck tingled under her touch. Knowing that underneath her skirts she had a very red bottom with his seed pressed into it didn't help. He really shouldn't have done that, but he hadn't been able to help himself.

It had soothed part of his possessive jealousy, as though he'd irrevocably marked her.

They'd have to have the wedding as soon as possible, he decided. He didn't think he'd last four weeks while the banns were read. Getting a special license would be the first thing on his to-do list. After speaking to his mother. And getting his little minx a ring.

******

Maybe this was a dream, Cynthia mused. Although she couldn't imagine how she would have fallen asleep at a ball. Or have conjured a dream of such a painful spanking. Perhaps the first part wasn't the dream and she had passed out during her punishment? Lowering thought. She'd always considered herself rather more robust than that.

She knew this really wasn't a dream, but she felt so deliciously hazy, so wonderfully muzzy... and the Earl wasn't behaving at all like himself. Everything felt rather dream-like. Well except for her throbbing bottom. But even that had been lessened by the incredible ecstasy the Earl's fingers had wrought in her. She wasn't entirely sure what had happened after that until they'd come into the house.

When she'd taken a peak over the Earl's shoulder on the way to the stairs, she'd seen Manfred glowering at them. Inwardly Cynthia sighed, knowing she was likely to get a lecture from the Countess tomorrow. Possibly two if the Earl told her what had happened at the Assembly rooms. Probably another lecture from the Earl and possibly another spanking as well.

She really shouldn't let the Earl be carrying her like this, but it felt so nice. No man had ever carried her. The muscles beneath his clothing moved and strained, and were so very attractive. It made her want to touch him, to run her hands over every part of him. The most she dared was his hair, which was soft and easily twined about her fingers.

How was she supposed to recover from this? Everything he did just made her further obsessed with him. Cynthia pushed the thought away, determined to enjoy being in his arms while it lasted and dealing with her twisted emotions on the morrow.

"In we go, baggage," he murmured as he pushed open the door to her room.

Silly chit, she scolded herself. *Baggage* was not a term of endearment, even if that was how her ear heard it.

Gently he laid her down on her bed, making her bottom twinge, although she didn't try to roll away. She finally dared to look up into his hazel eyes. For once they weren't hard, rather they were almost thoughtful, contemplative. Searching, rather than focused, as if he was trying to see within her rather than already knowing her thoughts – which he so often seemed to do. Heavy eyelashes blinked and then a slow smile spread across his face as he examined hers. Cynthia stared back up at him, eyes wide, waiting... but she didn't know for what.

He lowered his head and Cynthia gasped as his lips met hers. The Earl was kissing her!

A flash of desire shot through her, despite the fact she was sated. His lips were firm, coaxing, and she parted her own, inviting him in. Even if this was madness, she wanted it. And he kissed like a dream. There was no comparison to the other men she'd kissed in the past; this kiss made her feel so much more wanton, so much more wild and excited. The wet silk of his tongue danced with hers, exploring each other and he tasted like whiskey and spice. He kissed her until she felt breathless, her breasts becoming heavy and swollen, and her quim beginning to ache again. She barely even noticed how sore her bottom was as she lay on her back - it didn't matter if only he would keep kissing her.

When he pulled away, she was left gasping, her hands clutching at his jacket. Gently, he pried her fingers off as she stared up at him, trying to decipher what was happening. That kiss had already ruined her for any other man, why was he pulling away now? Why was he standing rather than joining her on the bed?

"Wait!" she cried out, pushing herself up to her elbows. "Where are you... why aren't you..."

The Earl chuckled, putting two fingers under her chin and tilting her head back. Leaning over her, his lips barely brushed against hers. It was less of a kiss and more of a promise. "You'll have to wait until after we're married to be completely ruined, baggage."

His lips pressed down again, this time kissing her more fully, although without his tongue, and then he was walking towards her door, leaving her feeling bereft and utterly confused.

"*Wait*!" Her strangled cry caught him in the doorway, and he turned to look at her. Darkly handsome, a devilish twinkle in his eye, and every inch the elegant gentleman. Except she'd already discovered, the guise of a gentleman only covered the true dominant male underneath. "Married?"

A little amused smile crossed his lips. "Of course. And don't you dare think about going anywhere *near* another man or I'll take a strap to your arse and I won't care about how red it already is."

The crudeness of his threat left her staring as he exited and shut the door behind him.

Married! To... to *him!*

A thrilled flutter went through her stomach even as confusion buffeted her about. Why on earth did he want to marry her? He hadn't said. Cynthia flopped back down on the bed and immediately turned on her side, hissing, as her bottom protested. Now that she'd been shocked out of her pleasant haze, her poor rear end was burning more than ever.

Think about another man? How could she?

Still, he didn't know he'd been consuming her thoughts. And if he didn't know, then she wasn't going to tell him. With a man like that, she needed every advantage she could get. Although she certainly wasn't going to test him by kissing other men. Not because she feared a spanking, but because she didn't want him to change his mind.

She would absolutely marry him. Even if he wasn't as easily distracted or influenced as other men she'd met. Even if he spanked her. Actually, she wasn't sure if spanking was a detraction or a benefit of marrying him.

Right now it certainly felt like a detraction, but she was quite sure she'd be disappointed if he never spanked her again. A little smile played across her face. While he might not be easily influenced, she was quite sure she could spur him into punishing her whenever she felt like. If nothing else, his last words to her had indicated a rather surprising possessiveness on his part.

Marrying the Earl was the only way to assuage her curiosity and the tingling excitement he created inside of her. The only way she could keep her heart from breaking as she watched him with other debutantes. None of them would have him, he would be hers. And, as he wanted her attention solely on him, she could demand the same in return. Cynthia had no qualms about that.

She just hoped his mother wouldn't be too upset.

Chapter 11

Knowing his mother's penchant for taking her breakfast in her room, Wesley asked the staff to notify him when his mother sent for her breakfast. That way he could go and speak with her before Manfred or any of the other servants would have a chance to.

When he entered the room, his mother was sitting up in her bed, taking a light repast on a tray. The bed curtains had been drawn fully back, as had the drapes, and light was streaming in through both windows. Wesley was suddenly forcibly reminded of many days when he was a child and had come up to see his mother during breakfast, just like this. When the old Earl was alive, the Countess never joined them for anything other than the evening meal, although her door was always open to her sons. He'd spent many a morning sitting on her bed and talking to her, even more so than either of his brothers. Smiling a welcome at him, she buttered her toast and waved him to come closer.

"Good morning, Wesley, to what do I owe the honor of a visit?" she asked, her voice light and a bit teasing. After all, it had been years since he'd paid such a visit to her over breakfast. This might have been one of the things he'd missed most about England when he'd been overseas.

Wesley cleared his throat, suddenly uncertain as how to broach the subject of his marriage with his mother. It had all seemed remarkably easy before he'd stepped into the room and actually faced her; just announce he and Cynthia were getting married, and that was that. Now, looking down at his mother, he found himself feeling rather young and awkward; neither of which he was accustomed to feeling. Would she approve? He certainly wanted her to, he realized.

To buy himself some time, he pulled a chair closer to her bed so he could sit facing her. She watched him, one eyebrow arching as if in amusement over his hesitance.

The dressing gown she was wearing over her night rail made her look softer, more approachable, and yet he was still having difficulties finding the correct words. After all, it wasn't something he had much experience in.

Clearing his throat again, Wesley reminded himself that he wasn't in trouble. "I ah... as much as I appreciate your um... enthusiasm for procuring a marriage for me next Season, I've actually decided I might want to marry ah... sometime before that."

There, that was a good introduction.

"Oh! Did you have someone already in mind, dear?" The Countess put down her toast on her plate, her forehead crinkling a bit in concern. Cocking her head at him, she studied his face. "I apologize, darling, I didn't even think to ask if you already had a *tendre* for someone, I just assumed..." Her voice trickled off as she waited for his answer, since obviously he'd told her just a few days ago that he had no interest in marrying, much less anytime soon.

"No! I mean, that is, I didn't..." Oh bloody hell, might as well just get it over with. Wesley braced himself. "I've decided to marry Cynthia."

"Wesley!" the Countess screeched. He ducked the piece of toast flung in his direction, wincing at the shrill tone of her voice. "You compromised her last night, didn't you?!"

"No!"

"You didn't?"

Wesley eyed his mother suspiciously, and not just because she was now holding a second piece of toast. Did she sound just a little bit disappointed? Surely not.

"No... well, not really. Not completely, but it could have had the appearance of... anyway, what I mean to say is

174

I've grown rather fond of the chit and I know she's been a handful to you, but I'll make sure she behaves herself from now on and..." His voice trailed off as he realized his mother was beaming at him. Did his mother really not care *who* he married as long as he married someone? Or was there more going on here than he realized?

Wesley had the sudden suspicion he'd been set up.

"This is wonderful! Marie!-" she called out for her maid. "Marie come here at once! I need to get dressed!"

"Mother..."

"Oh do be quiet Wesley and get out, there's a great deal to be done and I need to be dressed to do it!"

******

When Edwin and Eleanor arrived, after receiving Wesley's note, it was to a house clearly in turmoil. Eleanor could hear the strident tones of the Countess echoing down the hall, obviously setting her troops in order. Looking rather harassed, Manfred showed them to the library where Wesley was obviously hiding out; he looked like a man under siege. Rather than sitting down, he was pacing around the room with a large glass in hand – looking at the crystal tumbler, Eleanor blinked. She recognized whiskey when she saw it. Then again, going by the way the Countess sounded, he probably needed some serious fortifying.

"Wesley! Congratulations!" Edwin gave his friend a hug, and then Eleanor caught him up, laughing as Wesley squeezed her tight with one arm. The other was busy holding onto his drink. She hugged him back, adding her own congratulations to Edwin's.

"Thank you... welcome to the madness. I told my mother this morning and I don't know what she's doing exactly, but apparently there's quite a bit that needs to be done today, immediately, if I'm going to be married in two weeks." He looked rather exasperated and Eleanor had to snicker. Men. They just didn't understand the time it took to plan any event, much less a major one like a title Earl's wedding. She sighed a little. If she'd had the wedding of her dreams it would have taken far longer than two weeks to plan...

"What needs to be done today?" Edwin asked, looking equally baffled. Eleanor restrained herself from rolling her eyes.

"I have no idea, but my mother's been on a tear ever since I broke the news."

"I'm going to go see what I can do to help," Eleanor said, smiling. As much as she wanted to question Wesley, she was even more curious about what Cynthia thought of all of this. Despite Wesley's attempt at being exasperated, he looked remarkably cheerful under his harried exterior, so she knew he was happy about the turn of events even if his mother was driving him a bit batty. Besides which, she was spending as little time around Edwin as possible at the moment.

"They're in the drawing room. I think," Wesley called after her.

Eleanor shut the study door behind her and let out a sigh of relief. Being around Edwin was particularly hard right now because she was exhausted and doing her best to cover it. It had taken her longer than she liked to realize she was pregnant, although her fatigue had certainly been worrying; it wasn't until she'd begun feeling nauseous in the mornings and had counted back the days that she determined the cause for her symptoms. She was worried that if she spent too much time around Edwin, he would realize her little illness hadn't been any such thing and what the real issue was.

She didn't know how she felt about her pregnancy. Protective, certainly. She cherished the idea of the life in her belly and a part of her thrilled to the very specific idea of bearing Edwin's child. But she was also terrified. Edwin had been so attentive, so affectionate since arriving in Bath... but it's not like there was much here to distract him. The slow top still hadn't declared himself, so she was still feeling uncertain about his feelings towards her. And she was still a bit worried that once he knew she was with child, she would discover his love was the love one had for a friend. Not the kind of passionate, delightful and despairing love she felt for him. A pregnant wife wasn't much fun, and she knew, in many *ton* marriages, the wife's pregnancy usually heralded the infidelities on both sides of the relationship.

After all, he'd gone to the Assembly last night without her. When she'd plead fatigue, he'd insisted she stay home, but then he'd gone anyway. Ostensibly in case Wesley needed assistance watching over Cynthia, but Eleanor couldn't help but worry about the other ladies who were there. Granted, she hadn't seen any at the previous Assembly they'd attended whom she'd feel threatened by, but as the Season ended there would be more of the *ton* coming to Bath. What if just being tired, unable to attend the public events, gave another woman the opportunity to seduce Edwin? Part of her said she was just being silly, but another part of her was too terrified to take the risk yet.

So she was keeping the news to herself, which wasn't unheard of. After all, she could be mistaken. And, in the meantime, she was cherishing every moment she had with him, searching for some kind of verification he loved her the way she loved him. He seemed to, sometimes. But there was no proof, no certainty. The blasted man never said the damned words. Sometimes they almost slipped from her lips, but what if he didn't say them back? She'd be devastated.

Eventually she would run out of time, but right now she just wanted to keep pushing it back and back...

Entering the drawing room, she saw Cynthia sitting on the couch looking rather out of her depth, while the Countess had the servants bringing in various color samples.

"Eleanor, how lovely!" The Countess said, looking up and smiling with pleasure.

"Eleanor!" The relief in Cynthia's face was clear, she jumped up and ran to hug Eleanor.

"Cynthia!" Although there was a bit of reproof in the Countess' voice for Cynthia's brash behavior, there was no real censure. Eleanor bit back a laugh; Edwin had told her about his conversation with the Countess and her plans for Wesley to marry Cynthia. The fact that she'd actually been successful would probably mean a great deal of tolerance for Cynthia's behavior as long as it wasn't scandalous.

"I'm sorry, my lady," Cynthia said, pulling away from Eleanor but still clinging to her hand. In a lower voice, she said to Eleanor: "You have no idea how glad I am to see you."

"No, no, no, the cream and sage, not the cream and mint. She wants her gown to be rose pink and the mint will be too light to contrast nicely against that."

"I'm sorry, my lady, but these are what I could find," the exasperated housekeeper said.

"Oh dear... I hope they're not at the estates. I suppose I should go have a look." Turning, the Countess smiled at Cynthia and Eleanor. "Please excuse me, dears, I really must go look at the linens we have here."

When the Countess left, Cynthia sighed with relief and plopped down on the chaise in a distinctly unladylike position. Eleanor couldn't help but laugh as she seated herself on the comfortable couch across from her.

"She's a force of nature, isn't she?"

"Let's just say, I'm glad I don't have an opinion on what the color of the linens, and relieved she even asked me what color I would like my wedding gown to be!" Cynthia said, giggling a bit. She gave Eleanor a wry look. "I suppose you've heard?"

"Of course," Eleanor said, smiling warmly. "Wesley sent a note to us this morning telling us that, as of last night, you are engaged. I'm incredibly pleased to offer you my best wishes."

"I fear I may need them." Twirling one of her curls around her finger, Cynthia looked in the direction of the door the Countess had exited through. The gesture made her look rather younger and more unsure than she normally did. The morning dress of soft sky blue she was wearing only emphasized that. "I was worried she'd be upset. But if she was, she's hiding it very well."

"Why did you think she'd be upset?" Eleanor asked, rather curious. It appeared Cynthia had also been unaware of the Countess' machinations. Edwin had told her about them, of course, after they'd returned home from the first Assembly. Although that wasn't too surprising Cynthia was unaware; Wesley was not the type to go along easily if he thought he was being manipulated, and Cynthia didn't seem to be either. She didn't think Cynthia would have gone along with any plan of the Countess' if she'd been aware of it.

Cynthia shrugged. "I've been a bit of a trial to her, on occasion, I'm afraid." She didn't look particularly sorry about it though, Eleanor thought with amusement. "I didn't think she'd want me as her son's Countess, but she seems rather eager to become the Dowager."

"Well Wesley's been a trial to her his whole life," Eleanor said, smiling cheerfully. "And she still likes him. Perhaps she thinks he deserves you. Unless you're overcome by a sudden desire to behave now that you're going to be a Countess?"

To her surprise, Cynthia hesitated. Her hand rubbed the side of her bottom. "Well... not entirely. Although the Earl doesn't react quite like the Countess when I do."

Rather shocked at the revealing gesture, Eleanor stared at her. "Did he spank you?"

Somehow she couldn't imagine it. Oh yes, her brother had been raised to do so. And serious, dictatorial Edwin... it had been surprising but not entirely shocking he disciplined her in such a way - especially considering he was the man her father had chosen out for her. But charming, easy-going, good-tempered Wesley who was always quick with a joke? He had spanked his ward?

"More than once," Cynthia said rather ruefully, blushing although she appeared to be attempting to look nonchalant about it. "He ah... may have caught me kissing Mr. Carter last night."

"Oh dear..." Well, perhaps Eleanor could understand Wesley's reaction then; she'd seen the way he watched Cynthia. Still, it was hard for her to get her head around the idea.

It seemed Cynthia was eager to share, wanting someone to talk to about the experience, because she leaned forward so she could lower her voice a bit. "He spanked me in the carriage... much harder than he's done before. I'm still sore today but I can't let on in front of the Countess, I don't know what she'd think. But he spanked me and then he put his hand between my legs, which he'd never done before... is that usual? It felt wonderful but I'm a bit worried since almost immediately after he told me we would be married. Are you sure it's only a man's cock in there that can get a woman with child?"

Eleanor found herself at an utter loss for words. So many revelations she absolutely had not needed about her childhood friend! She turned bright red just thinking about him in such a way. It seemed he was more akin to her husband than she'd realized, despite their different temperaments. If Wesley had touched Cynthia like that then no wonder he had decided to marry her, although Eleanor was still shocked Wesley found such activities arousing. She didn't want to think about it, he was so much like a brother to her... did that mean her own brother-

Oh stop, stop!

She had to answer Cynthia's questions and halt that line of thought.

"My understanding is it must be a man's... ah... rod, because of the seed which is expelled from it," she responded, slightly dazed, in such a low whisper Cynthia had to lean even further forward to hear her. "His fingers can't... ah, won't..." Eleanor felt her face turning even brighter red. She shook her head, trying her best not to picture the situation in my mind, when something else Cynthia had said finally came to her attention. "Did you say he *told* you that you're getting married? He didn't ask you?"

Cynthia shook her head. "He took me to my room last night, after he spanked me in the carriage, but he didn't do anything but kiss me. I thought he was going to, but he didn't... and then when I asked why he didn't, he said I'd have to wait until we were married to be completely ruined."

Rubbing her fingers to her temples, which were suddenly pounding, Eleanor wondered what on earth was wrong with her male friends. First Edwin and now Wesley. At least her own brother had done the right thing and been betrothed and married in the proper way. Although it somehow seemed completely ironically appropriate that Wesley, great rake that he was, would insist on his bride being a virgin on their wedding night, to the point of refusing to do the deed himself. He could be surprisingly conservative in some ways. Even if he was rushing the wedding.

Of course, if he was amenable to bedding Cynthia before the wedding perhaps he wouldn't be in such a rush to get to the alter. Or perhaps he would be in more of one so it wouldn't be too telling to count back the months after her first child was born.

"Well he did the right thing in that regard. Although I can't believe he was so... so... bloody man, he should have *asked*."

As Cynthia burst out laughing at Eleanor's surprising cursing, she found herself giggling a bit as well.

"Would you have said yes if he asked?"

Cynthia nodded firmly. "Absolutely. He's... so very exciting isn't he?" she asked in a wistful voice. Eleanor heard the desire in her voice for something more than exciting, something more like the emotions Eleanor yearned to have from Edwin, but she didn't think Cynthia would have too much to worry about.

As far as she could tell, Wesley was well on his way to being in love with his fiancé. She'd never known him to lose control the way he apparently did around Cynthia. And if he didn't want to marry her, he would have never done so.

The Countess came swanning back into the room a moment later, causing Eleanor to give silent thanks she hadn't been in hearing distance of Eleanor's intemperate language mere minutes before. Beaming, the Countess showed them the sage and cream linens she'd been looking for and began chattering about the arrangements for the ceremony and wedding breakfast to follow.

Although she was already feeling exhausted, Eleanor pasted a smile on her face as she listened. Edwin was still with Wesley and she wasn't going to send to him to ask if they could take their leave, everyone would realize there was something wrong with her. Something more than just an illness.

Her hand wandered back down to her belly, stroking the fabric over it without thinking about it. Before she told Edwin she was with child, she would do everything she could to secure his affections and ensure he wouldn't be like other husbands, who lost interest in their wives once they were breeding.

And the bloody man better make a damned declaration sometime soon!

******

As soon as the library door closed behind Eleanor, Edwin's face broke out in the grin he was keeping constantly suppressed lately. Even larger and brighter than the one he'd given Wesley when congratulating him on his engagement.

"You must congratulate me as well," he told Wesley, his chest near bursting with the news. "Eleanor is *enceinte*!"

Wesley let out a whoop, splashing some of his whiskey out of his glass (not that either of them noticed) and the two men hugged each other fiercely, before Wesley broke away and shook Edwin's hand, congratulating him. "But why didn't she say anything while she was in here?"

"Yes well... I have to ask you not to share the news just yet," Edwin said, "as she hasn't officially told me."

"Then how do you know?"

Edwin snorted. "Please. You know how Nell adores social events, and yet she wasn't at the Assembly last night."

"I thought she wasn't feeling well."

"She hasn't been feeling well for quite some time, although she does her best to hide it. And she's been particularly unwell in the mornings, her maid told me. Besides which, I can count as well as the next man."

Grinning, Wesley went to his cabinet. "This calls for a special drink. The good brandy. Even if I can't congratulate you officially or mention it to her yet. Why do you think she hasn't told you?"

"Who knows," Edwin said, waving his hand. "I assume she's waiting to be absolutely sure... or perhaps she's worried I'll curtail our social activities if she tells me. Which she'd be absolutely right about, I'll be ensuring she doesn't wear herself out; I'm extremely relieved we're already in Bath where it's much easier to do so. Not that it was difficult last night, she actually asked to stay home."

"Well it's a good thing you already knew what was wrong, or you might have thought it was something serious," Wesley said, handing Edwin a snifter of his best French brandy. The situation called for it. Good grief... in two weeks' time, their entire little cadre would be married and one of them was already with child.

He wondered how he would feel when Cynthia carried his child. Proud, certainly. Would his eyes have the same radiance Edwin's did? The silly, soppy grin on Edwin's face should have made Wesley shake his head at the poor sod, as it would have a month ago. Instead he just felt glad for his friend and eager for the day when he might wear a similar expression. Gads, that was almost terrifying.

"So, decided you couldn't live without your ward, eh? Or was it your mother's practicing which tipped your hand?"

"Ah... well. Certainly my mother contributed, which I'm starting to suspect was her intention, but last night during the carriage ride home... well let's just say

184

matters progressed to a point where a marriage proposal would be expected, if not strictly necessary."

Edwin shook his head, laughing. "That is not in the least bit surprising. I wish Hugh had been here, we could have placed bets on when you would fall."

"I wasn't that obvious," Wesley objected, getting an arch look from his friend.

"I'm more surprised you're waiting two weeks to do the deed."

"My mother, you know," Wesley said with a shrug, looking faintly sheepish. "I knew she'd want to plan something and I found I couldn't deny her the opportunity. Still, two weeks is better than four."

Nodding, Edwin could only feel grateful his own parents had no taste for such events. They'd been overjoyed when he'd married Eleanor, eager for him to bring her to the Manse, but not at all put out that they'd missed the actual wedding. Although, he'd have to put off traveling there now for a bit longer, until after Wesley's wedding at least. His parents would understand. Still, he was looking forward to eventually being home, and his mother would be a solid support for Eleanor while she was breeding. He had no doubt Lady Harrington, and her possibly her husband, would join them there as well until it was Eleanor's time, which would also delight his parents. They did enjoy friends visiting, even if they preferred not to leave the estates themselves.

"I've written Hugh and Alex," Wesley continued. "And told my mother to include them on the guest list, but I wanted to ensure they'd be able to come. Figured I should inform them as soon as possible. Did Hugh tell you Alex is determined to reconcile with Lady Brooke?"

"Yes... I'll be interested to see how that plays out. Do you think he might bring her to the wedding?"

"Could be the perfect opportunity. Sentimental event and all that; women love that kind of thing. Besides which, I doubt he'll want to conduct his reconciliation under the eyes of the *ton* in London. Removing her to Bath under the excuse of a wedding and then going further afield would be a viable strategy."

"If he can get her out of London with him at all," Edwin mused, thinking about Lady Brooke's stubbornness. It rivaled his wife's. "Well, Eleanor would be glad to see Grace again, although I can't imagine what she would think about the circumstances."

Not to mention the other couple who would also certainly be attending the wedding. Thinking back to the last time Grace and Irene had been in the same room, Edwin couldn't help but wince a little. Although if Lord Brooke was going to reestablish his marriage, the women were just going to have to learn to get along.

He hoped.

Chapter 12

When the letter arrived, it was immediately taken to the study and read as soon as the master of the house was told the address from whence it came. And then Hugh laughed so hard he cried, leaning back against his chair and actually holding his belly. Hearing his laughter, his curious wife came in, having just returned from a visit with her mother. She didn't make them as often as her mother liked, and whenever she returned home she searched out Hugh from some much needed bolstering.

"Hugh? What is it?"

Still chuckling, Hugh waved the letter in his hand. "Wesley's getting married."

"Really?"

Hugh laughed again at Irene's obvious surprise as she approached his desk. He waved her closer and she smiled as she walked around the side. Today she looked particularly fetching in a morning gown of dark forest green which emphasized her green eyes and make her hair look even more coppery than usual. In the sunlight, her pale skin was almost luminescent. The soft folds of the gown clung to her slender figure and rounded breasts. Reaching out, he grasped her hand and pulled her onto his lap, which was where he liked her best.

"Hugh!" Irene fell down laughing, wriggling her soft bottom around on his thighs and stirring his interest as her feminine curves pressed against him. Looping his arm around her slim waist, he grinned as he realized she wasn't wearing a corset. She often didn't around the house, unless they were expecting guests or she was having an at-home. Hugh preferred it that way, and it wasn't as if she truly needed one. His wife had a wonderfully slight figure.

"See?" Hugh said, pointing at the pertinent section in the letter as Irene settled against him. "He's marrying his ward, Cynthia."

"The woman his mother described as a demon sent to plague her into an early grave? That's not very nice." Irene's eyes scanned the paragraph and blinked with surprise. "He says the Countess seems happy about it?"

"Apparently. Either she changed her mind about Miss Bryant being a demon, or she's just so relieved Wesley is to be married, she doesn't care to whom. Which I can understand, since I wouldn't have placed bets on him running to the alter anytime soon. They're to be married in two weeks. How would you like to go to Bath, sweetheart?"

"And miss the end of the Season? Oh tragedy," Irene said dramatically, pressing her hand to her bosom as she rolled her eyes. Hugh chuckled and kissed the upturned underside of her chin. Bath might not be the country, but he wasn't at all surprised Irene would still find it preferable to London, especially if it meant quitting the end of the Season early. And the way things had been going so far this Season, it wouldn't be a bad thing to end their Season early when it was for a socially acceptable reason such as Wesley's wedding.
Now that he knew how excitable Irene was, some months away from London where she could continue to build her confidence away from her mother and also learn to control her impulses, sounded extremely beneficial. She'd been thrust into the social scene as his wife largely unprepared, by next Season he was sure she'd be more comfortable in her position and with herself. But they couldn't have just left without a reasonable excuse or it would have set tongues wagging; however, Wesley's wedding was the perfect opportunity as no one would see anything strange in it. There would be no reason to speculate that the recent interaction with Lady Brooke had anything to do with their departure, for example.

In fact, Hugh wouldn't be surprised if quite a few members of the *ton* also left the capital early in order to attend the Earl of Spencer's wedding. Not just because Wesley was important as both an Earl and for business he created when he was in India, but because of his reputation. The dragons of the *ton* (many of whom were friends with the Countess) would want to see the downfall of a rake so they could crow smugly over it, the men would want to come and see what woman had managed to catch the notorious Earl of Spencer (and share a drink over another fallen comrade), and the young wives and widows would want to see if Wesley would remain true to his usual ways or if he had reformed. Hugh highly suspected those ladies would be disappointed.

Although Wesley's wedding certainly wouldn't deplete attendance of the Season. There was still the marriage mart to keep it going, those members of Society who never left London, not to mention the simple fact there were several major events upcoming which would have to be missed in order to attend the wedding. None of which was a concern for Hugh, but would be for many others.

"I wonder why the sudden decision," Irene said, as she finished reading the letter and shaking Hugh from his thoughts. "He doesn't say anything about how or why this came about."

"Probably compromised her beyond redemption."

"Hugh! What a thing to say about your friend!" Irene gave him a baleful look, lightly slapping his chest. "I'm sure Lord Spencer did no such thing." There was a hint of doubt in her voice, but not much. One thing Hugh had noticed was that Irene tended to take people at face value, which wasn't always wise to do but which he adored about her. She'd learn eventually, but he did enjoy her innocence for now, especially when it meant she hadn't seen Wesley for what he truly was.

"You have a very rosy view of my friends, sweetheart."

"Because you're all gentlemen and should behave as such," his wife said, rather primly. Hugh loved it when she was prim, it made debauching her so much more entertaining. It wasn't that she'd forgotten about when he had made love to her outside under the sun, or she'd forgotten the spankings she'd received at his hand, and she was a creative and passionate lover, but she held onto certain notions sometimes...

"If you say so, dear," Hugh said, leaning forward to nuzzle his face into the soft curve of her breasts. He breathed in her scent, lavender and woman and utterly intoxicating; he tightened his arm about her waist and brought his other hand down to clamp around her thigh.

"Hugh!" Laughing, Irene tried to push him away, but he just growled and held on more tightly, turning her slightly so he could bury his face between the delightful mounds. Her morning dress didn't show a lot of cleavage, but enough to tease him, enough to allow him to lick her skin in between her breasts. Sliding his hand up from her thigh to cup her breast, Hugh squeezed it gently, and she gasped, her voice lowering to a whisper. "Hugh, we can't! The door's unlocked!"

"Adds a certain flair to the situation, doesn't it?" He whispered back, teasingly as his fingers tweaked her nipple and then moved on to begin undoing her buttons at the top of her dress. He loved buttons down the front of a dress. "We could be interrupted at any moment and then someone would see me making love to my beautiful wife..."

"Hugh, no, stop," Irene whispered, giggling nervously, although obviously unsure as to whether or not he was serious in his intent. The little darting glances she gave at the door as a fiery blush rose in her cheeks, combined with her squirming bottom on his lap and her useless attempt to bat his hands away from her buttons, was delightful. Hugh's cock was pressed against the underside of her bottom, already achingly hard as he teased her. The sides of her dress fell open, revealing the creamy mounds of her breasts through the thin chemise she was wearing, with the rosy pink hint of her nipple.

"You don't really want me to stop," he murmured, pulling her down for a kiss as his hand slid into the top of her dress. Her breast was warm and heavy in his hand, the little nipple already hardening into a bud. The protest she tried to voice was muffled, first by his lips and then by his tongue as he thrust it into her mouth. Pinching her nipple, he tugged it fully to hardness, feeling her shudder on his lap as she moaned into his mouth.

Bending her back, so she had to catch his shirt to keep from falling back completely, Hugh deepened the kiss and took advantage of her precarious balance to more fully open her dress so that, other than the thin chemise, her breasts were bared to the air. He ignored her muffled protest. It was unlikely any of the servants would enter without knocking and he rather liked the idea of debauching his wife in the middle of the day, in his study, with an unlocked door. Especially since she obviously found it to be a scandalous proposition.

If anyone did see her in such a state he would be furious and jealous, but the idea that someone might walk in was rather exciting. And, despite her protests, he thought she felt the same.

Releasing her lips from the kiss, Hugh moved his mouth down her neck and to her breasts. Irene moaned as he closed his lips over one of her nipples, sucking on the hard little bud through her chemise. The wetted fabric clearly showed the rosy outline when he was done with it, and he transferred his attentions to the other. She whimpered his name and the blood in his body seemed to surge down to his cock, the hard rod pressing against the cheeks of her bottom as she squirmed and shuddered.

Her hands were now clutching at the lapels of his jacket and she'd stopped fighting him, all of her movements were those of an aroused, passionate woman. Exactly how he wanted her. Hugh wanted to drive his wife beyond the point where she cared whether or not someone walked in, to the point where her entire focus was on him and the things he was doing to her malleable body.

"Are you wet, Irene?" he asked, grasping her by the waist and lifting her to his desk. Seating her on it directly in front of him, he slid his chair forward to insert himself between her thighs, his hands on the inside of each of her legs to keep them spread. The front of her dress gaped, the unbuttoned flaps falling to either side, so she was only truly covered by her chemise. The wet fabric over her nipples clung to the hard tips, causing her to look even more provocative. Her face was flushed and her eyes had the shiny dazed look he associated with her arousal. She lowered her gaze and shook her head, unable to meet his eyes, and he grinned. "I think you might be lying wife... I suppose I'll just have to check."

"Hugh, noooo..." She looked over her shoulder at the closed door, her protest soft, as she tried to push her skirts back down from where he was lifting them.

Laughing at her, Hugh leaned forward so he could gently push her down until she was lying flat on her back on his desk, her legs hanging over the edge. With the top of her dress completely open and her skirt up around her hips, his wife looked more wanton than proper. His cock throbbed with excitement at seeing her laid out like this; in his fantasies she'd always been completely naked by this point, but the open clothing added a certain spice to reality that just couldn't be topped.

Pulling her legs up and over his shoulders to make her more comfortable – having them hang like that looked rather awkward - and so she couldn't close them, he grinned at her as he wrapped one arm around her thigh and laid his hand over her mound with its coppery curls, stroking one finger down between her folds. It came away soaking wet.

"You lied, wife."

******

Irene closed her eyes as the heat rose in her face at her husband's self-satisfied tone. When she'd come into Hugh's study this morning, this was the last thing she had expected - or she would have locked the door behind her! And at the same time, the possibility of being caught did, indeed, make this entire encounter even more exciting. It felt as though her pulse was pounding through her veins, her anxiety adding to the burning desire he had kindled in her. Her skin was buzzing with Hugh's touch, her nipples aching for more attention from his mouth and fingers, and the wetness between the folds of her womanhood was increasing with every second.

She moaned as she felt Hugh's fingers part those folds, his hot breath coming a moment before his tongue slid up the center and flicked against the little pleasure nub at the apex. Irene knew, in all propriety, she should resist further, she should at the very least close her dress back over her breasts, but she didn't. Instead she just moaned and threaded her fingers through her husband's hair as he lapped at the cream his ministrations had produced.

The chair behind him scraped on the floor as he scooted even closer, and Irene realized Hugh had seated himself comfortably so he could attend to her at his leisure. She knew her husband sometimes had desires that were nothing like she'd been prepared for, and she had to wonder if this was one of them... had Hugh sat in his study, wanting the chance to lay her out across his desk like this and use his mouth on her sensitive folds? It didn't seem at all unbelievable.

It felt like he was peeling back the petals of her body, taking his time as he nibbled each one and drew his tongue along each crevice. The sensations made her body tighten and quiver, but they weren't enough to bring her to the ultimate pleasure... no, he was teasing her, taunting her with his mouth, almost mocking her for her claim he hadn't made her wet.

"Hugh, please," she begged, gasping as his tongue actually felt like it slid inside of her. Her head thrashed back and forth on the desk, her hips moving up and down as she tried to force Hugh's head into the position she wanted. Needed. The pressure was building up inside of her and it had nowhere to go.

"Are you wet, Irene?"

"Yes!"

As if in reward for her honesty, his tongue slid back inside of her and out of her again, the same way his fingers or his rod might and Irene bucked and moaned. Her legs tightened over his shoulders, trying to draw him further into her body, needing him desperately.

"Do you want to cum, Irene?"

"Yes, Hugh, please, I want to cum," she begged, forgetting in her need to keep her voice down. Her movements were causing her breasts to jiggle, the nipples rubbing against the fabric of her chemise which felt rough and abrasive where it had been wetted by his mouth. The throbbing of those tender buds seemed to be pulsing in time with the needy clenches of her core. "Make me cum, please Hugh."

His tongue circled her clitoris, brushing against it, and Irene's hips jerked as she writhed with the ecstatic sensation. The pressure inside of her seemed to surge, but didn't break, as he dipped back down into her slit before coming back up to tease the swollen bud again. Irene tried to leverage herself to press the sensitive

194

spot more firmly against her husband's tongue, but it just circled and swept away again. The teasing was driving her out of her mind.

"OH! Hugh *please!*"

"Do you want me to fuck you, Irene?"

Irene moaned, the crude word making her shudder even as a surge of anticipation made her tighten. He'd heightened her passionate need to the point where she felt rather wild with it.

"Hugh, please..."

"Say it, Irene."

She opened her eyes as her legs were lowered and Hugh stood up. The hungry look he gave her as he began to unlace the front of his trousers left her no doubt he was just as aroused as she was. The position he'd left her in wasn't entirely comfortable, but she could see how it affected him.

Something new, something wicked, unfurled inside of her. She'd seen this look on his face before, but she'd never thought to use it. Now she wanted to make him feel as out of control as she did. Irene licked her lips, finding Hugh's gaze suddenly locked onto her mouth when she did so.

"Please Hugh," she whispered, bringing her hands up to her breasts, which were absolutely aching. It felt amazing. She ran her fingertips over the mounds, her back bowing a bit as the soft touch teased her nipples. Hugh's eyes flared with passion and she squeezed her breasts, watching him watch her. "Please..."

"Irene..." His voice sounded suddenly ragged, and she could tell he had frozen in place. It was as if a match had been struck inside of her head, igniting her, emboldening her. Irene did something she'd never thought of before; she released one breast and moved

195

her hand over the soft fabric of her chemise and the bunched skirts, down to her mound, and pressed her finger right against where she ached the most. It felt almost as good as when Hugh touched her there.

"Hugh..." Irene moaned, sliding her fingers over the wet flesh. "Please..."

"Dammit Irene..." Her husband's voice grated, a violent movement snatched her hand away, holding her wrist in his long fingers, and suddenly his rod was pressing against her, pressing into her.

For the first time, she'd managed to elude what he wanted in favor of what she wanted, by behaving like a complete wanton. It was empowering. Erotic. And the rewards were oh so wonderful. Not that she had any particularly strong feelings against saying 'fuck,' but denying him had been wonderful, teasing him even more so and this...

Irene gasped as Hugh thrust hard and deep, splitting her open quite suddenly. As well lubricated as her channel was, it was still a shock for those tight muscles to be so forcibly pushed aside as his rock hard length was buried inside of her. He hooked his arms under her legs, bringing them up so he could pull her into his thrusts, taking her more deeply.

It felt like he was filling her completely, harder and thicker than ever before, and Irene gripped the edges of the desk, next to her hips, as he began to pound in and out of her. Every time he used his arms to leverage her body into his, she groaned from the incredible sensation. His thrusts were wild, as if he was out of control, and the raw, animalistic passion she saw on his face was as frightening as it was exciting.

Crying out his name, Irene's body bowed and ached as he took her. The rough passion consumed her, the friction of his fast, deep thrusts making it feel as though she was burning inside and out. The pressure had built up inside of her, it swelled and pulsed until she thought she might go mad from it.

"Dammit Irene... Come for me... I want you to scream my name..."

And then Hugh leaned forward, his body pressing against her clitoris as he rocked against her, and Irene's body was engulfed in flames. The ecstasy burgeoned outwards, from a singular point deep inside of her, and filled her completely. She screamed her passion, not a single thought spared for the staff which might be passing by the room at any time.

Hugh's hands gripped her hips, pulling her even more firmly against him as his breathing grew more ragged. Bent nearly in half, her legs splayed and held tightly by his arms, Irene had no defense from the waves of pleasure that continued to swell and surge through her to the point of becoming almost painful in their intensity. She sobbed his name again, pleading with him to slow, to stop, to give her a moment to recover... but her pleas only seemed to increase his passion.

Irene couldn't even let go of the desk to try and use her hands to slow him, his thrusts were so rough, so strong, that she was hanging on for dear life, her fingers locked around the wood. She screamed, high and piercing, as he seemed to grow even larger inside of her and the burning, tingling rapture become too much to bear. Her womb contracted and she writhed, her breasts jiggling, and her body squeezing him tightly over and over again.

Tears leaked down her cheeks as the hardness inside of her became completely unyielding, and then Hugh bellowed his own triumphant ecstasy. Irene gasped for air as her husband rocked against her, the hard rod inside of her pulsing as he released his seed deeply within her. She could feel every spurt, every throb of his member, and she clenched around it, causing him to groan and close his eyes. Hugh's head tilted back as he filled her, his body slowly relaxing. Then his head fell forward again and the rest of his body followed it, leaning forward to rest his head on her breasts as the last of his climax shuddered through him.

"Mmmm...." Hugh rubbed his head against her breasts, making Irene gasp and clench around him again. Every inch of her body felt exquisitely sensitive in the aftermath of her orgasms. Unwrapping her grip from around the edge of the desk, Irene winced a bit as she flexed sore fingers and reached up to clasp her husband to her. Raising his head at her touch, he gave her an inquisitive look. "And where did all that come from, wife? Have you been touching yourself when I'm not around?"

She blushed hotly. Now that she was coming down from the heights of pleasure, her behavior seemed inexplicable and rather shocking. Although, she still had to admit Hugh's response to it had been very satisfying. "No, I've never done anything like that before. I'm not sure... I think... I don't know."

"Well it was delightful," he said, pulling back and pulling her with him as he sat down on his chair, her legs straddling his and her breasts directly in front of his face. Kissing her nipples, one after the other, Hugh grinned at her, looking nothing at all like the golden angel he sometimes resembled and much more like a self-satisfied and dangerous rake. "Anytime the notion takes you again, feel free to run with it."

He pulled her lips down, kissing her deeply, their bodies still joined together. When he finally released her, Irene began to squirm away from him as she remembered the door was unlocked and the servants might come in at any time. Especially now that there were no noises coming from behind the closed door.

Blushing deeply, although more than a little pleased and quite a bit emboldened by Hugh's obvious appreciation of her wanton behavior, Irene accepted his help in setting herself to rights. Sticky seed seeped down her inner thighs and onto the tops of her stockings, which Hugh wouldn't let her clean up.

"I like knowing it's there," he murmured, pulling her skirts down over her hips and kissing her again to stifle her protest.

Sighing, Irene decided to let him have his way for the moment. After all, as soon as she was alone she could wipe the uncomfortable mess away. And there was something strangely titillating about having his seed decorating her inner thighs, with no one the wiser. Hugh helped to straighten her rumpled skirts and hindered more than helped to button up her dress. He chuckled over the state of her hair, which caused her to scold him. He stopped her with a kiss, and was still kissing her when a knock came on the door.

Immediately, Irene pushed him away as her face flamed. Her hands flew to her hair, hastily pulling the rest of the pins out and pushing it into the semblance of a bun, so at least it wasn't a completely mess. The look her husband gave her was decidedly amused and she scowled at him.

"Yes?" Hugh said after a moment, even though Irene hadn't quite finished fixing herself up yet. She kicked his ankle and he wagged a finger at her.

The door opened to reveal their butler, Marling. He looked at them with a blank expression, not even blinking. The lack of reaction didn't stop Irene from feeling incredibly embarrassed, knowing she didn't look the way she should and it was very possible Marling knew perfectly well what had been happening in here.

"Lord Braithwhyte is here to see you, my Lord."

"Thank you, Marling. You may put him in the library, I'll speak with him in there." Reaching out, Hugh caught Irene's hand before she could leave and pulled her to him for another thorough kiss.

Beet red and yet glowing from within, Irene retreated from the study a few minutes later, avoiding the entrance to the library.

✳✳✳✳✳✳

Standing outside the stylish townhouse, Irene gathered her courage. After a few days to think things over, she had come to a rather lowering conclusion: she needed to apologize. In fact, she'd meant to be at this house earlier in the morning, when it was more likely Lady Grace would be home, but then her interlude in Hugh's study had distracted her as well as necessitating a change of her underskirts and a redoing of her toilette.

She hoped Lady Grace would be at-home, and hopefully not entertaining a large number of guests. If Irene's mother heard Irene had visited the scandalous Viscountess... well Irene didn't like to think how her mother would react. Although being Hugh's wife offered her quite a bit of protection, especially as her mother was so pleased by her daughter's current position in Society, she wouldn't be forgiving of anything that might endanger her position.

But Irene needed to do this. Not just because Alex was going to reconcile with Lady Grace, or because she and Eleanor were such good friends, but because it was the right thing to do. Irene had been immature and, when she thought about it, rather uncaring and cruel when Grace had only been reacting as any wife would in such a situation. In fact, Grace had been rather circumspect and tolerant. In addition, Irene needed to apologize for her physical attack, which had been completely uncalled for, no matter the situation.

Irene gathered her courage and walked up the steps to the house.

Knocking on the door, she held her chin up high. She'd dressed to help her confidence today, although she'd been steadily gaining in the commodity since being

200

married. Today she'd needed the little boost of her favorite bronze and ivory dress with its dark green trim; she knew she looked particularly well in it, and even if she wasn't as fashionable or sophisticated as Lady Grace, she almost felt like it in this dress.

When the door opened, Irene blinked. Had she knocked on the wrong door? "Peters?"

The man at the door looked rather startled, the first time she'd ever seen such an expression on his face. She hadn't seen him in years. This was certainly the last place she'd expected to find him, and was probably the last place he would have expected to see her. Although he'd never said it, Irene had always thought Peters knew more about what went on in the Brooke household and the extent of her feelings for Alex than anyone else. Of course, he'd been a footman then and not a butler, but she was sure he'd make a good one. His surprise was only evident for a moment, and then his face assumed the usual blank expression of the best butlers.

"Viscountess," he said with a bow.

Somehow it didn't surprise Irene that, even though he was working in Lady Grace's house where she doubted her own name was ever spoken, he knew of her marriage. Servants gossip, of course, the most reliable network of gossip which existed.

"Is Lady Brooke at home?" she asked, smiling warmly at him.

For the first time since knowing him, she saw Peters hesitate. "The lady is still in residence although she is scheduled to go out this afternoon, but... may I inquire as to the nature of your visit?"

Irene smiled, tilting her head. "Why Peters, that was almost bold for you. I'd just like to speak to Lady Brooke."

"I hesitate to inquire further, my lady," Peters said, every inch of his body managing to give off the impression of being both deferential and apologetic, yet protective. "Lady Brooke has had several visitors at times who wanted nothing more than to speak with her, but their visits were rather distressing to her ladyship."

Despite herself, despite knowing that, in many ways, Lady Grace deserved to be distressed for her behavior and treatment of Alex, Irene couldn't help but feel a surge of sympathy for the woman. It was one thing for her to be cut in public or be excluded from a guest list, but to hound the woman in her own home just seemed to cross a line. Yet it didn't surprise her that there were those among the *ton* who would do so.

Irene shook her head.

"Nothing distressing, I promise, Peters," she said, looking up earnestly at the man she'd known since she was a child, when he was a footman on the Brooke estate. A man who'd, more than once, help her sneak a pastry or tart from the kitchen. "In fact, I'm hoping to relieve some distress I may have caused her."

Peters studied her, as if trying to decide on her sincerity, and she realized if he thought she was misleading him, she wouldn't make it through the doorway. In fact, if he hadn't known her for so very long, that very well might have been the case.

"Very well then, my lady, please come in."

"I didn't realize you were working for Lady Brooke," Irene said, hoping Peters might give her some more information. Circumspection was part of his job, but perhaps he might give her a hint as to his change in loyalties.

"The lady needed someone to watch over her," Peters said, his expression blank, but his voice sounded sympathetic towards his mistress' position in Society.

Considering his devotion to the Brooke family, Irene found it rather curious he would choose to work for a woman who had betrayed Alex. Then again, perhaps his devotion extended to the entire family, including Alex's wife whether she was estranged or not, or perhaps he had seen something while working for Alex that caused him to choose Lady Grace over the Brooke family.

The idea was not a comfortable one for Irene, because it made her wonder what she didn't know about her childhood friend and his estranged wife.

Peters showed her to a beautifully decorated drawing room before retreating to see if Lady Grace might have time to see her before going out. Irene couldn't help but wonder where the other woman was going. During her own social rounds they'd never been at the same event. Then again, Irene was accepted by the high sticklers of Society and Grace certainly wasn't, so it really wasn't surprising they didn't run in the same circles.

Grace wouldn't be welcome there.

Even if Irene wasn't enamored of the social scene, at least she never feared being turned away from someone's home. No one turned up their nose at her or whispered behind her back or refused to acknowledge her. In fact, many of the women seemed to be envious and slightly in awe of her, since it was a well-known fact her husband was a former rake, their marriage was arranged, and yet he was - to all observers - quite reformed. Sometimes Irene was a bit in awe of herself. Lady Grace wouldn't even have the protection of Lord Brooke's name.

Although it did beg the question why she was received at all, in *any* homes.

The door opened again and Lady Grace swept in, beautiful and regal as ever. Irene had her usual reaction of feeling inferior in the face of such striking good looks, but then again, what had her looks gotten Lady Grace? She was on the edge of being an outcast, living alone, and her husband was publically unfaithful to her – as she was to him. Whereas Irene not only had a wonderful husband, she also has his devotion and the respect of the *ton.*

It was impossible not to feel just the slightest bit of pity, although she doubted Lady Grace would appreciate such an emotion on her behalf.

Standing, Irene nodded her head in greeting at the other woman. "Lady Brooke."

Crystal blue eyes, enhanced by the ice blue dress she was wearing, blinked in surprise. She was absolutely stunning in her light colored dress, which made her cheeks look even paler and her hair even darker; a vision of ice and beauty. It was the very first time in Irene's life that she'd called Lady Grace by her proper title.

"Viscountess."

Had that brittle wariness been there in the lady's manner before? Was it new, or was Irene finally noticing someone other than herself? Perhaps it was all her new thoughts about the woman which made her more attuned to her emotional state.

Despite their past, despite their recent contentremps, Lady Grace's manner seemed hesitant but civil. Rather like a puppy who was hoping to be petted, but had no reason to expect anything other than a kick. Irene felt another wave of shame and sympathy, and was shocked at her own reaction. Had she never seen Lady Grace clearly before, through the bias of her own determination to have Alex and to be angry at Lady Grace's treatment of him, or was this a result of Lady Grace's time in town and her position in Society? Irene had the unsettling feeling it was more likely the former. She'd always taken Lady Grace's haughty ways at face value and poured dislike upon the woman for them. Now she was starting to see the other woman in a new light and it was making her notice things she hadn't before.

Even more than before, Irene was determined to make things right. The woman in front of her may have betrayed her marriage vows, but Irene was starting to realize she couldn't possibly know the whole story. What kept Lady Grace going, despite the disapprobation of Society? What made this wary, imperious woman continue on her course when all she had to do to be welcomed back into Society was act the part she'd been given to play? Why didn't she just go to Alex and give him an heir, so she could resume her currently life as normal afterwards?

And why had Irene never wondered these things before?

Perhaps she was finally growing up.

Her next move was part of that. Irene drew a deep breath, feeling humbled and ashamed, and yet also feeling a small sense of relief.

"I've come to apologize."

Another one of those heavy blinks, a tilt of her head, and that same wariness. Silence descended and after a moment, Irene realized Lady Grace might not know how to respond. After all, Irene hadn't been very specific.

"My behavior the other evening was deplorable. I'm very sorry for what I did to your dress and I hope you believe me when I say I didn't intend... well, I didn't intend any of what happened." She drew in anther breath for courage as Lady Grace continued to stare silently at her, frozen in place. Irene had no idea how the other woman was taking her apology, but she was determined to finish it. "Even more so, I need to apologize for my behavior over the years. I was more than immature in my manner towards you after you married Alex, I was insulting and presumptuous. I understand now how upsetting that must have been for you, and you didn't deserve my scorn or my snide remarks."

Irene realized Lady Grace's blinking was so pronounced because of the long, heavy lashes which ringed her bright blue eyes. She shifted uncomfortably, having run out of things to say. The silence in the room was deafening.

"Would you like to sit down?"

Now it was Irene's turn to blink in confusion. "Pardon?"

"Would you like to sit down? I can ring a maid for tea." The offer was made somewhat tentatively, but it sounded sincere.

She only hesitated for a moment. "That would be lovely, thank you."

Staying for tea hadn't been in her original plan, but it seemed rude not to take Lady Grace up on the invitation. Besides which, the entire point of being here was to establish more cordial relations, and what could be more cordial than enjoying a cup of tea together? And with her newfound insights, Irene realized she was incredibly curious what a conversation with her ladyship might reveal.

Lady Grace rang for the tea and then waved to Irene to take a seat again. Lowering herself back onto the couch, Irene watched as Lad Grace sat across from her in a delicately carved chair. The easy, graceful manner in which she settled her skirts was something to be envied. "I must admit, when Peters told me you were here... this was not what I expected."

"I can only imagine," Irene said, smiling somewhat ruefully. How would she have reacted if Lady Grace had one day shown up on her own doorstep? What would she have thought? Nothing good, certainly.

"When you said you wanted to apologize," Lady Grace continued, as if Irene hadn't spoken, "I thought you might be trying to mend fences because of Eleanor. But that was a rather descriptive and sincere sounding apology."

"Because I mean it," Irene said earnestly. She felt slightly taken aback by Lady Grace's bluntness, but hadn't Irene been just as blunt in the past? And she could understand the lady's suspicions. Perhaps it was best to speak bluntly at this point, Irene certainly preferred that over speaking sideways around an issue. She respected Lady Grace was still unsure of Irene's motivations, and she did want lady Grace to know her apology was sincere, rather than taking it at face value and always wondering. "After marrying Hugh... well, let's say I've grown up a bit. At least, I hope I have. And I see quite a few things in a different light than I did before. Especially when it comes to the difference between a friendship between a man and a woman and the relationship between a man and his wife."

"Ah yes... Hugh, the entirely reformed rake despite the fact that his marriage was arranged and not a love match," Grace said, her voice light and almost mocking.

For a moment Irene bristled, but then she realized Grace wasn't even looking at her. Those bright blue eyes were unfocused as if peering inward, as if the comment had been directed more at herself than at Irene. Irene suddenly realized Alex had a reputation as a rake, yet obviously he wasn't reformed.

Irene had always taken Alex's word that Grace had separated from him without provocation, that he'd intended to be a good and faithful husband to her, but something about Grace's demeanor made her wonder... The woman sounded almost envious of Irene's situation.

The brittleness was back. As was more than a hint of bitterness.

And Irene didn't know what to say in response.

Fortunately the maid arrived with the tea then, and they were able to take refuge in the meaningless social chatter the tea service made possible. It was soothing, balancing. The appropriate topics were far away from Alex or Hugh.

"Where will you be going when the Season ends?" Lady Grace asked, perfectly cordial and poised. Irene wondered if she would ever be able to perfect that kind of social facade, the bland face which covered all manner of anxieties. She imagined Lady Grace must have had a lot of practice, in a manner Irene would prefer not to experience. "Hugh must be eager to return to Westingdon."

"Eventually," Irene said, brightening as she remembered they were leaving the Season early. "Next week we leave for Bath to attend Spencer's wedding."

Grace's eyes widened, her lips curving in an obviously unanticipated smile and then she threw back her head and laughed. It was a light, bright, tinkling laugh, one that wiped away her cynicism and made her look like a young girl. She absolutely chortled, and Irene watched fascinated. The reaction was so genuine, so unanticipated, and she couldn't help but grin in response. Hugh's reaction had been similar. Her smile faded a bit. How well did Lady Grace know Spencer? Had he been one of her lovers at some point?

That would not go over well with Alex at all...

"Oh dear... and the last of them falls," Lady Grace said, still giggling a bit as she composed herself. "I should have made a bet with someone that they'd all go down in the same Season, they always did everything else together until Wesley went to India."

208

Now Irene's smile returned to full force. It was rather amusing how the three friends would all married during the same Season. How often did such an occurrence happen? Especially when all three had reputations as firmly entrenched bachelors? She knew Edwin and Eleanor's wedding had been considered a surprise to many, even if Hugh's wasn't, and Spencer's was apparently even more so going by Hugh and Lady Grace's reactions.

"The three of them," Lady Grace said, shaking her head, now fully composed again although her eyes were still sparkling. She looked much less like an ice princess now and Irene suddenly wondered if this was the side of her Eleanor normally saw, the side the Hugh remembered. Was this, perhaps, the Lady Grace that Alex had met and proposed to? "And who is Spencer marrying? The last I heard he was running from Lord Windham, who was not nearly as accommodating as Lady Windham led him to believe."

The gossip had gone round the *ton* rather quickly, to the amusement of many. Of course, the only one damaged by it was Lady Windham, who had been hurried from the capital by her angered husband. Rumor had it he planned to keep her there until she was with child again, as she so obviously needed something to occupy her time. Still, it was the Lady's own fault for being indiscreet. Wesley had done the proper thing, which was why Irene had been so convinced, however he'd become engaged, it had been through the proper channels. That was just the kind of gentleman he was, no matter what Hugh had implied.

"His ward, a Miss Cynthia Bryant."

A little twist of those perfect pink lips made Lady Grace look almost as though she was sneering. "Another love match, I suppose," she drawled, sounding rather derisive. "How predictable."

This time Irene wasn't fooled at all though. She was becoming more and more convinced that, like her blank social mask, Lady Grace's cynicism, sarcasm and sneering remarks often covered her true feelings. It didn't make Irene like her, but she did wonder if buried under all that negativity might be a woman who was quite likeable. After all, Eleanor was very sweet and friendly, and she and Lady Grace had been friends for years, and Irene had gotten a glimpse of a woman she thought was very likeable for just a few moments. There must be some reason for Lady Grace's usual airs.

"The letter didn't say," Irene said. Then, hoping to get the conversation back to a more pleasant tone and away from Grace's negativity: "Hugh said he thinks Spencer must have compromised her."

That got another smile, although it was still a bit cynical. "That would do it. It must irk him considerably to be caught in the parson's trap. I do hope the poor thing is up to the challenge of being married to him."

"She certainly sounds like a bit of a challenge, herself," Irene said, which then led to an explanation of the previous letters sent by the Countess to her son. Grace derived quite a bit of amusement from the conversation and, subsequently, became quite natural and almost friendly in Irene's company. They passed a surprisingly pleasant afternoon, during which Grace ended up staying in with her, and by the time Irene left, she wondered if they might even be becoming friends.

Chapter 13

One week before her wedding and since the night her erstwhile fiancé had proposed, and Cynthia hadn't been so much as kissed!

Well that wasn't entirely true. The Earl had kissed her hand several times. And once he'd kissed her cheek. But nothing more. It was frustrating. Bewildering.

Downright infuriating.

He was a rake, this wasn't the way things were supposed to be happening between them! She felt as though she'd been given a glimpse of heaven only to have it snatched away from her. Suddenly the Earl was being as much stuffy starched shirt as when she'd first met him, with absolutely no bending.

And she didn't have time to make trouble and earn another spanking and some more alone time with him; the Countess was keeping her so busy with dress fittings, shopping for accessories and a trousseau, writing out invitations, planning the meal, and when Cynthia did have a moment to herself it was because she was visiting Eleanor. For once, she was too exhausted to make trouble. Besides, she didn't really want another spanking from him, because who knew if he would kiss her afterwards again?

Still.

If this was the way her marriage was going to be, she was no longer very excited about it.

"He hasn't been exciting at *all*," she said to Eleanor, rather aggrieved. "I thought he'd be doing all the things rakes do, whisking me away to dark corners, kissing me senseless and trying to get under my skirts. But all he does is stare at me. And he's never in the same room as me unless his mother is there!"

Eleanor laughed. Cynthia was glad to see she'd managed to cheer her friend up, even if it was at her own expense. When she'd first arrived to visit with Eleanor, the other woman had been looking rather wane. She had some dark shadows under her eyes and seemed a bit listless. But she'd insisted she was fine, when Cynthia asked, and sitting on a chaise and watching Cynthia pace and vent seemed to have instilled some life back into her.

"Honestly, I'm not surprised," Eleanor said, giggling a bit as Cynthia pulled a wry face. "He did warn you he wasn't going to thoroughly ruin you until after you're wed."

"Yes I know," she responded grumpily. Placing her hands on her hips she glared into the air. "But couldn't we do what we've already done? I rather liked that."

"Even the spanking part."

Cynthia shrugged. "If that's what it takes…"

"Well don't push him," Eleanor said sagely. "You're just as likely to get a spanking without any of the… ah… intimacies as you are to get both."

"That was my thought as well," Cynthia said, sighing as she slumped down in the chair across from Eleanor, tapping her foot on the floor. "He's not going to be like this after we're married, do you think?"

"I highly doubt it," Eleanor said. "Wesley's just a bit… um conservative in some ways. He lost control with you once, I doubt he's going to risk it again until after you're wed. Even if you did misbehave, he might very well leave the Countess to deal with you instead of doing it himself."

"Blast." Cynthia shook her head stubbornly. The Earl might be getting his way in many things, but she wasn't going to just dance to his tune all the time. "I'm not going to stand for it."

"What are you going to do?"

"I'm not sure yet, but I'll think of something."

******

Creeping down the hallway, which was almost pitch black dark, Cynthia carefully counted the doors she was passing. Of course she knew which one the Earl slept in, but it was much easier to determine which was his in the light of day. In the darkness, with only the barest light to guide her, it was more sensible to count the doors. Much better than making a mistake.

Cynthia wanted to know more about what life would be like with him, not just her daytime life but her nights and beyond. She wanted to explore those wonderful sensations he'd elicited with his fingers, wanted to do things with him that she hadn't done with Mr. Carter or any of the others. Surely the fact they would be married next week meant some of the standard rules could be bent. Besides which, she truly didn't like the idea of him thinking she would willingly bow to whatever decree he wanted to make.

And even if the Earl didn't agree, well surely a willing, naked woman in his bed would go a long way towards changing his mind. What man could resist? What sane man would want to?

As she'd told Eleanor that afternoon, she was willing to risk a spanking. Besides, after spending an afternoon with Eleanor, away from all the planning and fuss, she'd felt very much rejuvenated. Ready to make mischief and for whatever came after. Since they hadn't had an event to attend that evening, she was feeling all the more rested.

Holding her breath, she grasped the handle of his door and turned the knob slowly, to make as little noise as possible. Easing the door open just enough to allow her to slip in sideways, she paused as soon as she got inside the door, waiting for some kind of reaction. Waiting for the axe to fall.

Nothing.

Grinning in triumph, she very carefully closed the door. Moonlight trickled into the room and she gave her eyes a moment to adjust and take in what she could see. After all, she'd never seen the Earl's room before. Never seen a man's bedchamber at all for that matter.

The moonlight made everything look dark, but she could see he used much heavier furniture than she did. Big, intimidating furniture and a large heavy rug that took up most of the floor space. Despite the large size of the room, the bed in the center dominated it. A large four poster bed, the bed curtains were tied to the posts and she could clearly see the lump in the center of the bed which must be the Earl. Since everything was dark she couldn't see the colors, but she assumed they would be just as masculine as the furniture. The scent unique to him filled the air, as if his presence saturated every ounce of space he lived in.

There was only one small table between her and the bed, so she skirted to the side of it, tip-toeing as quickly as she could. Her breath was coming fast and it seemed so very loud in her ears, but the shape on the bed didn't stir. The silk wrapper she was wearing slithered around her legs, brushing against her breasts as they heaved in excitement. She was sure that at any moment he would suddenly leap up from the bed, shouting at her, but he didn't. When she finally reached the side of the bed, she paused to fully appreciate the view.

The Earl was laying on his back, gloriously nude. One arm thrown over his eyes, the other sprawled across the width of the bed. His blankets only partially covered him, one leg and hip and - of course - the area she was most interested in. But she could still see his muscled chest, the dark hair sprinkled across it and in a line down his stomach; his thighs were just as impressively muscled as his chest and she had to stop herself from reaching out and trying to touch him immediately. He was the most intensely masculine man she'd ever met, and even more so out of his clothes. The last time she'd seen a shirtless man it had been entirely on accident and not nearly this interesting.

She wondered if he always slept nude and what that might feel like. Perhaps she should try it sometime. He certainly looked comfortable.

Tugging on her sash, she pulled open the knot and let her wrapper drop to the ground. As tempting as it was to just sit and look at him, and not risk more, that wasn't what she'd come here for. Cynthia was determined to be quite thoroughly ruined before her wedding, no matter what the Earl had said. Or at least a bit more rumpled than her present state.

Patience was not a virtue, it was a sign of passivity. Cynthia preferred action.

Crawling onto the bed, on the side where his arm was flung outward, she pushed the sheets off of his body. The moonlight was just enough to allow her to see his rod, not quite as big as she'd imagined it; it was long and thick and laying against his body rather like a big, fat worm. Was this was seemed so fearsome when it was in men's breeches?

Reaching out with gentle fingers, she touched it - it was soft! And kind of squishy... she ran her fingers down the length and almost shrieked when it moved. It straightened, sort of, turning to point up towards the Earl's belly and it began to get longer and thicker under her fingertips. She watched, fascinated as it began to grow quite large indeed. Now it looked – well still not quite what she'd imagined, but at least it was more the size she'd imagined.

And this was supposed to fit inside her mouth? And her quim? She looked at it doubtfully; it was much larger than her fingers. Perhaps that would feel good, all the rakes had told her it would, but the proposition seemed a bit more intimidating now than it had before.

Putting more pressure on the turgid length, she felt it pulse and harden. The exterior was still soft, his skin there quite silky, but with a core of steel. At the base there was a wrinkled sack which hung between his legs, but that wasn't nearly as interesting as looking at and touching her first naked cock. Scooting a little closer, Cynthia's tongue flicked out and ran along the crown, which bulged at the end of his rigid staff.

The Earl moaned and she froze, but he didn't move. Wrapping her fingers around the thick staff of flesh, she drew it slightly upward so it was pointing more towards the ceiling. She wanted to put her mouth on it. If she could fit it in her mouth then perhaps it wouldn't be so intimidating to put it other places.

It tasted of musk and salt and flesh as she wrapped her lips around the fat mushroom tip, laving it with her tongue. The texture of his skin there was almost pebbled. This time when he moaned, she ignored it, too caught up in her own activities. Something sweet and a little salty dribbled onto her tongue and she immediately went questing for more, exploring the wet little slit with her own tip. It was slick inside, the same way she became slick, and it tasted interesting.

A sudden growling noise filled her ears as a rough hand grasped her hair and yanked her away. Shivering, she gasped and let go of his rod to reach for the hand pulling on her hair.

She found herself face to face with an irate and rather confused looking Earl. "Cynthia?"

216

"Good evening," she said, smiling and batting her eyes. With all the instincts of a true flirt, she twisted her body slightly so that if the Earl hadn't noticed she was naked already, his eyes were drawn to her bare breasts now. For a moment he was successfully distracted and she had the thrill of watching his eyes rove over her, his expression arrested. Her nipples hardened, her already slick quim grew even wetter with excitement, sure he was about to touch her. Ruin her.

And then he scowled again.

"What are you doing in here?" he roared. The erect staff of his penis didn't detract at all from his intimidating stance of outraged male.

"Shhh," she scolded, her heart pounding, but she refused to show how much he'd startled her. He was quite frightening sometimes, but it's not as if she could scurry away anyway; his fingers were all tangled up in her hair. And though she had a hold on his wrists, she didn't fool herself into thinking he would release her before he was ready. Still, it was quite exciting being held like this by him. "You'll wake the household."

The Earl's dark eyes narrowed, looking even more foreboding in the shadows created by the moonlight.

"You are going back to *your* bed. Right now." Releasing her hair, he pushed her in front of him, sliding them both off the bed and immediately saw her wrapper on the ground. Unabashed by his own nakedness, he picked it up and thrust it at her.

Cynthia had let him push her out of the bed, more because she hadn't been expecting it and he was much stronger than her, but she wasn't about to allow him to summarily dismiss her. She folded her arms under her bosom and smirked when his eyes immediately fell on the slightly lifted mounds of flesh. No matter what he said, his cock was still thick and hard, the way they got when men were aroused. Whether he was willing to admit it or not, he wanted her.

"No."

"Cynthia, you will leave my chambers *now* or you will be punished."

She bet his devastating, threatening tone of voice worked quite well on most people. In fact, she had to stiffen her knees against doing exactly what he ordered. Tilting her chin up, she glared right back at him.

"I don't want to be punished, I want to be ruined. What's the point of being engaged if you're not going to touch me? I've been fending off men from touching me anywhere beneath my clothes for years now and now I'm standing, *naked*, in front of you and all you'll do is look at me! Is this what our marriage is going to be like?"

"It better not be," he muttered, looking at her balefully and Cynthia huffed. She knew he meant her actions and not his lack of them, and she was getting angrier by the minute.

"Are you going to ruin me or not?" Taking a deep breath, she readied herself for his reaction to her next threat. Whatever she had to do to stay in the room. "If not, I'm sure someone else would be happy to!"

"That's it."

******

Grabbing the little minx by her bicep, Wesley hauled her up against him and kissed her. Possessive fury rode him, directing his actions, even though he was well aware she was making an empty threat. She gasped and then melted into him, all soft curves and woman pressing against him. Not that she was going to get her own way, but he needed her off guard for a moment.

218

He ended up taking much longer than a moment as he savored the kiss and the sweet taste of an eager young woman. While he believed her when she said she was untouched, he'd never met such a wanton virgin in his entire life. Not that he spent much time with the breed, but he was still convinced she was entirely an Original, in this as in other ways.

Pulling the silken sash from her wrapper, he looped it around her wrists before pulling away from the kiss, dropping the rest of the garment on the floor. She beamed up at him, looking rather dreamy, sure she had gotten her own way. He doubted she even noticed he'd tied her wrists.

Wesley would enjoy being married to Cynthia, he was quite sure of it. He liked her brazenness, her passion, her wanton ways - as long as they were confined to him, as well as her spirit, humor and intelligence, but he would be damned if he allowed his wife to prod him around or manipulate him the way she was trying to.

Tossing the long end of the sash over the top of his bed, so that it wrapped around the bedpost, he used it to haul Cynthia's arms over her head.

"Oh!" she said in surprise, looking up as her wrists were lifted. Wesley's cock, which was already hard and ready to sink into her, throbbed as fear flickered across her face along with some excitement. He wrapped the other end of the sash around her wrists and tied them tightly, leaving her bound to the bedpost and up on her toes - which made movement rather difficult for her. Her back was arched, thrusting her breasts and bottom out, temptation incarnate. "My Lord, how long do you expect me to stand here like this?"

Only the slightest quiver in her voice gave away her uncertainty and anxiety. Damn but she was bold. Which he normally appreciated, but he would appreciate much more after they were properly wed.

"Wesley," he said, pulling the special box he'd brought back from India out from under his bed. He'd given Hugh and Edwin each one for their wedding gifts and he'd kept one for himself. Of course, he hadn't truly anticipated ever using it for a wife, more likely for a mistress... he had no idea if Hugh and Edwin had used theirs but he liked to think they might have found an opportunity to at least utilize a few of the items. He was very much looking forward to how Cynthia would react to them tonight.

"What?"

He looked up at her, amused. "We're going to be married in a week, you might as well start calling me by my given name." Fortunately the length of cloth he was looking for was right on top. "Although perhaps not right now."

Before she could respond, he was standing in front of her and tying the gag around her head. He couldn't quite tell, since her face was fairly shadowed because of their angle, but he was quite sure she was glaring at him. As usual, her aggravation only made him feel even more cheerful. Especially now that she was bound and gagged and entirely at his mercy.

If she wanted to wake him with her mouth on his cock then he certainly had no objection to that, but not until they were married. Wesley had been doing his best to play by the rules, although if she'd chosen a different way of getting his attention then he might have succumbed to her persuasions and divested her of her virginity. But he wasn't going to let the little witch think she could just wake him in the middle of the night, catch him off-guard and get her way. Letting her push him around using sexual wiles would be far too dangerous a precedent to set.

Which, unfortunately, meant he wasn't going to sink into her hot, wet quim tonight either. But he could certainly satisfy himself, and her as well, without giving her what she had come for. Still, he intended to exact a certain price out of her hide for her attempt. And hopefully he wouldn't find her sneaking into his bed before the wedding night again if he made the lesson sharp enough.

From the way she was wiggling and the muffled noises she was making behind her gag, she obviously had more to say to him. She could wait. After attempting to force his hand, it would be good for her.

Grinning, Wesley picked up the little metal clips with dangling red jewels. He was quite sure Cynthia would have never experienced anything quite like them. At the time he'd chosen the red jewels because he liked the color, but he was looking forward to seeing them adorn her lovely nipples. The red would suit her; brazen and passionate, just like her.

"Hold still," he said, pressing her back against the post with his body, pinning her there with his hips. Cupping the heavy mound of one breast in his hand, he lifted it and lowered his head. His fiancé made a little moaning sound as his lips wrapped around her nipple, which was tightly ruched and ready for loving. Wesley sucked the little bud into his mouth and nipped at it, hardening it even further as Cynthia began panting.

He looked up to see her head leaning back, resting against the pole, as she arched her breasts out at him, her body begging for more.

Perfection.

******

The Earl - Wesley's (could she really become accustomed to calling him by his given name? She hoped so, he seemed to want her to) - mouth on her breast was heaven. Hot, warm, wet, and his clever teeth and tongue were playing with and pulling on her nipple, creating the most delicious sensations which went straight through to her pulsing core. It made her feel so empty and needy, so very tingly and wet.

She didn't like being up on her tiptoes and she certainly didn't like being gagged... but this might be worth it. Her utter helplessness had a certain appeal to it; the fact that the Earl could put his hands and mouth anywhere he wanted, do anything he wanted to her was wildly exciting. Especially because she never knew what he was going to do next - this certainly hadn't been something she'd expected. If being tied up to his bed and letting him have his way with her was punishment, she didn't think she was going to end up being a very obedient wife.

When his mouth switched to her other nipple, the one left behind was wet and throbbing, feeling the cool air even more acutely. The pole was wedged between her buttocks and she ground her front against the hard ridge of his cock, rubbing herself as much as she could when she could barely balance on her toes. It was absolute torture... exquisite torment. And more than anything it proved the Earl was the kind of man she desired.

So many men had tried to seduce her in order to pleasure themselves, although she thought they would have done their best to ensure she enjoyed it. The Earl, when presented with *fait accompli*, hadn't just fallen on her like a ravening beast; he was taking his time and pleasuring her as well. All of this remarkable man's focus was entirely fixed on her. Although with him she might not have minded the ravening beast.

Her nipples were aching, throbbing, and making the rest of her body pulse with need. The area between her legs felt like it had a burning, tingling itch that begged to be scratched by his fingers or whatever he felt like scratching it with. Even if she hadn't been stretched out and up on her toes, she would have been unbearably uncomfortable from the strength of the erotic desires coursing through her.

222

And she couldn't even beg him to touch her because of the gag in her mouth. The inability to communicate her need to him, being forced to wait for him to touch her, made her even wetter.

The Earl leaned back, looking down at her breasts as if to admire his handiwork. Cynthia looked down too, fascinated by the way her nipples had turned a darker pink under his ministrations and how prominently they stood out upon her chest. Grasping the first breast he'd suckled on in his hand, the Earl lifted it again, and this time she noticed that he had something in his other hand. It looked like jewelry, silver with a red jewel hanging from it.

Watching her face, the Earl closed it around her nipple.

Cynthia's eyes bulged in shock. Her head threw back, banging against the pole, but the brief flash of pain was nothing compared to the deep, sharp ache of her nipple being squeezed in an unforgiving grip by the silver clamp. It was like nothing she'd ever felt before. In the past she'd pinched her nipples rather hard, but this was more than a mere pinch - and unlike a pinch, the pressure didn't release when the Earl moved his hand away. It held on, crushing the poor, tender bud.

She tried to shake it off, her breasts jiggling, which only ended up increasing the pain as the little jewel bounced and tugged on the clip. Because of her position, she couldn't move much anyway, and she whined behind her gag as the Earl smiled wickedly, lifting her other breast. Cynthia was quite sure he knew exactly what the clip was doing to her and he enjoyed seeing her attempts to alleviate the painful pressure.

The pinching of her other nipple was both easier and worse. Worse, because now she knew exactly what to expect, easier because somehow having the pain balanced out made it slightly easier to bear. Her nipples throbbed in their confinement, seeming to be on a straight line down to her little clitty which pulsed in

223

sympathy. It wasn't like the pain being spanked, but her body had the same reaction - arousal.

Pulling away from her, the Earl spun her around, pressing her against the bedpost so it nestled between her breasts. The initial painful pinch of her nipples was slowly dissipating, and although she could still feel the awful pressure, it was beginning to feel almost good. Her body obviously had difficulty discerning the difference between pleasure and pain. Because of her position on her toes, she was now off balance and she found herself pushing her rump out at him. Cynthia moaned and wriggled, but her large breasts on either side of the post - not to mention his hand on her neck - kept her from being able to turn back around.

SNAP - CRACK

Pain whistled through Cynthia and she screamed behind her gag. Whatever he'd hit her with had left a thick line of unhappy, throbbing flesh behind across the center of her buttocks. She would have danced away, but she had no room to maneuver, and her jiggling was causing her breasts to bounce, which meant her nipples were being tugged by the weight of the jewelry again...

SNAP - CRACK!

She screamed again, this time before the crack of pain even bit into her flesh. The snapping sound was the wind-up, but it let her know what was coming a moment later. Tears sprouted immediately traveling down her cheeks to soak into the cloth gag as she ground her teeth against the burning lashes.

"You're lucky it's only my belt and not a birch," the Earl said, chuckling at her reaction. Cynthia tried to growl at him, but it came out more like a whimper. His belt! "Don't worry sweetheart, I'll have a birch made for you tomorrow, just in case you decide to be particularly naughty again."

This time Cynthia really did whimper. She'd never been birched before, but if it was worse than this, she didn't really want to try it. The two stripes across her bottom were already more painful than any spanking he'd meted out, almost obliterating the throbbing sting in her nipples which had either faded or was just obscured by the belt welts.

SNAP - CRACK!

The belt caught the underside of her bottom, causing her to jump slightly, which tugged on her wrists. Her breasts bounced even more, reigniting the flames in her nipples and Cynthia twisted and sobbed. The Earl's hand on the back of her neck wasn't punitive, but it did keep her from being able to move around too much - later she would realize this was in part for her safety - if she had managed to turn around the belt would be snapping against much more tender areas! But right now all she could focus on was trying to get away from the painful lash, not realizing he was doing her a favor by holding her in place.

SNAP - CRACK!

SNAP - CRACK!

SNAP - CRACK!

Her ears seemed to fill with the sound, the rounded cheeks of her backside feeling swollen and bruised from the punishing leather. Cynthia found herself doing a little bouncing dance she couldn't stop, even though it made her nipples and their clips bounce and sting as well. The gag was becoming soaked through with her tears where it covered her cheeks and she sucked on the cloth as if it could provide some sort of comfort.

Eventually, she couldn't say after how many strokes, it ceased. Cynthia slumped against the bed post, letting it take her weight as she sobbed. It felt like her bottom had been set in a fireplace and left there to roast! The

Earl's deep, crooning voice, murmuring that she'd been a very good girl, made her feel marginally better as he turned her around. He kissed her forehead and her eyes, ignoring the fact that her lashes were wet with tears.

Probably she should hate him, but Cynthia found his gentle hands on her hips and her sides comforting, his gentle kisses even more so. The expression on his face was softer than she'd ever seen before, warmer, and he told her that he was proud of her for taking her punishment so well. This was a side of him she hadn't seen before and it made her want to snuggle into his arms and just weep for the pain in her bottom.

Then the bastard unclipped the jewelry from her right nipple and Cynthia screamed again. It was much worse than when he'd put the jewel on. The release of pressure brought with it a rush of tingling sensation that was like little needles being pricked into the tender bud - a thousand of them, all at once. Lowering his head, the Earl took the tortured nubbin between his lips and sucked. The sensation was almost too much for Cynthia and she sobbed again, caught somewhere between intense pleasure and pain.

When she felt his fingers sliding over the curls of her mound, down to the lips of her pussy, she moaned. She hadn't realized it before, she wouldn't have thought it possible, but she was so wet the top of her thighs were slicked. The strapping he'd given her might be the most painful thing she'd ever experienced, but one certain part of her body had been highly aroused by it. Cynthia moaned as he suckled her nipple, soothing the biting flares of pain with his tongue, and one long finger probed between her pussy lips.

Looking pleased, he pulled away and watched her face as he reached for the other nipple. Cynthia shrieked into her gag, begging him not to with her eyes, as one long finger slid inside of her body between her legs and his fingers closed around the jewelry.

This time they could both feel her pussy clench as he removed the clip and the stabbing needles returned. The Earl lowered his mouth to this breast as well, suckling and soothing the tortured bud. She was on fire all over; her bottom, her nipples, and now between her legs where his finger was exploring her quim in a decidedly pleasurable manner. It confused her even more than the spankings had; how could such brutality inspire such a response? She was riding his finger, wanting more, despite her bottom banging painfully against the bedpost every time she moved her hips in an attempt to get it.

When the Earl finally lifted his head from her other sore nipple, he stood and wrapped his free arm around her body, pressing her against him. Her breasts were squashed against his hard chest, her sensitive nipples abraded by his body hair, and her netherlips forced even further open on his hand. Cynthia moaned and her hips jerked, tears springing to her eyes as her bottom throbbed painfully against the hard wooden post behind her. Blinking, she looked up into the Earl's eyes and realized he was watching her quite closely.

"You are perfect," he murmured, lightly brushing his lips over hers, even though he couldn't truly kiss her because of the gag.

******

The wet vise of Cynthia's cunt was squeezing his one finger so tightly it was a wonder his blood was still flowing. His cock seemed to throb in time with the pulse pounding through his hand, as if his finger was an extension of his manhood. If only he could replace one with the other.

But what he planned to do was going to be just as pleasurable, if not more, and it should make the hierarchy of power quite clear to his soon-to-be wife. If she hadn't gotten the message already. Grinning, Wesley reached up to loosen the gag and she spat it out

227

of her mouth so it fell around her neck. Her lips were swollen, her eyes red even in the moonlight, cheeks streaked with tears, and yet her spirit was unbroken.

As she opened her lips to say something, his mouth came crashing down on hers and he swallowed her words as he ravished her mouth with his own. He could feel her little whimpers, her squirming, as he pressed her back against the post. The clenching wetness around his finger pulsed and she rocked on his hand, all of her weight becoming supported by her hot quim as he forced his leg between hers and lifted her onto his thigh.

She was soaking wet, her juices coating his hand and now dripping down to his thigh. The little noises she was making could be of pleasure or pain, but it was more likely a mix of both.

Wesley groaned into her mouth, pushing harder against her. She was so soft and helpless, and so perfectly aroused by the situation. In his wildest dreams, he had never thought he'd find a woman who would complement him so completely. While he knew she was surprised by her body's response to any kind of punishment - that had shown clearly in her face - the fact was, some part of her loved it. Craved it. Needed to feel it in the same way he needed to dole it out.

And she still didn't seem to be able to keep herself from baiting him, which meant he should get to discipline her quite often. Something to look forward to.

Tearing himself away, he reached up to undo the sash around her wrists. She moaned a little as her arms were lowered, shrugging her shoulders as if the position had been uncomfortable. Wesley rubbed his hand up and down one of her arms, from her elbow to her shoulders, helping to restore the blood flow to her limbs; her head tipped back and she smiled up at him, licking her lips in anticipation. She wasn't going to get what she was obviously expecting.

Turning her around, Wesley pressed her down so her upper body was resting on his bed. Putting his foot between hers, he pushed her legs apart. She made a faint little sexy noise as her breasts squashed against the bed and he was sure her nipples would be feeling particularly sensitive after the clamps. The sheets on his bed would rub against them, arousing her even further. And tomorrow she would feel every twitch of her dress against the tender nubbins. The wet folds of her pussy glistened in the moonlight, deep shadows making the lips look nicely pronounced.

In this position he could truly appreciate what his belt had done to her luscious bottom cheeks; he could see the raised sections from the edges of his belt, the swollen redness of the rounded mounds, and the darker spots would be slightly bruised on the morrow. When he ran his fingers over some of the raised welts, Cynthia hissed and then moaned, her hips wagging up and down. And her sweet little cunt became even wetter, begging for his attention.

Instead of complying with her obvious desire, he put his hands just below those open lips and pushed her thighs even further apart, kneeling down and licking along the outside of her pussy. Cynthia gasped and then moaned as his tongue slid up her sweet center. She tasted of honey and musk, and it might have been his imagination, but her virgin cream was the sweetest he'd ever encountered.

He teased her with his tongue, not wanting her to find satisfaction yet... in fact, he wanted her to be wild before this next part. While he was licking and teasing her cleft, he was also pulling out the box of dilators from the Indian chest. Since she was holding her legs far apart for his tongue, he could use both of his hands for the next part of his preparation. Taking the smallest one, he smeared it with the oil he'd brought back from India. His cock surged as he stood up, placing his hand on the small of her back.

With both of his feet placed on the inside of hers, he ensured she wouldn't be able to close her legs against him. He pressed the tip of the narrow black rubber dilator to the crinkled rosebud of her anus and began to push in.

******

Cynthia bucked at the strange sensation of something touching her most intimate area. She'd been lost in a haze of pleasure as the Earl had used his mouth on her, eliciting sensations she'd never felt before. But now he'd stopped and he was trying to do something else entirely. In all the times she'd touched herself, all the time men had touched her, she'd never imagined and they'd never eluded to something like this!

"Oh stop!" she cried out, rather frightened. Whatever was pushing insistently inside of her was incredibly hard, and pushing back against it did nothing to dissuade its entry into her backside. "What are you doing?"

Bad enough he'd teased her into a quivery, wet mess of lustful need, now he was doing something completely unnatural which did nothing to quench the craving between her thighs. Cynthia's breasts rubbed against the covers, her nipples throbbing as they were rubbed, while she tried to squirm away from the Earl's hard hand on her back. He held her easily in place as the thing entering her bottom nudged deeper.

The tight ring of muscle stretched, and whenever she tried to push it out, it only burned worse and continued its path inwards.

"Just relax," the Earl said, almost soothingly. "It will make this easier. And if you're going to be constantly disobedient enough to earn more than a spanking, you'd best get used to this. Anytime you're naughty enough to merit being birched or strapped, I'm going to follow it by punishing you inside this sweet little arse as well."

Cynthia moaned as the thing seated itself snugly within her. For the first time in her life she felt embarrassed by something a man was doing to her... and yet not even that stymied the flow of wetness from her quim. It just excited her more that he was doing something so perverse, so unnatural, so... so... dirty to her and she couldn't do anything about it.

Then the thing began to move, withdrawing and pushing back in again, the same way his finger had moved in and out of her pussy earlier. It felt strange as it withdrew, and uncomfortable as it re-seated, and yet it wasn't entirely bad. There was something exciting about feeling it moving back there, the sense of fullness every time it was pushed in and the way her back passage burned as it was violated. Cynthia tried to relax, knowing she couldn't get away anyway as his hand pressed down on her.

Just as it was starting to feel almost good, as her hips were lifting up to meet the downward stroke, the Earl pulled it from her completely.

"Oh please," she said, the words spilling out before she could stop them as she lifted her hips.

She heard him laugh and she moaned with embarrassment, glad she couldn't see his face. "This isn't for your pleasure, minx, remember?"

Something hard and cold pressed against her lubricated channel and pushed in. Cynthia gasped as she was stretched wider. It felt like the same thing he'd been using before, but bigger and not yet heated by her body, which made it feel even more uncomfortable as it was pushed into her slightly stretched hole. She writhed, trying to escape the uncomfortable stretching, the muscles surrounding the area beginning to burn all over again.

It went deep inside of her, deeper than the first one, and stretched her so much wider. Cynthia groaned and twisted under the Earl's hand, impaled on the hard rubber probing her body. But she'd learned a bit from the first one and she forced her muscles to relax, making it easier for the thing to enter her and sink deep, without any extra burning.

But when he began to move it back and forth inside of her, she couldn't help but clench as the intense sensations washed through her, and her spasming hole made the probing burn even more. Cynthia moaned and squirmed, the unaccustomed sensations confusing her.

"Please... more slowly... oh... please stop..." she begged, shuddering and squirming.

"Shh, you can take this," he said. "I'm going to stretch this sweet little arsehole and get it ready for me." She didn't understand what he was saying, his words didn't make sense, but she did know the Earl seemed to delight in her begging and her useless attempts to squirm away. She didn't know why she didn't just reach back to stop him; perhaps fear that he might tie up her hands again and then she truly would be helpless against this assault on her privates. Just the idea made her body spasm again, but she wasn't willing to admit it.

As before, just as she was beginning to take the invasion more easily, the Earl set the thing aside and she found a third one striving to gain entrance into her tight hole. Cynthia cried out as it pushed past the protesting ring of muscle, her poor burning hole between her poor burning buns was becoming more than she could take, especially the way her body confused pain with pleasure.

She desperately needed to climax, the need growing with every violation, and yet there was no relief in sight from either her desperate erotic craving or the torture the Earl was inflicting on her backside. First he'd made her outsides burn, and now, as promised, her insides were burning just as much. The sensations were even more intense this third time around, she could feel every inch of the awful intruder as it nosed further into her body than she would have thought possible.

"Oh please!" she cried out again, begging him to stop. And yet, she didn't know what she would do if he did. Part of her didn't want him to.

There was no need to worry, the Earl was completely unmoved by her pleas as far as she could tell, firmly driving the hard rubber between her cheeks. Her poor hole was beginning to feel quite sore from the stretch and the friction, her backside was fuller than it had ever been before. Cynthia gripped the sheets, her toes curling as the strangest sensation went through her in a rippling spasm; it wasn't quite pleasure, but it definitely wasn't pain either. It left her breathless and panting, her quim clenching eagerly. In some ways it almost felt like when she rubbed herself to a climax, but it was different from that too.

The thick rubber prod withdrew and Cynthia moaned, in both relief and disappointment. Her entire body slumped over the bed as she panted. She felt horribly empty, and yet also hopeful the strange torment was over.

"There's one much, which is even larger, but I don't see the need for that one," the Earl said, shifting so he was standing directly behind her. Even though she couldn't see him, she could feel his movement and the heat of his body as it came closer to her beaten bottom. Cynthia started to nod her agreement, deciding she was relieved the ordeal was over, and then she shuddered as something new poked her newly stretched rear entrance.

It was hot and thick, softer than the things he'd been putting inside of her, and yet rigidly hard. When both of this hands grasped her hips, Cynthia realized it was his cock - he was putting his cock into her arse! Thicker than the prods he'd been using, hotter in temperature, and so much more frighteningly intimate, Cynthia

233

shuddered and moaned as the long shaft sank deeper and deeper.

If she'd thought she felt full before, it was nothing compared to now.

When his body pressed against her hot, battered cheeks, flames ignited across the sensitive surface of her skin, even as her hole clenched tightly around him. He groaned and twitched inside of her, rocking hard against her bottom and causing her to writhe for all new reasons. Of all the outcomes she might have expected when she'd dared to enter his room this evening, none of this had crossed her mind.

She felt him lean forward, bending over her, as one of his hands slipped around her hip and down to the front of her mound, the pads of his fingers pressing knowingly against her pleasure nub. The little swollen bud sparked to life, eagerly. The Earl shifted his hips, withdrawing slightly and then pushing back in; the same way he'd worked her tight hole with the hard prods, but somehow this felt completely different.

Despite the flare of fiery pain in her bottom as his body pressed against the beaten surface, Cynthia found herself rocking back against him, encouraged by the circular rubbing of his fingers over her clit. The wetness of her pussy was coating his fingers and it felt so delicious to be so very full in her backside while he played with her little pleasure nubbin. Delicious and yet also as though lightening was striking through her with every short hard thrust of his cock into her fundament.

This wasn't the marriage act; it was something depraved, something meant to punish but which also pleasured, a way of enforcing his dominance over her. Cynthia hadn't asked for this, wouldn't have wanted it if she'd been given a choice, felt rather embarrassed by her ardent response to it, and yet the Earl was forcing her to pleasure anyway, even as he ravaged her most intimate area.

And it felt wonderful.

Terrible.

Life altering.

Cynthia cried out, her back arching upwards as the Earl's fingers rubbed out an intense orgasm from her. The pleasure felt doubly intense for the amount of pain it had to overcome, making her feel almost floaty as the rapture trembled through her limbs. It was a strange climax, involving her rear channel as much as any other part of her body, which made the pleasure feel much fuller, much more rounded and complete, like she was being fully satisfied for the first time.

Almost. The channel of her womanhood still felt empty, but it didn't diminish her ecstasy at all. She was wild with it, her body trembling and spasming, riding his fingers for all she was worth.

Then the Earl's fingers pulled away, his body did as well, and Cynthia was suddenly being pounded into his bed with long, forceful strokes. Now that she'd gotten her pleasure, the Earl was taking his. Both of his hands gripped her hips, and, as he was no longer hunched over her body, the Earl was able to withdraw much more of his cock before slamming it back into her. She shrieked at the intense sensations, especially as his body slapped against her reddened buttocks, as if spanking her all over again.

Something smacked into her wet pussy lips with every thrust, her flesh jiggling, her abused hole protesting; and yet the pleasure went on and on. It was as if she couldn't stop cumming once she started, no matter what he did to her. Cynthia bucked beneath him, clenching and twisting in her passion. Pressing her mouth against the bed, she screamed his name as she felt her entire body begin to curl, from her toes, to her arching back, to her gripping fingers.

******

Bloody hell...

His fiancés' tight arsehole was like a bloody vise... and the vision of his slick cock disappearing between those beautifully reddened cheeks only inflamed Wesley further. He was going to fill her backside with his seed in an embarrassingly short amount of time. Having wrung Cynthia's reluctant pleasure from her sopping wetness, he felt no compunction about taking his own, as roughly as he desired.

Although it did seem as though she was still enjoying herself anyway.

Wesley lost himself in the intimate, depraved act, and his fiancés' wanton response to it. Her hot, tight hole was gripping him over and over again, the flesh of her welted bottom jiggling and rippling every time he slapped against it. As her moans and whimpers filled his ears, he reveled in his choice for bride. If this was any indication of what their love life would be like, it would be no hardship to cleave to his wife and no other.

Gripping her hips even more tightly, he shouted something... he didn't even know what... and nearly felt his knees buckle as his cock began to throb inside of her. He covered her body with his own, burying himself as deeply in her ass as he could, shuddering as she clenched his cock and milked the seed from his balls straight into her dark channel. Every jet of cum into her backside had him jerking and rocking against her hot buttocks until he lay, spent, atop her, lazy with sensual satisfaction.

Eventually her soft whimpers and small movements recalled him to himself.

"Are you alright, sweetheart?" he asked, softly into her ear, concerned he'd perhaps become too rough at the end. While it had been perfection for him, he didn't want to scare her off from such relations and now that he was more in control of himself he worried he'd pushed her too far.

Cynthia shuddered beneath him, clenching again and Wesley moaned as he rocked against her. The spasms made his sensitive cock jerk and he pulled away, gasping. The air felt cool against his groin, no longer nestled in the warmth of her body. Her face was turned to the side, but he could see enough of her expression to realize she was in a bit of a daze - unsurprising considering everything he'd just put her through.

Not that she hadn't deserved it.

Quickly cleaning himself off with a cloth, he then cleaned the seed which was beginning to leak from the tiny crinkled hole, which had tightened back to its original proportions, and her thighs of her juices. To his satisfaction, he saw her little rosebud anus was quite pink but otherwise quite unscathed. The dilators had done their work very well in preparing her for his cock.

Donning his own dressing gown, Wesley dressed Cynthia back in her wrapper, handling her like a life-size doll. She smiled up at him, rather dreamily, and then shivered. When he pulled her up into his arms, she snuggled right into him with her head on his shoulder. Sighing rather regretfully, as he would have preferred to keep her with him for the rest of the night (a rather surprising sentiment, but at least he knew Hugh and Edwin were the same way so he wasn't alone), Wesley opened his door, made sure no one was in the hall, and began carrying his burden back to her own room.

He looked forward to after their wedding, when he could keep her beside him in bed, within easy reach whenever he wished. No wonder his friends preferred to share a room with their wives. Wesley would be following their example.

Chapter 14

Eleanor's tapping fingers couldn't completely distract her from the nausea that had been threatening all morning. She felt distinctly green. Even the tea the Countess of Spencer had given her wasn't helping very much. The Countess' sharp eyes had seen more than Eleanor would have wanted; she only hoped the Countess didn't share her suspicions with Eleanor's husband.

Although Edwin had been most attentive lately, Eleanor still hadn't told him of her condition. Every day it became a little harder to admit it, as if by waiting she was risking more, although eventually she knew it would become obvious even if she said nothing. Especially since they shared the same bed every night and his passion for her hadn't diminished. The small changes in her body were becoming more and more noticeable, and while they could be hidden by clothes, there was no way to hide them from his hands or his eyes when they were in their marital bed.

"I think Wesley's done something to Cynthia," Edwin murmured into her ear, jerking her out of her thoughts. Eleanor blinked and refocused. She had been invited over for tea with Cynthia and the Countess, and Edwin had insisted on accompanying her. She was rather grateful for his presence, because she was having trouble concentrating and he'd been remarkably adept at dropping hints along the conversation to help her. Still, it had been rather unexpected, and it meant Wesley had joined them as well.

Looking over at Wesley, she couldn't imagine what Edwin was referring to and she looked up at her husband, raising a questioning eyebrow.

He nodded at Wesley, and then at Cynthia. Wesley was standing next to the mantle, one elbow casually resting on its surface, watching his bride who had been wandering around the room and recently come to a stop beside the window which looked out over the street.

The Countess had been in and out of the room as various details for the upcoming wedding required her attention, and was currently speaking with the housekeeper about the menu.

Eleanor realized the entirety of the noise level in the room was that conversation; neither Wesley nor Cynthia had said a word in ages. Besides which, they'd barely seemed to interact at all. Not at all what she might have expected between an affianced couple, no matter what Cynthia had told her about Wesley's current hands-off approach.

"He looks far too satisfied, when just yesterday he was rather on edge, and now *she* looks anxious and she hasn't sat down once since we've been here," Edwin said, sounding rather amused. Eleanor found it more worrying than amusing, although as she looked at Cynthia it didn't seem as though the young woman was afraid of her fiancé.

Just nervous.

Which was odd enough, considering it was Cynthia and so far Eleanor hadn't seen anything which fazed the young woman. Not even being spanked. So what had Wesley done to her? Or, rather, what had Cynthia done and how had Wesley reacted? Yesterday she hadn't worried when Cynthia had said she was going to do something to prod Wesley, now she wondered if she should have questioned the other woman more closely.

Eleanor was going to have to get her alone and ask. It would be impossible to do so today, she couldn't get Cynthia alone without being rude. Perhaps after Irene arrived; then Cynthia would have more than one well-disciplined wife to speak with. And Irene and Hugh seemed to have resolved their differences, going by the letters Eleanor and Edwin had received since arriving in Bath. So perhaps Irene would also have some advice. Although neither she nor Eleanor courted their husbands' displeasure the way Cynthia did with Wesley.

She couldn't imagine Irene deliberately misbehaving. But at least she would be able to add another perspective to the situation.

******

"Irene!"

"I'm coming," she called, hurrying down the hall. Hugh's demanding tones didn't cause quite the same reaction as her mother's always had, but she still couldn't help the little knot of anxiety coiling in her stomach.

It disappeared the moment she reached the top of the stairs and looked down to see him smiling up at her. No matter his impatience, he didn't scold or chide her the way her mother would have if she'd been kept waiting. He was fashionably but comfortably dressed for traveling. They were going to be arriving in Bath a few days before the wedding so they could meet Wesley's fiancé and spend some time with Eleanor and Edwin. Irene was wildly curious about Miss Bryant, as well as eager to see her sister-in-law again.

She was wearing her riding habit, although she wouldn't be able to ride until they were out of London. But Hugh had promised her that once they reached the country he would allow her to ride her horse rather than be stuck in the carriage, even though it was rather out of the bounds of propriety. It was something her parents had never permitted and she was extremely grateful her husband wasn't so bound up in the rules of Society as they were.

Indeed, marriage to Hugh had turned out to be much more satisfying than she could have ever imagined. A thought which he confirmed when he caught her up in his arms and gave her a very thorough kiss, ignoring the titters of the staff in the hall. When he released her, Irene was bright red but beaming with happiness.

Offering her his arm, he walked her out to the carriage which was waiting for them. Seating herself facing forward, she settled her skirts around her legs, already eager for when she could quit the confines of the carriage. She looked at her husband in surprise when he climbed in after her, seating himself across from her.

"Aren't you going to ride?" she asked, curiously.

Hugh smiled at her, the sunlight trickling in through the window and making his golden hair look even brighter. "Once you can, I will as well. Before that, I thought I might keep you company if you have no objection."

"No objection at all," she replied, smiling brilliantly.

Love surged in her heart for her caring, generous and all-too-wonderful husband. Irene didn't know how she'd gotten so lucky. While Hugh might discipline her when he thought she required it, he was also the most thoughtful, giving man she'd ever met - and that included when compared to Alex. The way Hugh had forgiven her transgressions, the way he continued to care for her, the happiness he'd brought to her life on a daily basis, when she'd thought she'd have to hoard and snatch small bits for herself... it was more than she could have ever imagined or asked for.

Thank goodness she hadn't married Alex. While she loved her friend, she also knew if Alex wanted to ride, he would do so, even if Irene was stuck alone in a carriage. She had never expected to feel sorry for Lady Grace, but right now she did. How awful to be trapped in a marriage with a man one didn't love when she obviously craved that; Irene could no longer imagine it.

And yet Alex was supposedly determined to reconcile. Irene no longer knew what might be best for the estranged couple, but she could only wish they found even a fraction of the happiness she had with Hugh.

Epilogue

Peters showed Alex into the drawing room. He looked around, noting the bright colors and feminine touches his own house lacked. Compared to Grace's rooms, his own residence was downright dismal and had been that way for as long as he could remember.

"May I say it's good to see you again, my Lord?"

"Thank you, Peters, it's good to see you as well," Alex said. The man hadn't changed much over the years, and he was still one of the most trusted servants the Brooke family had ever had. Peters' father had served Alex's, his grandfather, all the way back at least four generations. He was the only man Alex had trusted to send with Grace when she'd left. "Will her ladyship be down soon, do you think?"

The butler hesitated. "Lord Conyngham has yet to depart the premises this morning, my Lord, but Lady Brooke has summoned her maid and I believe they should be coming down to breakfast shortly."

"Thank you, Peters." Alex ignored the disapproval in the other man's face, knowing it was for himself and not for his wife or her lover.

After all, Peters knew it was his fault. It was Peters who had informed him that the rumors surrounding Grace and her 'lovers' were untrue when she'd first left him; she'd been having flirtations but she hadn't betrayed him. And Alex, proud idiot that he was, had retaliated by initiating his own flirtation. But Grace had had no way of knowing it was only a flirtation, unlike him who had Peters to inform him of the truth of the matter. She had not known that the rumors he'd acquired a mistress were false. It was only after she thought Alex had taken a mistress when her lovers had become so in truth, and he blamed his own prideful folly for that.

At first he'd been furious she'd taken the final step and retaliated by going through a veritable gauntlet of

242

women, rather than thinking through what she must have been feeling. Then he'd started hating himself for his behavior, as he had never been one to enjoy multiple partners, and he kept his affairs to one woman at a time, becoming more circumspect and choosing the ones who would be discreet and wouldn't flaunt the affair in front of his wife. But the damage was already done. By the time he'd swallowed his pride and recognized his own fault in their current situation, by the time he'd finally tried to approach Grace again, she'd hated him and he couldn't honestly blame her.

If only he hadn't let his pride and temper get the best of him, if only he'd gone after her when she'd first left, when she'd started her first flirtation... or even if he hadn't compounded the problem by beginning his own.

The only thing he'd been able to do for her was ensure she maintained a place in the *ton* rather than being driven away from it completely. A quiet word here, a word there, and only the highest sticklers wouldn't have anything to do with her. The others knew they would court his displeasure by openly shunning her.

And he kept her accounts at the various shops open, so she could buy whatever she needed. At least this way she remained in London rather than disappearing to who knows where and with whom; she would never be driven to desperate straights or end up relying on another man for her livelihood. He'd hoped that eventually her fury would cool, that she might see how he was still providing for her, and she might come back to him, be willing to talk about why she'd left him in the first place, but she never had.

For a while he'd even forgone his mistresses, although that hadn't seemed to help as rumors had continued to swirl regardless, and after a year he'd stopped denying himself when she obviously wasn't. Even though he never had to see her, he still heard about her lovers and it grated. At least she only had one at a time and they always lasted for a long period. Truthfully, Alex preferred it that way, he didn't like to think she wouldn't be constant once their relationship was finally repaired.

At one point he'd thought they might have a chance at something more than the usual *ton* marriage. Their honeymoon had been blissful. Grace had caught his eye when he'd begun looking for a wife and the first few weeks after their wedding had seemed to confirm his choice. A large factor of their marriage had been the business deal between himself and her father, but he'd rather enjoyed Grace for herself and he'd especially enjoyed her warmth and vibrancy, her openness.

Then, after they'd returned to London, it was as if the sun had gone out and Grace's personality had snapped shut. He'd come home from his club one afternoon to find her packed and ready to leave, when he'd tried to stop her she'd railed nonsensically at him, something about both of them being foolish, and then she'd gone.

Everything had disintegrated rather rapidly, leaving Alex feeling as though she'd taken all the light in the world with her. And once his pride and anger had worn down, months later and far too late, he'd realized he'd behaved remarkably stupidly.

But he was determined to change that now. He wanted his wife back and he was tired of waiting. It was time to stand up and fight for what was his.

******

The two men faced off, Conyngham rather warily. After all, he wasn't quite sure what to expect; Lord Brooke wasn't behaving the way most husbands of the *ton* did, whether or not they were accommodating. An accommodating one would have left as soon as he knew his wife was entertaining, to continue the illusion he was unaware she was doing any such thing. An unaccommodating one would already be either brandishing pistols or calling for them.

244

Alex was leaning against the doorway of her drawing room as if he had every right to be there, watching them come down the stairs. He wasn't shouting or retreating, he was just standing there, observing. And as much as Grace wished she could just see Rupert off with his usual kiss and promise of a later engagement, she didn't think she could pull it off with her husband standing there. Her stomach churned with nervous tension even though she didn't look directly at him.

Rupert reached the bottom of the stairs before her. "Lord Brooke." He nodded his head in greeting, still wary but apparently determined to be civil. "What an unexpected surprise."

Ah yes. And this was why she'd fallen in with Conyngham. He was never at a loss for words, unlike herself. He always managed to find something civil to say; it was a talent Grace wished she had. That and he made her smile, which was hard enough to do these days.

Grace felt like Sisyphus, and the great stone of her marriage was about to roll over her and crush her flat.

Divorce.

It had finally come. She'd wanted it, waited for it, planned for it... and yet now that Alex was standing here in her home, finally ready to deliver it, the pain in her chest was so great she thought her heart might actually be falling into tiny pieces. Not for the loss of Alex, she told herself, but for the loss of what might have been. The marriage that could have been. The girl she had been, before she'd spent years estranged from her deceiving, philandering husband.

"I need to speak with my wife," Alex said, almost affably.

Grace tensed at hearing her described in such terms. Surprisingly, Rupert didn't, and neither did he completely abandon her. Instead he straightened, looking Alex directly in the eye. "I would like your assurance that no harm will come to her from you."

Tears sparked in her eyes. Rupert cared. He didn't love her and she didn't love him, she knew that, but she did care for him and enjoyed his company, but she hadn't truly known how he felt about her. Whether or not there was more to their relationship than her affection for him and his desire for her. But he did care; for the first time in her life she was actually hearing a man stand his ground for her, for no reason other than to ensure her well-being. He was standing up to her own husband for her. And it shocked her nearly speechless even as it made her want to cry out with gratitude.

Alex looked back at Rupert, just as serious, his face as stone-like as ever, and nodded. "On my honor."

Rupert nodded back and looked up at her, she was only standing a few stairs above him. "My dear... I'll call upon you this afternoon."

To check on her. To ensure Alex had followed through with his word. And suddenly Grace knew that if she asked, Rupert would stay.

As practiced as her social mask was, she could feel it cracking and saw Rupert's eyes widen as he took in her watery smile. Despite his willingness, she knew he had things he needed to attend to this morning, and she didn't truly want any witnesses around for her conversation with Alex or the immediate aftermath. As wonderful as Rupert had been, and as good a friend as he was in addition to being her lover, she doubted he would quite understand her need to mourn a marriage which had been effectively over for years. Seeing him this afternoon would be soon enough, after she could compose herself again.

"Thank you, Rupert," she said, the warmth in her voice completely sincere and not just a show for Alex. "I'll see you then."

He took her hand and kissed it, rather than the usual kiss on the lips; apparently she wasn't the only one feeling stymied by Alex's presence. Then he left, leaving her alone with her husband for the first time in years.

Blinking away the tears Rupert's stalwart support of her had engendered, Grace swept down past Alex and into the drawing room, trying not to tense as she passed by him. It wasn't exactly easy to pretend he wasn't there, when he took up nearly half the doorway with his muscular frame, but she managed well enough.

Firmly entrenched in the middle of one of her favorite rooms, Grace took a moment to gather herself before turning to face him, her expression as blank as she could possibly make it. She wished she'd had more time to prepare, but she hadn't realized Alex was here so she was wearing a soft pink morning gown that was more comfortable than flattering, and her hair was curling down her back rather than being tidy and up. It made her feel at a disadvantage when he was looking so splendid, but that couldn't be helped. She didn't realize how warm and beautiful she looked in the soft pink, or the way her dark hair framed her face and shoulders, or how the fabric clung to her curves.

Raising her chin stubbornly, she forced herself to calm, hiding her clenched hands in her skirts. "I assume you're here about a divorce?"

If she couldn't manage relieved, at least she sounded indifferent if rather brittle. But there was no point in tip-toeing around the issue, she wanted it right out in the open so she could get through this part of her life and move on.

Alex raised one eyebrow, and Grace's stomach seemed to drop somewhere around her knees. Just one look and she knew she had assumed incorrectly.

"No Grace, I'm here about a reconciliation."

******

Claiming His Wife, the final book in the Domestic Discipline Quartet is now available!

******

About the Author

About me? Right... I'm a writer, I should be able to do that, right?

I'm a happily married young woman, no kids so far, and I like tater tots, small fuzzy animals, naming my plants, hiking, reading, writing, sexy time, naked time, shirtless o'clock, anything sparkly or shiny, and weirding people out with my OCD food habits.

I believe in Happy Endings. And fairies. And Santa Claus. Because without a little magic, what's the point of living?

I write because I must. I live in several different worlds at any given moment. And I wouldn't have it any other way.

Want to know more about my other books and stories? Check out https://goldeniangel.squarespace.com/ or http://goldeniangel.blogspot.com/.

Thank you so much for reading, I hope you enjoyed the story... and don't forget, the best thing you can do in return for any author is to leave them feedback!

Stay sassy.